MARY FITT

Death and
the Pleasant Voices

DOVER PUBLICATIONS, INC.
NEW YORK

This Dover edition, first published in 1984, is an unabridged republication of the work first published by Michael Joseph Ltd., London, 1946.

Manufactured in the United States of America
Dover Publications, Inc., 31 East 2nd Street, Mineola, N.Y. 11501

Library of Congress Cataloging in Publication Data

Fitt, Mary, 1897–1959.
   Death and the pleasant voices.

   Reprint. Originally published: London : M. Joseph, 1946.
   I. Title.
PR6011.I787D4   1984   823'.914   83-20637
ISBN 0-486-24603-5

*Death and
the Pleasant Voices*

PART ONE

I HAVE never seen such lightning or such rain in all my life. As I drove, the rain swept towards me in great grey sheets, so that the macadamed road was awash, and the lightning danced in quivering perpendicular lines just ahead of me. I cowered behind my low windscreen as if to avoid a blow; and over the sound of the engine I could hear crash after crash of almost continuous thunder. The sky behind, before, above, closed down over me; it was far darker than the surface of the road. Unable to think, and scarcely able to see, I steered along, doggedly and slowly, wondering what it would feel like when the inevitable happened and the car was struck: is there, or is there not, a moment of awareness before death and oblivion, even when the manner of death is so complacently said to be instantaneous? I wondered then, and I wonder now.

I came to a fork, and took the right-hand road. There was no means of knowing which was the correct one; the only thing to do was to go on. I had not gone more than a mile when I realized that I must have chosen wrongly: this was no longer the macadamed surface of the main road—itself a very third-class road with an enormous camber at each side, such as they still have in the country, where carts come before cars, and drainage before safety—this was a lane, with a fairly good but untarred surface, one of those delightful lanes which are the same red colour as the ploughed fields behind their hedgerows. There was no room to turn; there was a ditch and a steep bank on either side, and the ditches, like the lane, were running with water. One could do nothing but press on in the hope of coming to a gap or a gateway, or perhaps a house or farm where one could take shelter. I pressed on, therefore; and I was not made happier to find that I was now coming into an avenue of immensely tall elm trees. I knew all about the dangers of elm trees in

5

a storm. The dark green tunnel swallowed me up; it seemed to shut out some of the lightning, though the thunder still crashed unrelentingly overhead. And then, with a sputter and a sigh, my engine died.

I got out. It was useless to attempt repairs, useless to open the bonnet even, while the rain streamed down, making bad worse. I pulled up the collar of my storm-coat, and bowing forward, began to walk on along the lane; the elms groaned and creaked and soughed. The lush dark green grass in the hedgerows was uncut and thick with chervil, and the ditches ran gurgling like mountain streams. I could not believe that this lane led anywhere; and certainly there was no hope that any other motorist would pass this way and rescue me. Yet for some reason, or none, I did not think of turning back. I went on, as one does sometimes, sure that it was the right thing to do, though I could not have said why. I was not altogether surprised, therefore, when I came to a wide opening: a curved gravel space leading to a gateway, two tall moss-grown pillars with animals on the top—monkeys, I saw they were, at a second glance, and thought what a curious choice—and, wide open, the two halves of most exquisitely wrought-iron gates, all tendrils and vine-leaves and bunches of grapes, with a touch of rather faded gilding here and there. The gateway was set sideways, not parallel to the lane, so that one saw the open halves of the gate against a background of green shrubbery. There was no lodge; but the drive curved round invitingly, between rhododendrons and pines. Again, without hesitating or even making a conscious decision, I went forward as though the gates had been opened for me. In fact, I realized later to my amazement, I did behave and feel exactly as if I had been expected.

When I came to the end of the drive, though, and the long mansion stood before me, I thought at first that it looked deserted. Certainly in these times it could not be wholly inhabited. It was not beautiful, or handsome, or even very old; but it was imposing. It was built of some dark grey stone, and no imagination had been wasted on its design. It was simply a massive oblong structure with four tiers of windows, those on the ground floor being the longest and most ornamented, and those at the top the shortest; round the roof ran a stone balustrade. But there was no sign of life: no chimney smoked, and many of the windows had their white blinds drawn, giving the whole place an eyeless look. Standing there on the broad terrace, I thought that the place looked forbidding and forlorn, but, on second thoughts, not deserted: the lawns below the terrace were beautifully kept, the hedges were trimmed, the gravel of the drive was clean and weedless. And anyhow, I could not go back. Again I bowed forward and pushed on, round the side of the great house, past a group of massive cypresses, to the front entrance, and with some misgiving, climbed the stone steps to the pillared porch.

The brass handle of the iron bell-pull was highly polished, yet when I pulled it, it hardly seemed to move, and I had little hope that it would work. But in a very few moments, slow footsteps approached, the door was opened, and before I had time to formulate a question that would account for my presence, I found myself handing my coat to a manservant, and following him across the hall, wiping my wet hands as I went. He asked no questions, not even my name. He seemed to expect me, and wondering, I accepted the rôle.

The door he held open for me was the door of the drawing-room. I took it in at a glance. It seemed to me to be a very large room containing several groups of people dressed for dinner; but my impression was vague, as I stood there still trying to dry my hands on my handkerchief, for I was dazed by the storm, and the thunder reverberated in my ears. They had all been absorbed in conversation until I entered. Then they all turned and stared, in a way that struck me as unusual, although I was a stranger who had no right to be there. Their looks were hostile and forbidding, like that of the house—so much so that I withdrew a step in surprise. Then a fair-haired young woman in a yellow frock detached herself from the group standing near the fireplace, and came forward with outstretched hand and dazzling smile.

'Good evening,' she said. 'What a terrible storm, isn't it? We thought perhaps the train would be late. I'm afraid you are rather wet. Did the car miss you? By the way, I am Ursula.'

She smiled again, brilliantly. I took her hand in my still rather damp one, and released it quickly, as I felt sure she wished. Her voice was very pleasant. Hers was the first of the pleasant voices that I heard, though there now seemed to be an equally pleasant

7

murmur of welcome rising up behind her. She laid her hand lightly on my sleeve, and was about to lead me forward to the group she had left, when I came to my senses with a jerk.

'Excuse me,' I said, 'I must explain——'

Ursula laughed merrily. 'There's no need of any explanation, Hugo!' she cried. 'You are here, and we must all get to know each other as soon as possible. Mustn't we?' she said to the others. 'Explanations can come later, if at all.'

She moved, taking me with her, towards the group standing beside the fireplace, where a rather damp-looking fire of logs was smouldering under the high, wide chimney. And I, not quite able and not at all willing to break the spell of this curious dream, moved with her, conscious of my wet shoes on the pale buff Chinese carpet.

The first person to detach himself was a man, short, broad-shouldered, with black hair brushed smoothly back from his broad high forehead, and, like Ursula, smiling.

'This is our friend Dr. Parmoor,' said Ursula.

Parmoor took my hand in a hearty grip, and said in a strong, pleasant voice, 'I've heard a great deal about you,' which I suspected wasn't true; but he gave my hand a second reassuring shake as if to say, "Don't be alarmed: they won't bite," and smiled more broadly still. I noticed that his teeth were much filled with gold. Before I could recover sufficiently from his impact to announce my identity, Ursula had turned me to the next person, also a man, a tall, fair, sullen-looking youth who leaned against the chimney-breast with his hands in his pockets, and was studying me with undisguised dislike. I was not at all surprised when Ursula said, 'This is my brother Jim.'

Jim nodded disdainfully and said, 'How do you do?' He did not take his hands out of his pockets; but his voice too was pleasant in itself, a light tenor that went with the little fair moustache of which he was probably so proud. There was another girl in this group, a small dark girl who looked on silently and did not smile; it was clearly her turn next, but before Ursula could speak, we were all interrupted by an imperious voice from behind. The group nearest the bay window had broken up and was bearing down upon us, headed by an impressive-looking grey-haired woman with a very red face and

8

a very sour expression. Her green eyes were fixed protuberantly on me, and her small white hands, folded on her well-corseted but still conspicuous stomach, revealed by indefinable small movements that she was angry, angry with me for intruding. Those movements of her hands, slight as they were, were as significant as the twitchings of a cat's tail.

'I am glad to see you, Hugo,' she said sourly, and the tips of her fingers moved. 'I do hope you will settle down here and get used to our ways as soon as possible.' She smoothed back the white lace cuffs at her wrists. 'It should not be difficult, though of course it will require an effort at first—from all of us.' She spoke as if she were a headmistress receiving a very tiresome little boy at his first school.

'This is Aunt Susan,' murmured Ursula in my ear, and there was a hint of laughter in her delightful voice. I turned and smiled at her. I was now counting the seconds, watching for the right opening when I could reveal myself without instantly shattering the occasion and finding myself shown out of this room, out of this house, into the real world and my own hum-drum existence again; but Ursula's murmur in my ear made me want to prolong the dream for another few moments, at whatever cost.

Over Aunt Susan's shoulder, and in strange contrast to her round red face, there now appeared a long white face with drooping grey moustache, and a soft though rather lugubrious voice said:

'Don't expect too much from the boy, Susan. After all, he's never been used to English ways.' The speaker stared across her shoulder at me; it was a prolonged, unoptimistic stare, and his mouth was slightly open, but he did not address me directly. In fact, I never heard him address anyone directly unless he was absolutely obliged to do so through being left alone with him; if it was at all possible, he always spoke through and across Aunt Susan.

'Uncle Biddolph,' murmured Ursula in my ear. I could see somebody else coming towards me, from the alcove at the back of the room. Suddenly I felt desperate. The whole room with its chairs, china cabinets, pictures, tables, lamps, knick-knacks and people, spun round, upward and over my head, like a great

9

breaker forming, curling over me, preparing to crash down. . . . The episode had taken only a few minutes, yet it seemed as if I had stepped into another world, an enchanted world, a world where anything might happen, where one could lose one's identity and never be seen or heard of again. No doubt I was overtired and overwrought because of the storm that still rumbled, though it was no longer overhead; and it cost me a mighty effort to turn to Ursula, and to those still standing behind us near the fireplace, and to say calmly:

'I am very sorry, but you really must let me explain. I am not anybody you are expecting. My name is Seaborne—Jake Seaborne—and I came here because my car has broken down near your gates and I was caught in the storm.'

The moment's silence that followed was like the interval between the lightning and the thunder. Then I heard Aunt Susan say, 'Well, really!' in outraged tones, and Uncle Biddolph add, 'He's not at all what one expected.' In my confusion, I had addressed myself principally to Ursula's brother; I had not dared to look directly at Ursula herself. But Jim remained as he had been, contemptuous, indifferent, equally sure that, whoever I was, I must be a cad, because everybody is, really, and might as well admit it sooner as later. Rescue came from an unexpected quarter.

'Did you say your name was Seaborne?' said a pleasant male voice behind me. I turned in surprise, because this voice sounded genuinely friendly and normal and reassuring, like the voice that wakes one up from a nightmare with one's morning tea. The speaker was tall, very tall, taller than anyone else here; old enough to be my father, yet without pomposity of manner, though an eyeglass hung from a thick black ribbon down his white shirt-front, and he had the air of one who cares about the cut of his clothes.

'Have you a brother called Oscar?' said he.

'Yes,' I said.

'Seaborne isn't a common name,' said the tall stranger, holding out his hand. 'I've heard Oscar mention you. I knew him when he was a medical student. You're a medical student too, aren't you?'

I gripped his hand gratefully. By now the others had more or less closed round us in a circle, like the wolves round the prairie fire, leaving Ursula and me and my tall friend in the centre. But now I felt protected: my identity had been restored to me. I was no longer Hugo the undesired, but Jake Seaborne, medical student, rather damp and dishevelled, but nevertheless with a family, a background of my own.

'My name's Lawton,' said the stranger, and while I was still gaping—for I knew the name—Ursula's murmur in my ear came with welcome confirmation: 'Sir Frederick Lawton.' It was the hero, the great surgeon, my brother's paradigm, the undisputed master of the craft we were all feebly trying to attain. My position was secure. They could not turn me out now. As Sir Frederick drew me away with kindly questions about my brother, I could not resist flashing back a look of triumph at Ursula. She would not have dropped my damp red hand so quickly if she had known who I really was, and that I had friends. I had forgotten already that Ursula did not know or care who I was: that she had believed me to be Hugo.

Ursula was not troubling even to watch me. She was looking at a pale pink rose in the carpet, pointing at it with the tip of her yellow satin shoe. As Sir Frederick carried me off to the library for a talk, I heard Ursula say, 'But where *is* Hugo?' And as the door closed behind us, I knew that they had regrouped themselves just as before, in silent expectation, in hostility, against Hugo.

2

Sir Frederick poured me out a very small pink gin, and himself a whisky and soda; then he came and sat down in one of the deep leather chairs, crossing his long legs and smiling at me, while I watched him with an awe I tried hard to conceal. The library was one of the old-fashioned sort, not a lounge with a few bookshelves running round it. It was an immensely lofty room with large windows coming almost to ground level, yet nevertheless it gave an impression of scholarly obscurity. The books rose right to the moulded ceiling, and one would require to use the long ladders that leaned against the walls, if ever one needed any of the leather-bound volumes from the topmost shelves; but the books, ranged in their sets, looked as if they were never moved. Their ranks were broken here and there to admit forbidding-looking grey busts of bearded ancients. I recognized Euripides, whom I had often seen in my own University library, looking depressed and with a card saying SILENCE leaning against his sternum. I always had thought he looked tubercular, but now I decided his trouble was gastric.

'So your arrival here this evening was quite by chance?' said Sir Frederick, smiling at me benevolently and dangling his eyeglass between finger and thumb as people always do.

'Yes, Sir Frederick,' said I. 'It was simply because of the storm.'

'Strange!' said he. 'It only goes to show what I've often thought: that coincidences often look like design.' His eyes ran over the lofty shelves speculatively. 'It's a branch of research that has never been properly—that is, scientifically—explored. People think it is tainted with magic—humbug like telepathy, and quackery of all sorts. But nevertheless, I believe from observation that there's something in it. I am thinking of Democritus and the atomic theory, Democritus *che il mondo a caso pone.*'

I watched him as he obviously pursued some favourite train of thought—watched him, liking him enormously, yet still too much impressed by him to be natural.

'However——'—he came back to me—'*your* arrival was a true coincidence.' There was still a hint of query in his tone, though not enough to be offensive.

I swallowed my gin hastily. 'I suppose it couldn't have happened at a more awkward moment,' I ventured. I knew I ought to add, 'and now I'd better go.' But I was still unwilling to say the words so obviously expected of me. Instead I found myself blurting out my thought: 'Who *is* this chap Hugo they're all expecting? Am I his double or something?'

'I should think it most unlikely,' said Sir Frederick, dangling his eyeglass at me: he rarely used it in his eye, but kept it to play with. 'However, I don't know. I've never seen him. Nor has anyone else here.'

'Oh!' said I. 'I see what you mean. He was expected, and I walked in.' I paused for a moment. I was rather disappointed to think that I was not his double after all. Then, seeing Sir Frederick still smiling benevolently at me, and apparently in no hurry to urge my departure, I went on boldly: 'Rather a chilly reception, sir, I thought.' And then, as he said nothing, I made a great effort, sprang to my feet, and said, 'Well, I suppose I should be going now.'

Sir Frederick did not move. He seemed to be listening for something not in the room. But there was no sound except the distant rumbling of the thunder. It was growing dark again, and there was an occasional flash of lightning.

'Sit down, my boy,' he said. 'You can spend the night here if you want to. This is not my house, you know, but I can assure you that nobody will mind whether you stay or not—and you might even be useful.' He glanced round at the great windows: 'The storm is coming back.' The first large drops of the new downpour were already beginning to blur the panes.

I did as he bade me; it seemed inevitable, and it did not seem to matter in the least that I had not yet heard the name of my unwitting host or hostess. Sir Frederick leaned forward, looking down at his clasped hands, and raising his thick grey eyebrows as he glanced up at me.

'No,' he said. 'Nobody has yet seen Hugo. Nobody had even heard of him until three weeks ago. Yet he is the legal owner of this house; and all these people who thought themselves securely in possession for the rest of their lives are now going to be dependent upon the caprice of this young man. And as none of them has ever had to earn a living, none of them will have the slightest idea of what to do if Hugo decides that he doesn't want their company. So you see, the young man will walk into a rather ugly situation when he does arrive—and he is expected at any moment.' He leaned back, hands on knees. 'That's why I'm glad you've come. It has relieved the tension somewhat. They can't get themselves quite so much worked up a second time.'

'I see,' I said. 'I've been a sort of lightning conductor.' By now, I was as much interested in Hugo as if my own fate depended upon him. My interest was not merely curious; already it was acquiring a protective quality based on sympathy—the sympathy of one who had already faced that barrage of pleasant voices and hostile eyes. I warmed towards Hugo; I was his champion and friend. He was going to need a friend, of that I was very sure. Sir Frederick was saying:

13

'The situation has some rather odd features.' His manner was quietly diagnostic, and as such it compelled my attention. 'The family that owns this house and land is called Ullstone. They have owned it since about 1780, when an Ullstone inherited a fortune in Indian trade from his father. The Ullstones have always had connections with India.' He dangled his eyeglass. 'The young lady who received you in mistake for Hugo is Ursula Ullstone. She and her brother Jim are twins. Until three weeks ago, when their father died in a London nursing home, they thought they were his sole heirs, and the other people you see here thought so too. But——'

'What did the father die of?' I could not help interrupting.

'Cerebral tumour,' said Sir Frederick. 'Poor fellow. There was a long history of headaches, and latterly crises of rage followed by weeping; I think they all thought he was going out of his mind. The night before we operated, I had a long talk with him. Interesting man: he had seen much of the world and had many strange adventures. He insisted on confiding in me; and as I knew he hadn't one chance in a hundred, I let him talk. He asked me to do him a service. I don't know why he chose me.'

'I do,' I said, but not in a voice that Sir Frederick was bound to hear. I think he did hear, however, though he went on as if he hadn't.

'I never saw him before in my life. Still, I felt obliged to agree. He asked me, if the operation proved fatal, to break some bad news to his family: oh, not the news of his death, he said—he didn't think that would upset them unduly. No, but—and then he told me about Hugo.'

I leaned forward, eager to hear at last the truth about my unknown protégé.

'He said that twenty-five years ago, when he was in India, he fell in love with and married a high caste Indian woman—call her a princess if you like. She gave birth to a son, and died. Then Ullstone came straight home and married the girl to whom he had been engaged before he left—"a dear insipid English girl," he called her. He had meant to tell her about his previous marriage, but when he saw her again, he realized that this was quite impossible. So, as he wanted to marry and found a family, he squared his conscience by some convenient theory such as that

14

one was entitled to conceal the truth when to do so would be for everybody's good; and that people could be told only so much truth as they were capable of hearing, or would allow one to tell.' The eyeglass swung to and fro like a pendulum. 'I was greatly interested,' said Sir Frederick. 'Such theories arouse endless speculation in the mind.' He lay back in his chair and smiled up at the bust of Euripides, which gazed sourly down upon him.

'Well, sir, but what became of Hugo?' I said impatiently.

'Hugo?' Sir Frederick came back with a jerk from his happy contemplation of Mr. Ullstone's sophistries. 'Oh, he survived all right. The father had some difficulty in getting him away from his Indian relatives. One would have thought that Ullstone would have done better to let them keep the boy, and himself make a fresh start. But he was not like that. I gathered that he really had loved his Indian bride, and that the boy was precious to him as being all he had left of her. Difficulties and inconveniences did not trouble him where his own wishes were concerned: he was obviously a very self-willed man. He therefore found a nurse for the boy, and arranged to have him brought up in Paris. There he has grown up, with, of course, English tutors and everything else necessary to turn him out a perfect specimen of frustration and discontent. No expense has been spared. He has been allowed to travel—always with his tutors, naturally—and even to visit his relatives in India. But on the whole he has lived in Paris.'

'Lucky devil!' I murmured.

'Well,' said Sir Frederick, regarding me with an indulgence I found a little embarrassing, 'I agree with you that for people of mixed blood, Paris is the best place, the only place to live, if one must live at all. But you see, with the usual perversity of the young, he had other ideas.'

'Do you really think, sir,' I said, 'that the young are more perverse than the old or the middle-aged?'

'No,' said Sir Frederick blandly. 'It was a cliché, like your assumption that the man who lives in Paris must be a lucky devil. As I was saying, he had other ideas. For instance, he would have liked to live in London.'

'In London?' said I. 'Why?'

'I suppose,' said Sir Frederick, 'because it was the one place where he was not allowed to live—that he was not allowed even to visit. His father would not let him come to England, for obvious reasons. It was too dangerous. Having married again, he did not wish his second family to know anything about his first. In this he was completely successful, his second wife being, apparently, a model of uninquisitiveness.'

'Did Hugo know anything about this second family?' I asked.

'That I can't say,' said Sir Frederick. 'I know only what my patient told me. He said that having settled Hugo in Paris and arranged for his education, he thought little more about him, and didn't often even go to see him. He was quite content with his English life and his new family, for many years. His wife gave birth to twins within a year of their marriage, and all went smoothly until his wife died a couple of years ago. This, for one thing, brought him more closely in contact with his children, Jim and Ursula; and I gather that the experience proved something of a shock, though he didn't tell me how, and my own impression was that he must have been a difficult man to live with. Then again, I gathered, his house was invaded by all kinds of people who had had no footing when his wife was alive: relatives with axes to grind, friends of the children, and so on. He discovered that his home was no longer his own, and his children no longer children. This set him thinking of the past: of India, and his Indian wife, with nostalgia. Of course, a good deal of this was due to his physical condition—profound depression, irritability and the rest. But still, the form it took was this particular kind of nostalgia. It led him to do something which to a sane man must seem the result of severe pressure on his brain.'

'He made Hugo his heir!' I said triumphantly.

'He left him the bulk of his property,' said Sir Frederick, 'including this house and land. He left Ursula and Jim each an annuity of three hundred pounds a year—a sum that to most of the inhabitants of this island would seem to give freedom from financial anxiety for the rest of their lives. But to Jim and Ursula it means a fall from their world into one of which they know nothing and which therefore terrifies them. They quite understand that the advent of Hugo means a sort of eclipse for them, and they have no idea how to supplement their incomes, and no wish to work or to be useful or anything tiresome of that kind. One must not be censorious. That is how they have been trained to think. They are conditioned, quite as much as the people whom you youngsters probably still call wage-slaves—or is that expression already out of date?'

He paused, smiling, as if he expected me to answer. I said, nettled at being classed with what he considered my mental age-group:

'At least they are ornamental, so perhaps they're entitled to be kept, for the enjoyment of the rest of the community.'

Sir Frederick laughed: 'So that's the latest line! Well, I'm old-fashioned, and I think it doesn't do anyone, however ornamental, any harm to do a little work. If they don't work, they'll put on flesh and lose their figures and their good looks. However, their future doesn't concern us. What their father asked me to do was, first, to break the news to them. This I did the day after he died. They took it very well indeed, outwardly, especially Ursula: her behaviour was a credit to her training. Secondly, he asked me to contrive to be present when Hugo arrived. I said I would do my best, and here I am, on the evening on which he is expected. But my time is not my own. I must be back in town to-morrow. If Hugo doesn't arrive to-night, I can't postpone my departure. And even if he does—you are on vacation, I presume?'

'Yes,' said I. 'I had intended to take the car——'

'How long have you got?'

'Ten days.' There was no resisting him.

'Well, now, I want you to do me a service. Take my place. Act as a sort of buffer for this young man, at any rate for a few days. You can do it better than I: you're nearer his age, and he'll feel happier if he has a companion. Be his bodyguard—oh, I don't mean that they have any sinister designs on him—such things don't happen in English country houses—but I speak metaphorically. You won't lose by it: the situation is psychologically interesting, and you need to learn how to handle live people as well as how to dissect corpses. Medicine is still an art, and always will be in the last resort, however hard they try to turn us into mechanics. Moreover'—he leaned forward with his most engaging smile—'come and see me when you're in town and tell me all

17

about it, and I'll give you a dinner you'll remember all your life—worthy of Paris.' He drew out his watch. 'In fact, if you'll agree to take over, I could catch the nine o'clock train up this evening, and get a good night's sleep. What do you say?'

I stared at him, open-mouthed. I knew I would do as he asked. He was painlessly robbing me of my ten days' vacation, and making me feel that it was for my own good—that I should be much better without it. I knew I would agree, but as a last gesture, a salute to my vanishing freedom, I said:

'But sir, these people here—what earthly reason can I give for staying on? They don't want a stranger in their house. What if they ask me to clear out, as they're quite entitled to do?'

Sir Frederick was now standing, looking down benevolently on me, the poor rabbit. 'Oh, that will be quite all right,' he said kindly. 'This house is always full of people coming and going. It's a house famous for hospitality. I doubt very much whether anybody remembers how some of the guests come to be here. Just take your place—no one will mind, I'm sure. In fact, they'll be glad of your company. And'—he stowed away his eyeglass in his waistcoat pocket—'remember it's really Hugo's house. If you get on well with him, no one can touch you.'

He patted me a couple of times on the shoulder; and as he walked away, I realized that he had not only made me agree to stay, but had made me sound as if it were by my own wish.

Hugo's house! I looked round the gloomy library, to the rows and rows of untouched books, the busts of bearded Greeks, the dark furniture, the leaden sky outside. What would Hugo, fresh from Paris, and with his oriental background, make of this? Well, I at least was disposed to be friendly, which apparently was more than could be said for anyone else here.

3

The evening passed uneventfully. It was just as Sir Frederick said: everybody accepted me without question. By now it seemed to them that I was his protégé; in fact, I think they thought that he himself had sent for me, to act as his locum. We dined in a long dark room lit rather dimly with yellow electric light, manufactured on the premises. The whole thing was rather dim to me, dazed as I was by my new situation. There were several more people present than I had noticed in the drawing-room, but they appeared to be neighbours, dinner-guests only, and I did not fully take them in. The only person who was as yet perfectly clear to me was Ursula, in her yellow shining frock, with her shining blonde hair and sparkling manner. She really was quite dazzling. I was able to watch her to my heart's content, because she had forgotten my existence, or at least had accepted me as a quite negligible young man. She was not beautiful, not really; but she had all the prestige of the genuinely yellow-haired, and she knew this to the full.

I thought to myself that at eighteen I would have at once fallen in love with her, if only for a brief while. But now, I thought, 'No—no.'

4

Hugo did not arrive till the following afternoon. I had spent the morning getting my little car to go, drying out the engine; and when at last I managed to start her, I had gone off for a drive, and had had my lunch at an inn, in order not to make myself too conspicuous in the house where I still felt I had not the smallest right to be. It had been refreshing to rush through the country lanes and forget all about the Ullstones and their problems. At one time I wondered if I had better go straight on, just as if chance had never led me to their door, and allow the episode to take its place in my experience as a strange and pleasant dream. But in those days I still had a ridiculous and schoolboy-like sense of honour: I felt that the great Sir Frederick had honoured me with a sacred trust, and that I ought not to let him down, since I had made no effective protest at the time.

Besides, I wanted to see Hugo.

When I got back and drew my little car up before the front of the house, there was a large limousine standing ahead of me, and the chauffeur was carrying luggage up the steps of the porch. The luggage was that of someone planning a long stay: there were several trunks and cases, covered with bright labels, and the man carrying them in seemed to find them heavy. I ran up the steps, passing him, and made my way into the drawing-room.

Hugo was standing there, alone. This time, there was no reception. Everyone had gone out walking, or playing golf, or had retired to sleep. He stood at one of the round tables, with one hand in his pocket, and the other fidgeting with some small object that lay there. He looked frowning and sullen and at a loss—not in the least like one who has come to take possession of his inheritance. When he heard me, he looked up sharply with his right hand still poised over the table, like one detected in an act of petty pilfering.

'Hullo!' I said. 'My name's Jake Seaborne. I believe you're Hugo Ullstone. You've just arrived, haven't you? I'm sorry there's nobody here to meet you. They were all here last night.' I was aware of the fatuity of these remarks, and of the false position that I, a total stranger, was getting myself into by presuming to welcome the master of the house; but after all, somebody had to do something.

Hugo put down the small ivory box at which he had been looking, and came towards me. He was a handsome creature. With a thrill of pleasure, I saw that I had not wasted my time in waiting for him. He was of medium height, and as graceful as a sea-gull in flight; yet there was nothing affected in his walk, his figure, or his way of standing, or even in his clothes. It was just that in his movements he could not go wrong; and so it was with him in all his outward behaviour: he could not go wrong. He came towards me and held out his hand—a finely-shaped, strong-looking brown hand—and with his head a little on one side, studied me for a moment with great earnestness and attention. I saw his dark eyes glance up at my flaming red hair, and a faint twitch at the corners of his fine lips told me that he found it odd but not distasteful. Then he looked earnestly at *me*, at my eyes, as if to read there whether I were friend or foe; and what he saw satisfied him. I could see that, from the sparkle of light in his own eyes, and the smile he gave me as our hands met.

'I am very glad to meet you,' he said in a soft yet distinct voice, unlike any I had ever heard before. If his English sounded at all odd, it was not because he had any foreign accent, but because it was purer and more formal than we natives with our slipshod ways are accustomed to hearing. 'Yes, I am Hugo

Ullstone.' He smiled, most engagingly. 'Excuse me for the question—but are we related? You see, I have been away all my life, and I don't know the members of my family.'

I laughed, relieved at having the chance to explain myself. 'No, no,' I said. 'You don't need to bother about me. I'm not a relative. I'm a stranger. I have no right to be here, and I'll go at once if you want me to.'

Hugo was listening to me with great attention, still with his head slightly on one side.

'You know Sir Frederick Lawton?' I went on.

Hugo frowned. 'He is the surgeon, is he not?' he said. His voice was still soft, but it had developed a threatening note. 'He is the one who operated on'—he paused—'my father. Unsuccessfully,' he added, hissing the word softly but with venom.

'Yes. I mean to go and see him as soon as I am established here.'

'My dear chap!' I said, shocked to the core. 'Do you realize that your father had a cerebral tumour—that to remove a cerebral tumour is one of the most difficult operations in the world—that Sir Frederick Lawton could have done it if anyone could? Your father went to him of his own choice, and he was given the best possible advice. He would have died anyhow——'

'But not then!' interrupted Hugo.

'Maybe not—but inevitably quite soon. He took a chance, as everybody must: either a complete cure, or—— He was unlucky. But you can't blame the men who take the responsibility for trying to save you ungrateful blighters.' I was getting heated myself now, and I heard my voice rising.

'He was well paid,' said Hugo through clenched teeth. I fancied that his pleasantly-coloured face, in which red or pink were always lacking, had gone a shade paler.

'No more than his time and skill were worth,' I retorted angrily. 'He didn't guarantee a cure. If your father wasn't prepared to take a risk, plenty of other people were. Sir Frederick could have left him to die in his own way——'

'And killed off somebody else instead, I suppose,' said Hugo. The words were still provocative, but to my surprise his tone had changed: he could almost be said to be teasing me. The moment before, we had been on the verge of a violent quarrel; now, his

21

mood had suddenly changed, and my anger fell too. He watched me, saw me relax, and added with a smile, 'I see you also are a member of the profession. I understand: you are all in league against us.'

I explained hastily that I had not yet earned that privilege, and to avoid further misunderstandings I told him how Sir Frederick had intended to be here to meet him, and how my chance arrival had given him an opportunity to get away. I slurred over Sir Frederick's request that I should take Hugo under my wing: it did not seem to me that Hugo would take at all kindly to that idea. I wound up by saying blithely, 'I expect he'll be back quite soon to see you, and then I can go.'

Hugo turned away, broodingly. He paced several times up and down the room, while I stood there wondering what he was thinking. At last he came back to me, and fastening his dark eyes on my face in a way that made me rather uncomfortable—for I fancied he would know how to detect any deviation from the truth—he said:

'You have already seen the people here—my family, I mean. Tell me, what are they like?'

'Oh,' I said, shuffling a little and avoiding his look, 'they're all right, you know.'

'Who are they? How many are they? What do they look like?' he pressed me.

'Well,' I said, glancing behind me, 'first, there's your half-sister—Ursula.'

'Yes?' he said eagerly, leaning forward from the waist. 'Tell me about her.' And, seeing my hesitation: 'Don't be afraid. I shall not betray anything you tell me. You can count on my honour.' There was that in his tone which warned me not to show any sign of mistrust unless I wished to offend him mortally. I plunged on, therefore, though not without misgiving:

'She's all right—a very pretty girl: fair hair, blue eyes——'

'Ah!' he sighed, raising his eyes to the ceiling, as if the picture depressed him. 'Bread-and-butter, miss.'

I laughed loudly. I fear that "guffaw" best describes the sound I made—partly at the quaintness of his expression, partly at its incongruity, and above all, to relieve my own discomfort at discussing his relatives with him. 'By no means!' I said. 'She's full

22

of character—what sort of character, don't ask me. I'm no judge, and besides, I only saw her for a short while in company.'

He leaned forward again from the hips, with that graceful snake-like movement of his, and said quietly: 'You are in love with her?'

Again I laughed loudly: 'Don't be ridiculous! I saw her last night for the first time. One doesn't fall in love at that speed, at least——'

I checked myself. I had been going to say, 'not over here,' but I remembered that he probably would not care to be reminded of his mixed parentage, however little I might mean to offend.

He said gloomily, 'One either falls in love at once or not at all.'

To that there seemed to be no reply. I changed the subject: 'Well, anyway, I think she's the most important person here, if one wants to get on well in this house. Her brother Jim is very like her in outward appearance, but he's too lazy and contemptuous of everything to be of any great importance.' A sudden wave of sympathy for Hugo swept over me. I blurted out: 'What on earth made you come back here?'

He sat down on the arm of one of the larger chairs, and swung his well-shod foot to and fro, staring at the carpet: 'Do you consider it very foolish?' he said.

'Well, rather strange,' I said diffidently.

'Yes. Yes,' he said. 'It is strange, and probably also foolish.' He thought for a while, as if he were going over his reasons before uttering them. 'But you see, I have always had a desire to see my father's house, my father's people. He would never let me come here. He had his English wife, his English children. What could he do with a son like me?' He jerked up his head and gazed at me with an expression of infinite sadness. 'You know, my dear fellow'—he spoke the words carefully, as if it were the first time he had actually said them, though he had been practising them for a long while—'you people whose position is sure can have no idea what it is like to hover as we do between two worlds. Both worlds are all right if you belong to them; but how formidable, and yet how desirable, they become if you can't get into either! I've tried my mother's race. Now I'm trying my father's.' He sprang to his feet, his face

23

suddenly convulsed with passion: 'I have a right to be admitted somewhere! I will be! They shan't keep me out! If they try to, it will be they who will go, not I!'

'Steady, steady!' I said, terrified, lest he was going to burst into tears, or smash some of the furniture; but he did nothing except stand there with clenched hands and rigid body, as if fighting an inner enemy. As he slowly relaxed and was about to turn away, I was horrified to hear a light male voice behind me saying, 'So sorry to break in on your conversation—but may I hear what it's all about?'

I turned round to see Ursula's brother Jim, in riding-kit, sauntering across the room with his hands in his high breeches pockets and an even more pronounced sneer than usual on his face. Hugo turned sharply to me:

'Who is this?' he said.

'Your half-brother, Jim Ullstone,' I said, and turned to go.

'Stay here, please!' commanded Hugo, so urgently that against my inclination I stopped.

'Well!' said Jim, looking Hugo up and down with his most scornful air, 'so the new master is already giving his orders! I say, you know, I think you might let the family into your plans before you start telling them to every stranger.' Then he stepped back a pace, and favoured me with a similar scornful scrutiny. 'And by the way, don't you think it's time you moved on, you know? We don't know you. This house isn't an hotel—or even a Youth Hostel.'

A moment before, I myself had been of his opinion, that it really was time I moved on. But in the face of his insolent puppydom, it became a point of honour with me to hold my ground. Besides, there was still Hugo. I felt myself getting rather red, and I answered more or less at random:

'I don't think *you're* in a position to decide about that.'

We glowered at each other like two terriers bristling before a fight. Obviously the next step *was* a fight; but neither of us wanted this, especially in the crowded drawing-room, and yet neither of us was willing to give way. It was Hugo who put an end to the ridiculous situation. He stepped up to us and said:

'All right, leave this to me, please. This house is mine, and'—he turned to me—'*I* invite you to stay. From now on, you are my

24

guest, and you have as good a right here as anyone.' He bent his dark eyes on Jim, who was beginning to waver. 'You and I had the same father,' he said in a low but quite firm tone. 'Can you not remember that when you look at me? For the present, that is all I ask of you. We shall get to know each other, I hope, very soon. Then we shall know if we wish to spend more time in each other's company.' There was a moment's silence, while the effect of his strange and dramatic words sank into us. Jim looked down, biting his lip, and Hugo studied him still more earnestly, as if looking for anything in him to which he could address a further appeal, or with which he could establish any sort of communication.

'I doubt if we have much in common,' he said at last, as if thinking aloud. 'But please don't alter your ways at all for me. I don't really wish to interfere. I have come here rather to look on than to——' He stopped, and turned away. I thought I heard him sigh.

We were still standing like this—Jim like a sulky schoolboy who has received a rebuke from a junior master for whom he has no respect, Hugo once more fingering the ivory objects on the round table, and I somewhat bellicose and enjoying Jim's discomfiture—when again the door opened, and in came Ursula, all bright, sparkling and gay, wearing a light green dress very clean and stiff and uncrumpled, and carrying a large bunch of flowers, scarlet poppies and marguerites.

'Oh, there you are!' she cried, taking us all in with her beaming glance and brilliant smile as she stood on the threshold. She moved quickly towards Hugo and held out her hand. 'You must be Hugo. I saw the car arrive. I am *so* sorry none of us was here to welcome you. We expected you last night, you know.'

Hugo straightened himself, took his left hand out of his pocket, put down the ivory piece he was holding in his right hand. Every movement was graceful and deliberate. One can't often say that the spectacle of two people shaking hands is at all thrilling or comparable to a poem or a piece of music; but in this instance it was so. She stood waiting, with her hand extended; he seemed to be summoning all his hidden strength, as if to meet, not a welcome, but some new form of attack. And yet I had the feeling that he, after all, was the stronger.

25

He took her white hand in his brown one, which was no less finely-shaped than hers; and it was clear that he grasped it with a quite British warmth; in fact, I thought she winced a little, though she gave no obvious sign, and her smile remained fixed.

'Ursula,' he said in his pleasant, vibrant voice, as if he were practising the name. 'It is very kind of you to receive me like this. I am aware that my arrival may put you out a little. But I assure you, I have no wish to do so. Your brother seems to think otherwise. I am sorry for that. I am sure that *you* will help him to understand me a little better.' He smiled, and his smile, though melancholy, was no less dazzling than hers.

'Well, yes, Hugo, of course!' she cried, perhaps with more heartiness than she felt. 'You are most welcome here—I mean, we are very glad to see you. You must excuse us if at first we don't—quite——' Her voice grew meditative. Then she brightened again: 'I'm sure you understand! We are so used to regarding this place as our home that we can't quite get used to the idea that we're welcoming you not as a visitor, but——'

Hugo checked her with a slight gesture of his fine hand. 'My dear Ursula,' he said, and his voice, though authoritative, was not without feeling as well. 'I'm very grateful to you for your frankness. It is what I have hoped for, from the English side of my family. I want to be equally frank with you.' He motioned her to a chair. 'Shall we sit down?'

He himself sat down, on one of the uncomfortable settees, and remained for a moment or two looking sideways at the beflowered carpet. He took no further notice of Jim, who stood there glowering as though he had received his dismissal but was determined nevertheless to stay. I too stayed, though I kept myself at a distance. I was aware that for some reason neither Ursula nor Hugo wished me to go. Perhaps they found it easier to talk with me there; perhaps they did not yet want to face each other alone.

'You may wonder,' Hugo began, 'why I have chosen to come here and disturb your happy life together. You probably think that the life your father arranged for me, with its centre in Paris, was more suited to me than this.' He glanced round at the high windows. The lawns were green and sparkling after the rain, and to the right the shrubbery edged with rhododendrons was gay with colour, amethyst and rose. 'Well, perhaps that is so. But, you see'—his face contracted with a spasm which I was already beginning to recognize as the presage of a storm—'your—my father made one great mistake: he refused to let me come to England. England was the forbidden country. He gave me everything except that. And so, of course, that became the only thing left that I wanted. I have come here to break the spell, as it were.'

Ursula was smiling sympathetically and soothingly, as if she were listening to a child. But there was a hint of eagerness that I thought ill-advised in her voice as she asked: 'Then you don't intend to make your home here? I mean, you've come here just to see what it's like—for a holiday?'

'That I can't yet say,' answered Hugo coldly.

'Oh, please don't misunderstand me!' said Ursula. 'Everything I say must sound a little suspect to you, I know. But I really was thinking of it from your point of view. I can't help thinking that the life here won't come up to your expectations. It's so dull—so quiet and countrified—so different from everything you must be used to!' She laughed. 'I assure you, you won't find the society round here very amusing! The vicar, the local farmers, their wives and daughters——'

Hugo's tone was still reserved, and he did not smile. 'It is you who misunderstand me,' he said. 'I am not looking for amusement—for what you call fun. I am looking for—peace of mind.'

If he had said that he was looking for the philosopher's stone, I could not have been more surprised, the statement was so utterly incongruous with his appearance, his manner, with everything about him. I could not help stepping forward out of my discreet background, and saying incredulously, 'Peace of mind? At your age?'

Hugo turned sharply on me with a look of annoyance, as if my incredulity offended him; but as he regarded me, his look softened and grew wise. 'At my age!' he repeated, gently and ironically, nodding his head. 'You think, because you and I are the same age in years, maybe, we have the same needs. But you forget what I am!' His whole frame stiffened as he spoke these words with a violence so sudden that I withdrew a step again in sheer surprise. 'Do you think that I can look forward as you can to a happy normal life, with a wife and children to work for, with a definite place in the community—in any community? Where is there in the world any community which wants or needs me?'

'You could take up some kind of work,' I muttered, 'a profession——'

'A profession! Ha!' answered Hugo vehemently. 'And why should I? You would like me to take up medicine like yourself, I suppose—to heal the sick and benefit humanity. Why should I? Tell me that! Why should I force myself upon some society which doesn't want my services, to earn money which I don't need? No, no! There are better ways of passing one's life—of killing the time between now and the grave! From all that I have heard, I have gathered that your life here is peaceful and tranquil—that it goes on, day in, day out, without change. I have heard that the life of an English country gentleman is the best in the world, if you know how to savour its extraordinary monotony.'

Ursula laughed. 'Did my father tell you that?' she said.

Hugo nodded. 'I did not know what he meant. But what he said appealed to me. I begged him to let me come over here to live. He never would agree. But now that he is dead, he has made the *amende honorable*. He has laid his command on me—and it is sacred—not only to come here and live, but to take his place.'

'That you could never do!' broke in Jim savagely. Ursula turned her bright eyes upon him, but she did not intervene.

'——as head of this house,' said Hugo, deliberately, as if he had not heard. 'There is no need for any interruption of its quiet ways. All can come and go and stay as before—provided that they accept me as—as my father's eldest son, as the master. I want nothing else. In fact, I want to be left alone. I don't want your affection or even your friendship. But respect for my wishes there must be—and what I chiefly wish is,' he said, eyeing me defiantly, 'peace of mind. If I find that the disturbing elements are too troublesome'—he turned to Jim—'I shall have to make other arrangements.'

'Why not make them now?' sneered Jim, coming a step nearer. Hugo's answering look made Jim quail. Yet he spoke quietly:

'You misunderstand me, once again,' he said, addressing Jim directly for the first time since Ursula's entrance. 'I do not mean that I shall go. I mean that *you* will.'

Ursula intervened. 'Please go, Jim!' she said. With a last violent glance at Hugo and at me, Jim went, slamming the door. Ursula turned back to Hugo: 'Do please have a little patience with him!' she pleaded. 'His position *is* rather difficult, you know. He has had all his own way—as a matter of fact, so have I, but women are so much more practical and accommodating than men, don't you think? He is much, much younger than I in his mental outlook. I hate to say it, but I think that our father was a little to blame, for not telling us anything about each other. It *is* rather a shock to think yourself the son and heir, and then find——'

Hugo sat back in the corner of the settee, holding his forehead, which was rather high, in his hand, and shading his eyes. One could not tell if he were listening or not to Ursula's diplomatic babbling. But I thought I could discern—for I imagined I knew him backwards already—that he had been deeply hurt and angered by what had happened. The fact that it was only to be expected did not alter his reaction; he had somehow persuaded himself that in this house he would be accepted, given his rightful place, without a struggle. At last he drew his hand slowly back over his dark hair, and said:

'Maybe I *had* better go.'

'Oh, no, no, you mustn't do that!' cried out Ursula, with such verve that I almost believed her—or was it that I put into her protest, insincere as I knew it was bound to be, something of my own desire that Hugo should not slip away from us yet awhile? 'Oh, please, Hugo! This is your home, and we have all been longing to meet you.' She turned to me, of all people, for confirmation. 'Jake knows that we were all waiting here last night to receive you. Why, when he came in, we thought at first that he was you!'

She laughed merrily, and I fancied I could detect in her laugh something of her regret that it had not been so—that she had to deal, not with the clumsy red-haired medical student which was all she saw in me, but with this enigmatic creature, sometimes fierce, sometimes gentle, and quite outside the range of our prediction. She sprang up, and went towards the door: 'I'll get them to take your things to your room. And then we'll have tea. I'm sure you're ready for it.' She talked herself out through the door, while Hugo still sat brooding, and gave no sign that he had heard.

When all sound had died away, and nothing was to be heard except the rustling of leaves in the trees outside, Hugo looked up at me with a smile, and said in that intimate tone of his, as if he had known me all his life, 'What do you advise? Shall I go, or shall I stay?'

I sat down abruptly, on one of those armless chairs which are so much lower than one expects them to be. Suddenly I felt terribly responsible. I wanted time to think, for I believed that he would do what I suggested: not so much because he trusted me—it was not likely that he trusted anyone—but because he was too contemptuous or too fatalistic to care. He was using me as if I were a dice-box, that was all, and whatever opinion tumbled out of me would serve to save him the trouble of making up his own mind. To this day I cannot account for the answer I gave. I only know that, with his serious dark eyes fixed on me, I said what I thought, and what I had not known till then that I was thinking.

'*I'd* like you to stay,' I said, 'whoever else would or wouldn't. But—don't you think there's danger in it?'

'Danger?' Hugo's whole attitude changed, from the pose of weary nonchalance to a tense alertness, and his eyes flashed. 'Danger? For whom?'

'I don't know,' I said, thumping my forehead as I always do when I'm worried by an idea I can't account for. 'But your presence here is like a charge of electricity, or like a grain of radium wandering round. When you come up against these people, they'll disintegrate. Who is going to suffer most—you or they—I can't tell. The sensible thing for you to do would be to go away—go back to Paris, or London if you like, and run this place through your lawyers. There's no need for you to relinquish any of your rights. But if I were you, I wouldn't stay here—not if I wanted peace of mind, at any rate.'

'Ah!' said Hugo. Suddenly he switched himself round, and lay at full length on the settee, with his hands behind his head, gazing up at the moulded ceiling with an ecstatic look. 'Peace of mind! How could *you* understand what I mean by that? I don't mean your bovine contentment. To someone like me, peace of mind comes only from the mastery of the will, over people and things. *I* can find peace of mind only in difficulty and danger——'

'But you said just now——' I began, bewildered.

He waved me aside impatiently: 'I know, I know! I don't claim to be consistent. I find truth only in contradiction—the harmony of opposites. I come to this quiet place, seeking—I don't know what. And you tell me there is danger. I think you may be right. Perhaps I suspected it all along. Perhaps that's why I came!' He sounded exultant, boyish.

'Not you!' I said impatiently in my turn. 'You brought it with you, if it exists. There's nothing mystical about it. For God's sake—can't you see these people's point of view? They were secure in their lives—in their heritage—until you came. And now, that's all over unless they can get rid of you. They'll never rest until they have. They'll make it so uncomfortable that you'll have to go, unless you drive them all out first. And then you'll have the whole countryside against you. Nobody will work for you, nobody will recognize you, nobody will——'

Hugo leapt off the settee and sprang erect, with his hands to his ears. 'Stop! Stop!' he almost shrieked at me, his face contorted with rage. 'This is my house! I *will* stay! I will make them do what I wish, or——' His hands dropped to his sides, and he sat down limply, yet still gracefully, in an attitude of despair. 'At least, there is one thing they can count on,' he said between his teeth. 'I shall never have an heir.'

'Oh, rot!' I said, startled. 'Why shouldn't you?'

'Because I am vowed to celibacy,' he said passionately. 'Do you think I want to propagate my species—to be responsible for another human being as miserable and as divided as myself?'

'Well, I don't know,' I murmured ineffectually, taken aback by finding myself in agreement with him, and yet loth to concede him his despair. 'Surely there must be some way out. Man wasn't born to live alone, you know. Sooner or later you'll find some girl who'll fall in love with you, and then it won't matter.'

'It will always matter,' said Hugo. 'There is no answer. Any woman who really loved me would be accursed. If ever I allowed

31

that to happen, I would deserve to be shot—unless I shot myself first.'

He looked up, and no doubt caught me staring at him open-mouthed. 'Don't worry,' he said in a quite different tone, and with one of his most dazzling smiles. 'You mustn't take me too seriously. Perhaps it is not quite as bad as I say. In fact——' He drew towards me, and I had the impression that he was going to confide something to me; but at that moment, a maid entered and said that his rooms were ready and that his tea was served.

5

Ursula had tactfully arranged that Hugo should take tea by himself upstairs this first time. She had given him the best suite of rooms in the house. His sitting-room was enormous, with a great fireplace, the overmantel of which was a sinister-looking scene in Dutch plaster of what looked to me like a multiple hanging, though perhaps that was only because the figures were not in perspective and therefore appeared to have their feet off the ground. The carpet was rose-pink and very thick, and I could see from Hugo's walk as he crossed to the window that the feeling of the pile under his feet gave him pleasure. There were heavy curtains of some brocade-like material at the windows and else-where in the room; and there was one window that jutted out in a semi-circle and was completely cut off from the rest of the room by these sumptuous curtains, so that it formed a little separate room—the powder-closet, Ursula explained. The view from the windows was, to English eyes, delightful: nothing but lawns and trees and flowers, and the blue haze of the hills in the distance. Whether it was to Hugo's taste or not was a different matter. He hardly looked at the view, but he seemed to take great pleasure in the room.

'I'm so glad you like it!' said Ursula as he murmured some few words of praise. 'And remember, you have only to ring the bell and someone will come.' At that moment the maid entered with the tea-tray, and set it on a table near one of the lofty windows.

'Oh!' said Hugo, disappointed. 'Am I to have tea alone?'

'I thought you'd prefer it, just for to-day,' said Ursula

hastily. 'I assumed you'd be tired—you wouldn't want to meet *every*body *all* at once.'

Hugo regarded her with his head on one side. 'I understand,' he said. He turned to me with an appealing gesture. 'But you'll stay with me? You're a stranger here too.'

I shook my head. I thought it wiser to refuse. For one thing, I did not want the family to group him and me too closely together; I did not want to seem too obviously on his side against them. For another thing, I was curious to know what they would say. So I shook my head, and Hugo turned away with a disappointed look, like a child.

'Come!' said Ursula, laying a hand on my arm while I still hesitated. We left him there, staring out of the window, but, I am convinced, still seeing nothing of the view.

6

'He's rather sweet, isn't he?' said Ursula as we walked slowly down the corridor together. She still kept her hand on my arm, and I remember thinking that the red carpet with its black border was like the kind they lay down in front of church doors at weddings. 'Poor boy! I feel so sorry for him, coming among us like this. I do wish, for his own sake, it hadn't happened.'

She sounded most sincere. I glanced sideways at her: the expression on her face corresponded with her words. Yes, I supposed she *was* sorry for him in a way—sorry to think of what they were going to do with him. She knew well enough what he had come there for—in the absurd hope of finding somewhere to strike roots in, some people to whom he could say he belonged. We both had known this when we had left him there, staring out of the window at the prospect which already seemed desolate, no doubt, to his eyes. And yet, in spite of this, she must in the nature of things be out to circumvent him: in what way I did not know, nor perhaps did she. All I knew what that it involved keeping him here for the present, perhaps for a long time; at any rate, until in some way I could not pretend to guess, he no longer counted—no longer stood in their way.

Her fingers pressed a little harder into the rough tweed of my coat as we went along the corridor and down the broad stairs.

'I'm so glad *you*'re here, Jake,' she said, as if she had known me all her life and I had always proved a tower of strength in times of family trouble. 'It helps us all a good deal—and it will help poor Hugo too, I'm sure.'

'Oh, Hugo's all right,' I muttered perversely. 'He doesn't need anybody's help. He can get along all right alone.'

She turned wide, innocent eyes upon me. 'Oh, do you think so? He struck me as being very lonely, poor boy.'

'Of course he's lonely,' I said rather roughly. 'He's bound to be, coming here into a nest of——' I nearly said "vipers," but I recalled the word and substituted "relatives." '—relatives who can't possibly do anything but look upon him as a disaster. He's sensitive, you know. Anyone can see that at a glance.'

'Oh, do you think so?' she said again, as if my opinion were of the greatest importance. 'But surely——'—her fingers pressed more closely into my arm—'he was bound to find it a little difficult to fit in, wasn't he?'

We had reached the door of the drawing-room, and I could hear the tinkle of cups and the murmur of voices inside as I held open the door.

'Do you know,' Ursula went on, 'I don't think a really sensitive person thrusts himself in where he hasn't been asked, and can't be wanted—do you?'

She gave me a dazzling smile, and before I could answer she had preceded me into the room. I shrugged my shoulders, and followed her.

7

There they all were: Aunt Susan, Uncle Biddolph, Dr. Parmoor; Jim standing by the window, and the small dark girl whom I did not yet know sitting in the window-seat near him, looking up at him with an expression of anxiety. They were all, as I had expected, discussing Hugo. Jim was talking big, straddling across the tiger-skin that lay with snarling mask at his feet.

'Either the fellow's an impostor,' he was saying, 'or if he's genuine, my father was out of his mind. We can challenge his credentials, and if he's no good, we can challenge the will. I can get plenty of people here, on the estate and in Chode, to say how

34

queerly my father was behaving in the twelve months before he died.'

'He always did behave rather queerly,' said Uncle Biddolph, looking at Aunt Susan and lugubriously stroking his long moustache. 'I never thought him quite normal myself, even as a boy.'

'Be quiet, Biddolph!' snapped Aunt Susan. 'Please remember it's my brother you're speaking of.' She tossed her head, and her red face settled into grim lines, as if she were determined to regard that as the final answer. 'But still——'—she relaxed a little at the thought—'we have to bear in mind that he was ill in the last twelve months, otherwise I'm sure he would never have done such a thing. And what settles it to my mind is, he never gave instructions to the other solicitors to destroy the old will. He went furtively, just before he entered the nursing-home, to solicitors who didn't know him, and he didn't even tell them there was a long-standing will in existence. Now doesn't that look like a sudden whim—a mental aberration?' She sat back triumphantly. 'If the operation had been successful, he would have come to his senses, and we should never have heard of this new arrangement. For my part, he told me long ago what he intended to do for me. It was little enough, but he always behaved as if he expected gratitude, and of course I gave it. I can't think he took all those thanks under false pretences.'

Dr. Parmoor spoke in his soft deliberate voice, bowing a little over his cup of tea as he stirred it: 'But you know, Mrs. Biddolph, you really have no case. Mr. Ullstone took the precaution of getting protection against such a scheme.' He hissed the s's softly, and seemed to delight in choosing sibilant words. 'He got the best of all witnesses on his side in advance: Sir Frederick Lawton, a famous specialist in brain surgery. No, I don't think you have a leg to stand on there.' He gazed, smiling maliciously, down at Mrs. Biddolph's swollen ankles. 'You'll have to think of some other way.'

His look now turned on Ursula, and I saw then what I had not noticed before, that there was what is called an understanding between them. I wondered what she had seen in him, a soft-spoken, soft-handed, softly-smiling man of over forty. Clearly he would have the better bargain, provided he could afford her. And then I realized that up to a couple of weeks ago, she would have brought her own price with her. Now, she had a good deal less to offer, and she was still herself with all her extravagant tastes and love of excitement—unless, of course, they could get rid of Hugo.

'Oh, rot!' said Jim, swaggering. 'The thing is to throw the fellow out, and argue afterwards. What do you say? Shall I go now and tell him to clear out at once, or had I better wait till the morning?'

The small dark girl half-rose in her seat, and her hand went up in a gesture of protest, but no one seemed to be watching her except myself. She sank back into her seat, and the look of anxiety deepened into pain and fear; but she remained silent. I decided, as I had just decided over Ursula and Parmoor, that there was something between these two; but in this instance, I thought, it was genuine on one side at any rate: she must be in love with that little brute Jim, or else why did she watch him so anxiously?

I studied her more closely. She was not bad-looking: she had a rather thin face, with good features and dark blue eyes, and hair growing to a peak on her forehead. Her mouth was well-cut, and very expressive—more expressive even than her eyes. But it was her hands that gave her away: they fluttered about like frightened birds as she watched Jim and listened to his ridiculous boastings. She did not touch him—as if the birds were too frightened to alight anywhere—nor did she raise her hands to her face; but their movements, their hoverings between him and her, told of her anxiety more clearly than any words could have done. Jim, of course—the poor fool—ignored her.

A strange fancy crossed my mind: I thought, "That's just the sort of woman I would choose for Hugo. She would be devoted to him. They could go away somewhere, to some South Sea island perhaps, where the exact colour of your skin and your children's skins doesn't matter, and they could be happy." I decided that I would put this idea to Hugo some time—tactfully, of course. This was before I knew who she was or what was her name. I got the impression that she was a poor relation, perhaps because of the contrast between her and Ursula; and I could not believe that Jim Ullstone intended to marry her. Jim's future could be easily diagnosed, or so I thought: he would pass his time in riding and drinking and affairs with women, until he was about thirty-five and getting a little too fat and red in the face; then he would decide that the time had come to settle down, by which he would mean that he wanted a woman to look after him and to introduce some order into his life. He would choose what he considered to be a sensible woman, with money of her own, not extravagant, and somehow combining devotion to himself with an understanding of his peculiar ways, so that he could give himself a break sometimes and go off, leaving her to run the household and look after the children—for there would be children, two or three, whom she would bring up in all daily matters, while he made the major decisions regarding their destiny. Yes, I could see Jim, in fifteen years' time, a good-looking fellow still, but a little troubled with his digestion and his increasing weight. I could even hear his laugh, with a tremor of nervousness in it, as he consulted his doctor. Jim would always be one of those who exchange a suit of gold for a suit of brass.

Ursula was now talking: 'Don't be absurd, Jim! Hilary's right: we can't upset the will, with Sir Frederick against us. Of course, if he could be made to see—but I doubt it. No, my dears, I think we have only one course open to us: we must make a friend of Hugo. And then, when he has come to see our point of view, I'm sure he'll do something about it.' She clasped her hands together as if with a sudden impulse to be sincere: 'I *like* Hugo. I think he's a perfect dear. And I'm so glad, now he's come, that he's here. At first I naturally felt, like you, that it was a break-up of all we'd known and cared for. But now I feel it's simply providential that he has come right into our midst and given us a chance to know him and let him get to know us.' She turned sharply to her brother: 'I do think, Jim, you behaved very stupidly this afternoon. We ought all to be as nice as we can to him, and make him want to stay. So long as we have him with us——' She broke off, I think because she remembered that I was there, and said girlishly, 'What we should do is to find him a wife.'

'That's impossible,' snapped Jim. 'He won't get anyone here to marry him.'

'I'm not so sure,' said Ursula. 'He's very attractive, you know.

If we don't find him someone, he'll go back to Paris and——'
She shrugged her shoulders.

'But I say——!' said Uncle Biddolph dubiously towards Aunt
Susan, stroking his moustache.

'Be quiet, Biddolph!' snapped Aunt Susan again, as if he had
said, or were about to say, something improper. She added
sharply, 'Whom are you thinking of, Ursula? You obviously have
someone in mind.'

'Well,' said Ursula good-humouredly, 'as a matter of fact, I
was thinking of Evelyn.' She looked towards Evelyn, laughing,
and they all turned to stare at the small dark girl, who stared
back at them, motionless now, like an animal at bay, whose
only hope lies in absolute stillness. Even her hands had ceased
to move, and lay on her knees. Jim looked down at her, swaggering a little and twisting his small fair moustache:

'Well, Evelyn,' he said complacently and teasingly, 'what
about it? We've got to keep this property in the family, you
know. After all, you needn't—er——'

At that, Evelyn turned slowly and looked up at him. At
Ursula's suggestion, her face had turned a dark red. Now she
was pale again, paler than before, and in her eyes there was a
look of such bitter reproach that it silenced even Jim for a moment.
He recovered, though, after an embarrassed silence, and said
with a laugh: 'Think it over. But I still say my idea's the best—
throw him out first, and then contest the will.'

I had been staring so intently at Evelyn that I, like the others,
had not noticed the opening of the door. It was, in fact, the
change in Evelyn's expression that directed my attention to what
was going on behind us. She had withdrawn her reproachful gaze
from Jim, and was now looking past us all, with a new fear in her
eyes. I was the first to turn and see Hugo.

He stood looking on, with one hand, his left, in his pocket, and
the other balancing a small dagger which he had picked up from
the round table near the door. The expression on his face was of
one who wondered whether or not it was worth his while to deal
with his enemy now or later—whether he should, with an easy,
quick, contemptuous gesture, throw the thing at his enemy's
heart and have done with the matter, or whether perhaps it was
not worth the trouble and the disturbance. His face was very

pale, and he drew in his breath through his teeth, but his pose was nonchalant. A cold shiver ran down my spine as I wondered how much of the conversation he had heard. Before anyone could speak, he turned to Ursula with a quick movement that made her start:

'I gather that these too are my relatives,' he said in his clear pleasant English that made ours sound so slipshod. 'Won't you present me, please?'

He turned back to the round table, and carefully laid the small dagger back on its glass surface among the other knick-knacks. The silence was so profound that we heard the click of the steel on the glass as if it had been a pistol-shot. Then he came forward gracefully, still keeping his other hand in his pocket, as if he had something concealed there which he could and would use if necessary. He stopped inquiringly before the bulky figure of Aunt Susan, and bent down a little in an ironically polite bow. Ursula came to life with a jerk:

'This is Aunt Susan, Hugo,' she said brightly, 'our father's sister. And this is Uncle Biddolph.' There was no need to add "her husband." Biddolph's pose behind Aunt Susan's chair, and his obvious dependence on her, made their relationship clear. I admired Ursula's aplomb. I could imagine her describing the scene later to some of her friends and saying, 'My *dear*! I never was so embarrassed in all my *life*! But I had to do *some*thing!'

Aunt Susan, confused but inexorably hostile, bared her small white teeth in a grimace meant to take the place of a smile; her red face was a shade nearer purple. Hugo raised his black eye-brows as he looked down at her, like Debussy's fawn finding, on his afternoon's adventure, a large coarse deity in granite, and unable to believe his eyes. He did not speak, and neither did she; but the smile that curved the corners of his mouth was eloquent comment. Then he and Biddolph exchanged a stare, while Biddolph stroked his moustache at him; and Hugo moved on.

He stopped next in front of Dr. Parmoor. Parmoor blinked his eyes rapidly and cleared his throat. He would apparently have liked to say something hearty, but no words came. Hugo glanced inquiringly at Ursula:

'This is Dr. Parmoor—not a relative, just a friend. He looked after our father until he had to go away.'

Hugo gave Parmoor one of his searching looks. 'I should like to have a talk with you some time,' he said slowly. 'I am deeply interested in all that concerns—my father. I should greatly like to know more about him. I did not see him very often. But I loved him very much, and I find now, he must have loved me. I did not know this while he was alive. Perhaps he didn't know it either, until the end.' He gave Parmoor another long appraising look. 'Did *you* know he was going to die?'

Parmoor looked disconcerted. 'Well, no, I'm afraid I didn't,' he said. 'Cerebral tumours aren't easy to diagnose. The symptoms often look like mere psychological derangements. It takes a specialist——'

Hugo rounded suddenly on me: 'Would it have made any difference if it had been discovered earlier?'

'Don't be an ass,' I said irritably, annoyed at being made conspicuous among all these people. 'I've told you already, nothing could have been done, no matter when it was discovered, other than what was done. If you knew the first thing about medicine, you'd realize how difficult it is to spot such a thing at first.'

Hugo turned away. A grateful nod from Parmoor rewarded me. As Hugo approached the window-seat, Jim drew away from him to one side; but Hugo ignored him completely. Standing on the centre of the tiger-skin, he stopped in front of the small dark girl.

'*You* are a relative?' he said gently, and for the first time a real smile crossed his lips. Evelyn smiled back, and I was surprised to see that her eyes were full of tears.

'No, I don't think so,' she said, 'not exactly.' Her voice was what one expected, low and a little hesitant, as if she were seeking the right words, yet musical, and to my ears, then, the pleasantest of all those pleasant voices. 'My mother and Jim and Ursula's mother were sisters. So I'm their cousin. But I'm not really related to you.'

'Your name?' said Hugo. His eyes were fastened upon her with an almost hungry look, as if at last they had found something good to rest upon in this den of thieves.

'My name is Evelyn Ross,' she said, looking up at him with growing confidence, and with liking too, I could see.

'Evelyn—Ross.' He repeated the names softly, like a charm. 'And you are not a relative.' He bent forward suddenly with one of those graceful movements of his, and took her hand. 'I am so very glad to see you here. I hope you will stay a very long time.'

Again, Evelyn blushed a dark red. The blush spread down her throat, and mounted to her hair. 'You are very kind,' she said faintly.

The silence in the room was complete. We were all on tiptoe, because we simply did not know what Hugo would do next. It would not have surprised me if he had suddenly turned and clapped his hands and told us all to go. I shall never forget, as long as I live, the picture of those two gazing at each other, Hugo bending down from the waist as if he were about to invite her to dance, Evelyn looking up at him with parted lips as if half-eager, half-afraid. There was something alarming in the spectacle: it was too sudden, too unexpected, too unconventional, for the tempo of this house, like a scarlet cactus-flower bursting into bloom among a bed of primroses.

It was Jim Ullstone who broke the spell. He had been standing there scowling and pulling his small fair moustache, in undisguised rage. I had found time to glance at him, though nobody else was bothering, and I wondered when he would explode. Hugo was still holding one of Evelyn's hands when Jim said roughly:

'Come along, Evelyn—get ready.' He glared round at the company. 'We're going for a walk.'

Evelyn looked at him uncertainly, and then up at Hugo. She was, as I have said, rather thin-faced, and this gave her a pathetic, waifish air, like Cophetua's beggar-maid, and there were dark rings under her eyes; it was the kind of face that appeals to poets and painters, and perhaps to romantics generally, though to me it also suggested under-nourishment. But still, I thought as I watched her, it had a certain beauty, because the features were good, especially the clear-cut lips and chin, the fine nose and the high cheek-bones. Before she could answer, Hugo intervened, speaking only to her:

'Please don't go yet, Miss Evelyn Ross.' Again, it was startling to hear him use her full name. 'I should like to talk to you for a while.' He sat down beside her on the window-seat, and prepared to devote himself to her to the exclusion of the rest of us. As for her, she too seemed to have forgotten us; her glance fluttered away from Jim, and she turned to Hugo with that look of expectancy which he had roused in her from the first, and gave him her whole attention, while we all stared as if a miracle were happening under our eyes.

Jim said chokingly, 'Aren't you coming, Evelyn?' But there was uncertainty in his voice now, as well as rage—uncertainty and a vast surprise.

Evelyn smiled. 'No, thank you, Jim, I don't think I will,' she said in her pleasant, soft voice, 'not this evening.'

Jim gave them a last savage glance, and made his way out of the room, almost kicking the furniture as he went. Hugo and Evelyn, their faces close together, talked on softly. We all turned our backs on them—it seemed only decent—but I knew that however hard we talked, we were all trying to overhear the conversation of those two on the window-seat. I myself couldn't help pricking an ear whenever the gaps in our conversation allowed. But I could catch no words, only a low murmuring, and once or twice I heard Evelyn laugh. It was a musical laugh, and it was surprising, because she did not look like one to whom laughing came easily. When those laughs came through to us, I saw Ursula glance at Parmoor, and Parmoor with raised eyebrows return the look, while Aunt Susan sniffed loudly and Uncle Biddolph cleared his throat. At last, when we were all completely distracted with our efforts to hear, and our talk had reduced itself to jerky sentences separated by longer and longer silences, the two on the window-seat rose and made their way to the door. They took no notice of us. Shortly afterwards, we saw them pass the windows, walking along the gravel path towards the shrubbery, and disappear among the rhododendrons. He was much taller than she, and he was leaning over her solicitously; she was gazing ahead with the rapt expression of a Rossetti heroine, and listening.

We all watched them till they were out of sight.

8

Aunt Susan, followed by Biddolph, had waddled off to take

yet another of her between-meal rests. Ursula, Parmoor and I were left together.

'Well,' I said to Ursula, 'your plan for Hugo's future looks like succeeding rather more quickly than you expected.'

Ursula turned to me with even more than her usual vehemence: 'My dear! Wasn't it amazing? Evelyn of all people—such a quiet little thing! Of course I was only joking! I didn't mean a word of it! You see, Evelyn is so devoted to Jim——'

'Is she?' I said rather maliciously.

'Well, she was, until now,' insisted Ursula. 'Wasn't she, Hilary?'

Parmoor nodded. Ursula turned back to me.

'I keep forgetting you don't really know about us, Jake,' she said in her most winning tones. 'You seem to be so much one of us already.'

'Does Evelyn live here?' I asked, my curiosity now thoroughly roused. I suppose, at that time, I was already feeling what is called a transferred interest in Evelyn: Hugo's *empressement* had communicated itself to me, until I scarcely knew which were my feelings and which were his. I had even felt a twinge of jealousy, I had to acknowledge, as they had moved off together towards the rhododendrons.

'Yes, she still does,' said Ursula, 'though really I think it's time she began to think of leaving. But the trouble is, she has nowhere to go to.'

'She's your cousin on the mother's side, isn't she?' I said.

Ursula said quickly: 'She isn't really even that. She's an adopted child—adopted by my mother's sister when she, Evelyn I mean, was about fourteen. My aunt couldn't leave her a penny —she married a man who ran through all her money—and so Evelyn has been homeless since my aunt died a couple of years ago. So when my father began to get ill, it seemed a splendid idea to get Evelyn to come and look after him. I mean, I really couldn't cope with him myself, you know: we never did get on frightfully well together. He had all sorts of old-fashioned ideas about daughters, and I'm no good at playing companion and nurse. Evelyn was used to it: she had nursed my aunt through her last illness——'

'Poor Evelyn!' I murmured.

'—And we thought that my aunt would leave her comfortably well off, and Evelyn thought so too. Well, so she did, on paper; but when her affairs came to be straightened out, it was found that there wasn't a bean even to pay the debts. So Evelyn took a job of some kind, I forget what. She seems to have been very unhappy in it. She was very glad to come here to a comfortable home and comparatively easy work. And it answered very well at first, didn't it, Hilary? My father took to her at once, and of course it relieved me of all anxiety.'

'Yes—yes,' said Dr. Parmoor meditatively. 'I think she made most of his last year of life quite happy. He came to rely on her a good deal. She's the sort of girl one *would* come to rely on, if one needed companionship and sympathy.'

'Oh, you men!' cried Ursula. 'You love these modest violets, don't you? Evelyn is the sort of girl that gives me hives, if you must know: she simply cuts the ground from under our feet.' She laughed. 'I know I sound an awful cat, but I must say I think they have a pretty good idea of what they're doing, you know; but you simpletons can never see it. Myself, I soon noticed that Daddy was coming to rely on her too much altogether: for a time, it was clear he thought of marrying her. Think of that! But then that phase passed. I suppose he saw it would be going too far to marry a third time, and moreover, a girl of the same age as his daughter. Of course we didn't know about Hugo's mother then; but he did, and so perhaps he thought he had gone often enough to the well.' She laughed again. 'Actually, what put a stop to the idea was that Jim cut him out.'

'Oh!' I said. Again, I felt a twinge of jealousy. 'So your little Evelyn had to choose between father and son, as in Turgeniev. But she preferred the son, it appears.'

Parmoor said sibilantly, 'The scheme was yours, Ursula, wasn't it?—though I know Evelyn wasn't averse.'

I turned on Ursula in disgust: 'You surely don't mean to say you planned to use your brother to get Evelyn away from your father? By jove, I think that was going rather far!'

Ursula gave her high, pleasant laugh. 'My dear child! Where have you lived? Naturally I didn't want a step-mother—least of all Evelyn Ross. What do you take me for? I think I was perfectly justified. My mother would have turned in her grave at the idea.

Anyone would have felt as I did about it, though not everybody would have been frank. I acted for the best—for everybody's best in the long run——'

I cut her short: 'Well, what happened? Evelyn fell for your brother, I gather. What about him? What did he feel about it all?'

'Well,' said Ursula doubtfully, 'I never was quite sure about Jim. He always assured me that he wasn't serious, but sometimes I wondered. So did you, Hilary, didn't you?'

'I certainly did,' said Hilary.

'But the one thing we hadn't counted on,' pursued Ursula, 'was Daddy's reaction. You see, he was in an extremely nervous irritable condition already, because of his illness, though we didn't then know what was wrong. He couldn't bear to be thwarted in any way; and he always was very perceptive and quick. Somehow he got to know of our plan; and he never forgave us. It was from that time onward that he grew so very much worse—wasn't it, Hilary?'

Hilary nodded agreement.

'He began to have storms of weeping and sudden rages,' went on Ursula. 'As for Jim and me, he developed an absolute phobia towards us. He was always gentle and docile, comparatively, with Evelyn, though he bore her a grudge too, I think, and one could see that he had dropped all idea of marrying her. But with Jim and me—especially me—he was rabid. There were some terrible scenes—weren't there, Hilary?—in which he called me everything. He also said he wished he had never come back to England, but had stayed all his life out there. I didn't then know what he was thinking of—what pleasant little revenge he was planning—because I didn't know of Hugo's existence. I daresay I should have acted differently if I had known.'

'My dear, you had no choice,' interposed Hilary. 'If you had done nothing, he would have married Evelyn, and you might have had another little half-brother on the way by now.'

'Oh dear!' said Ursula, half-sighing, half-laughing. 'Life is so complicated sometimes, isn't it?' She turned to Hilary: 'You know, darling, now that Jake is so far in our confidence, I think we might as well tell him the rest.' She took Hilary's stout arm and folded her two slender hands over it: 'Hilary and I intend to get married as soon as he's free,' she said.

45

I glanced at Parmoor: he looked far from pleased at the revelation, but he took it with as good a grace as he could. 'My dear,' he said mildly, 'aren't you a little too proud of your frankness sometimes? Doesn't it strike you that Jake, for instance, may not be quite as much interested in our affairs as you assume?'

'Oh, not at all!' I said, no less awkwardly than ambiguously. Ursula went on unheeding:

'And that was another thing that made Daddy furious. I told you he was horribly perceptive. He knew perfectly well what was happening between Hilary and me, and it made him—well, I suppose one could say, jealous. Hilary was his doctor, and he wanted all Hilary's attention for himself and his illness. He used to get impatient if Hilary didn't call every day at least once and often twice; and he objected if Hilary stopped to talk to me too long on the way up. I suppose,' she went on meditatively, 'he wanted us *all* to dance attendance on his illness, as if it were some heathen god that had to be propitiated. And then again, he didn't believe in divorce. He had very strict views on marriage, as you see from his own history. So I was completely out of favour. And Jim—well, poor Jim had never been much in favour. Daddy and he never did get on very well. And he disliked all our friends. And so between us, Jim and I threw him into the arms of Hugo, who wasn't even a name to us. It was bad luck, wasn't it? Or perhaps you don't think so?'

Her tone was mocking, and I could see that she thought I would be a prig if I saw anything odd in her conduct. So I merely made a non-committal sound, and said:

'Do I gather you aren't altogether pleased with the way things are shaping now?'

'Oh, I don't know,' said Ursula, wrinkling up her smooth forehead. 'What I really think is that Hugo shouldn't get married at all.'

'That's what he thinks himself,' I said quietly, 'or so he says.'

'Does he really?' Ursula seized on this with avidity. 'Then don't you think you could——'

I interrupted: 'No, I don't! I think it's entirely his business, and that of the girl he wants to marry. I wouldn't dream of interfering.'

Ursula was persistent: 'But don't you think that for Evelyn's sake, one could point out to him——?'

I was beginning to be exasperated. 'I tell you I'll say nothing.' I almost shouted. 'Up till this afternoon I'd never seen him. Up till yesterday I had never seen any of you. Why the devil should you expect *me* to go sticking my fingers in the fire? He'd knock my teeth down my throat, and with good reason too! If you want anything said to him, why don't you say it yourself?'

Ursula's smile was undaunted. 'I will,' she said. 'Thank you very much for having shown me the right lines to go upon.'

Before I could protest, she had hurried out of the room, leaving Parmoor and me very much disconcerted.

'I say,' I asked him anxiously, 'you don't think she will, do you? Hugo might take it rather badly if she started preaching to him about duty and so on. What *is* her idea, do you know at all?'

Parmoor blinked his brown eyes with the yellow sclerotics, and passed a heavy white hand over his square chin. He looked wretched. 'Ursula intrigues,' he said, 'for the sake of intriguing. I don't think she always quite knows herself what exactly is the point of her different moves. She ought to be the ruler of one of the Balkan states. Her objective is clear enough: she wants what we all want—to keep the good things we've got, and get as many more as we can.'

'Did her father really want to marry Evelyn?' I said.

He sighed. 'I don't know. I suppose so.'

'Is Evelyn engaged to be married to Jim?'

For the first time, he gave me a shrewd, sharp look; but his answer was still guarded: 'I don't know. I don't think so. Jim's rather a difficult lad, you know. He's the kind of chap who wants what other men want, and cools off when he gets his own way. I think perhaps the hesitation, or apparent hesitation, may not have been wholly on his side. And now—well, I'm afraid there'll be trouble, between him and this fellow Hugo. Jim is like his father in that he hates to be crossed.' He shook his head gravely Then he gave me another sharp look from under his brows: 'It was rather indiscreet of Ursula to tell you what she did—about her and me.' He paused, and added in lower tones, 'Especially as that is by no means the whole story.' He looked up again at me: 'I hope I can rely on you not to let it go further.'

I nodded, embarrassed. 'Are you in practice here?' I asked, to change the subject.

'Well——' He looked down again. 'I have a practice in Chode. But I'm afraid I've neglected it lately. I gave a good deal of time to Ursula's father. And since he died'—he gave a self-conscious laugh—'I might almost be said to live here.' His self-confidence seemed to have oozed out of him as he talked. Then he pulled himself together with an effort, and laid a powerful hand on my arm: 'It's a mistake, my boy. I wish I could get away. But then, all my life has been one big mistake—and it hasn't ended yet.'

He gave another deep sigh. His breath was heavy with stale smoke and the effects of too-frequent tots of whisky. I withdrew a step.

'Why don't you get back into harness?' I said, not too sympathetically. 'It's a dog's life without work.'

'I know, I know,' he said. 'Easy for you to talk: you're young. I'm not so old as all that—but I'm bone lazy. I wasn't always—but—well, I've frittered away everything, my knowledge, my skill, my will-power. I've still got my health—but for how long?' His large hands went to his head. 'I daren't take my blood-pressure. I've got noises in my ears. Sometimes I feel as if my head were bursting. But I don't do anything about it. I don't diet, I don't take exercise, I don't stop smoking and drinking. I just sit about here and play cards and rot a little more every day. And yet I was quite good at my job once. My God, how I envy you!'

I didn't know what to say, I suppose because anything I could have said would merely have confirmed him in his despair—for I didn't honestly see any hope for him. What made it all the more hopeless was that he spoke quite quietly; he didn't rant or rave. I had met such men already, and I have met many more since; nine-tenths of them can't be cured, because they don't want to be. Their disease is a disease of the will, just as real as if it were their spleen or their lungs that were attacked by a deep-seated inoperable malignancy. It's all the same to them whether you try to brace or try to soothe: whether you sympathize or remonstrate. They can do all that for themselves—they see themselves quite clearly—but it makes no difference. They cannot alter, and if you could hand them a prescription, a magic formula, that would lead to a cure, they wouldn't take it. That's their tragedy.

'And now,' he said with a smile, 'I'm going to get a drink. Would you care to join me? No, I thought not. I won't try to persuade you.' He came close to me again. 'Do you know the one thing I regret above all?—that I didn't spot that cerebral tumour. It was pretty obvious, really. And I'll tell you something else: I shall never marry Ursula. Poor girl, it's a lucky escape for her. I think she's genuinely fond of me, heaven knows why. But that's because she's never seen anybody else she could like. Actually my wife would never divorce me, and she'll almost certainly outlive me.' His hands went to his head again. 'I wish I had the courage to take my blood-pressure.'

'Shall I take it for you?' I said. I was officious in those days.

'No, no, my boy,' he said hastily. 'If I knew what it was, I'd probably shoot myself. We'd all probably shoot ourselves if we knew what unpleasant surprises our physical mechanism had in store for us.' He patted my arm. 'Good luck, and long life to you, and don't be afraid to use me as a warning. Like that, I might do some good after all, like the fellows who leave their cadavers to hospitals and medical schools.'

He went off, leaving me marvelling: then, I thought, it's not enough to know oneself? But I could do nothing for him. I went back to the window and looked out, towards the long dark line of rhododendrons, blazing with clusters of pearl, amethyst and ruby. No one was in sight.

9

I spent the time before dinner in the billiard-room alone, knocking balls about the table. I have read somewhere that Mozart used to do this when he was working out something in his mind, and I have always found it a good idea. It's an odd fact that in order to concentrate on a problem, one must have also some minor activity that keeps the superfluous bits of one's intelligence from straying and dragging the rest of one's attention with it. So as I watched the red and white balls rolling so slowly and steadily over the green surface, my thoughts took a dive into the depths of my mind.

The inner voice that said, "What business is all this of yours?" was growing fainter and fainter. I told myself that I could not possibly leave here until Sir Frederick Lawton returned. But the truth was that any slight inclination I might have had, any remaining notion of leaving, had been finally annulled by the sight of Hugo and Evelyn walking away together towards the rhododendrons. The picture was sharp and clear; and somehow I didn't like it. In so far as I asked myself why, I got several answers: for instance, that Hugo should not be so sudden in his actions, that he ought not to show his preferences in that blatant way: it was not fair to Evelyn, especially since he had declared that he was determined never to marry. It was wrong of him, I assured myself, to take her from Jim, who might marry her; and certainly it was foolish to make an enemy of Jim, who already had such good reason to resent his coming. Further, Hugo ought to pay a little more attention to Ursula: after all, she was his half-sister, and she might take it rather ill that almost as soon as he had arrived, he had singled out and was paying marked court to a girl whom Ursula regarded as a poor relation, and a rather dangerous one at that. Doubtless Ursula exaggerated about Evelyn, as women do when their personal interest, especially their prestige, is involved; but all the same, there might be something in her view that Evelyn had had designs on her father—for clearly that was what Ursula thought, though she hadn't said so openly.

Ursula's hostility to Evelyn was understandable, I thought. The balls rolled about the table, cannoning gently and doing all the odd things that billiard-balls do when you set them moving, looking almost as if they moved with purpose and of their own volition. Ursula saw in Evelyn a girl outwardly much less interesting and attractive than herself, and yet with the power to win men in key positions in Ursula's life: first her father, then her brother, and now the new master of her childhood's home. True, Ursula had—or thought she had—the man she loved—or thought she loved; but might that not be one of the reasons why she was so much concerned at what was happening? Parmoor wouldn't be able to support her unless he changed his course, which he seemed incapable of beginning to do; and he would be an impossible luxury on her future income of three hundred a year.

Yes, I could see why Ursula feared Evelyn—Evelyn, who

seemed always to be looming up as the mistress-designate of her home. I didn't blame Evelyn: I thought it probable that, like most of us, she was mostly a victim of circumstances; but I wished to blame someone for something that I disliked and disapproved of; so I concentrated on Hugo. It seemed to me that he ought to have shown more tact; and since I was here to look after him, it was my place to tell him so, as gently and firmly as possible, for his own sake above all.

When I went down to dinner, I felt considerably cheered and braced by this resolve; but as soon as I entered the dining-room, I realized that Hugo and Evelyn were not there. The party looked glum, all except Ursula, who talked as brightly as usual, but, I thought, with an edge to her voice. As for the others, they made no attempt to support her. Jim ate his dinner in silence, answering in monosyllables only when Ursula spoke to him. Parmoor, having by now thoroughly saturated his system with half-hourly doses of alcohol, was sunk in his usual evening mood of muzzy gloom, which would lift a little when the food and the coffee had had their effect. Aunt Susan, fiery-red with indigestion and lack of exercise, grumbled about the food while eating heartily; Biddolph stroked his long moustaches between the courses and watched her with doleful apprehension. After the soup had been removed, Aunt Susan said harshly:

'What has happened to the young man? Did he decide to have his dinner upstairs? It's going to make a great deal of work, Ursula. The servants won't like it. They don't like extra journeys up and down stairs, especially in these times.' She ran her glance round the table at us, and her green eyes rested for a moment on me with sow-like hostility; then she passed on, fixing them on Jim:

'What's the matter with Evelyn this evening?' she said. 'Has she got another of her headaches? I shouldn't wonder. You went too far with her this afternoon, Jim. Not that I approve of your marrying that girl: she's got no character, and her health isn't good enough.'

Jim glanced up at her from his plate as if he would have liked to empty the contents over her head. He was as red in the face as she was, but, being young, he could take it better than she. Ursula interposed:

'I think Hugo and Evelyn have gone into Chode for dinner.

They have taken the car. I hope Hugo can drive. I'm afraid Jenkins will be furious when he finds out: the car will be muddy, and Jenkins had washed it and put it away. He hates anyone else to touch it.' She rattled on.

So that was it! They had gone off together. I didn't know why, but I too felt a wave of resentment. I suppose I felt that he ought to have told me, ought even to have asked me to join them; for hadn't I been his only friend just now, when he arrived in this house that hated him? I bolted my food, and excusing myself as soon as I could, went off and left the party to their long dull evening of bridge and grumbling.

10

I ran up the wide staircase, taking the shallow steps two or three at a time. There was still a chance that Hugo might be in his own room by now. At any rate, I felt impelled to find out. I tapped at the door: there was no answer. Cautiously I opened it and looked in. There was no sound, nobody in the sitting-room. I could not investigate further, of course, but by now I did not need to. I was convinced that the rooms were empty.

I closed the door softly again, and crossed the landing to my own room. My impatience had mounted to an extreme irritation; I could not rid myself of the feeling that Hugo had done me a personal injury in going off for the evening with this girl. I wondered if I should kill time by going off somewhere myself in my own car; but the independence which yesterday had seemed so precious had now turned tedious, and I could not face the prospect of a long drive through the country lanes alone. I would have liked, if I had dared, to go into the town myself and look for them, perhaps join them for coffee and a drink after their meal; there weren't many places in Chode where they could have gone, and I could easily find them. But a moment's thought convinced me that dignity must come first.

I paced about my large room, unable to read or write. I had left my door ajar, so that I could hear when they returned. At last, when it was quite dark, I heard a car drive up, and car doors slamming; and after a while, I heard voices and laughter as Hugo and Evelyn came up the stairs.

52

I could not see them. I did not try. But I knew by their tones that they were still engrossed in each other, and that the evening they had spent together had been more than satisfactory. There was now a new confidence in Evelyn's voice and in her low laugh as she answered something Hugo said to her; and I knew exactly how he looked as he walked beside her, bending a little towards her, enveloping her with that feeling women love, of being treated like a queen. It was his way. He had learnt it in Paris, no doubt, and it would be bound to go to the head of a girl like that, used to taking last place everywhere. My moral indignation mounted: if things went on like this, I thought, I would have to warn her too.

They stopped outside his door, and I heard him asking her, in his gentle, considerate, infinitely caressing and flattering tones, whether she wouldn't come in for a moment and talk. She refused. She must surely have shaken her head, for I did not hear her say "no"; but I heard her say, 'It has been a lovely evening,' and I knew from the pause that followed that he was gazing at her, holding her hand.

'Well, good night then,' he said with a sigh, and she whispered back, 'Good night.'

I heard his door close; and I opened my own door and stepped into the corridor just in time to see her turn the corner at the far end. She looked appealing and pathetic, walking down the long corridor alone; and I had an impulse to run after her. But next moment she was out of sight.

I stepped across and knocked at Hugo's door.

11

'Come in!' he called.

I entered. He was in high good humour, I could see that. He was humming to himself, and pacing lightly about, and his whole being radiated happiness. He looked so handsome and gay, and somehow so disarming, that my resolve to give him a lecture momentarily faded. But I pulled myself together, and began:

'Where did you get to? You might have told me you wouldn't be in to dinner.'

'My dear fellow!' Hugo stared at me, half-annoyed, half-amused. 'What on earth had it got to do with you?'

'Oh, nothing, of course,' I said, still absorbed in a resentment which wasn't lessened by the fact that I could not give it rational expression. 'But don't you think it was rather cool of you to go off like that on your very first evening here, without a word to anybody, even your hostess?'

'My hostess?' Hugo gave me a queer sidelong look. 'Is that how you see her?'

'Oh, of course, actually she's your guest, I know,' I said impatiently, nettled by the absurdity of my position, but unable to get out of it, and still determined to convey displeasure to Hugo. 'You needn't labour the point. But you can't expect her to see things like that so soon after your advent. It's just flaunting your position in their faces to behave like that. They know you're their master, without your telling them. And besides, you needn't drag that girl into it. She was almost a dependant of theirs until you came. And now you're making them *her* enemies, too.'

Hugo crossed the room slowly towards me, and stood in front of me with his head on one side, and with that deep questioning look in his eyes which meant that he was paying me his most special attention.

'Ah!' he said with maddening certainty. 'I see! So you too have noticed Evelyn Ross, and she interests you. You are more perceptive than I gave you credit for—though of course you arrived before I did, and so you have had more time. You know, my friend, you should examine your motives more closely before you begin interfering in other men's affairs, especially if you want to be a doctor. A physician must at least be sound himself, if he is to heal others.'

His tone was offensively patronizing and cool. I tried to keep my temper, but I felt myself going red to the roots of my hair. Hugo drew a thin gold cigarette case out of his breast pocket. I noticed the monogram H. U., and the fine chasing of the background. He flicked it open and held it out to me. I waved it aside. He took one of the oval cigarettes and lit it, and the pleasant, aromatic smell of some oriental blend of tobacco reached my nostrils. Smiling, he waited for my answer; and when I said nothing, he began again, with the same maddening assurance:

'It's no use your standing there like a bull waiting to gore me,' he said. 'The truth is, you are jealous. Evelyn Ross is just the kind of girl you like, the sort that knows when to speak and when to be silent, and how to make you feel, while you're with her, that you're the only person in her life. You would like just such a woman for yourself, my friend, though you don't admit it. So you followed us all evening in your mind.'

'I don't know what you're talking about,' I said. 'I've no time to think about women—not with a view to marriage, anyway. I'm not even qualified yet. It'll be years before I can keep a wife. But fortunately I know it. What I can't understand is how you, having vowed you won't marry anyone, can lead a girl on like that and take her away from someone who wants her. Do you think that's fair? I don't.'

Hugo walked to the great fireplace, flicked his cigarette ash into it, and stood looking down, as if studying the plaster-work with its grim hanging figures.

'Spare yourself the trouble of protecting her from me,' he said sombrely. 'I shall tell her the whole truth about myself, if necessary. Perhaps I have done so, already. In any case, it doesn't matter. I shall not be here for very long.'

'What!' I said, astonished, and very much taken aback, for I knew that when he left my own reason for being there would cease to exist. 'But you said earlier on that you intended to stay. What on earth has made you change your mind?'

He smiled enigmatically, and obviously rather pleased at my bewilderment. 'I'm afraid I have deceived you,' he said. 'It is quite a harmless deception. You will understand it all quite soon, if you care to. Meanwhile, Miss Evelyn Ross is quite safe from me. I believe she regards herself as pledged to Jim Ullstone, blackguard as he is. But she is a girl of strong loyalties. Still, if *you* can make her change her mind, go ahead. It's every man for himself in such matters.'

I opened my mouth to protest at the absurd idea, but no words came. As I stood staring at him where he leaned against the plaster-work of the fireplace, suddenly everything shifted a little: his face seemed to grow longer and more pointed, the dark hair seemed to recede, the smile to widen and the eyebrows to take an upward tilt. The very figures in the relief behind him, grotesque as they were and already seeming to dance in mid-air, came to life and jerked as if at the end of ropes for a brief few seconds. Then all grew normal again: Hugo became himself, and the dancing figures ceased to move.

I left him, and went back to my room and to bed. There I was a prey to nightmares, in which Hugo retreated with Evelyn Ross into a forest, where the branches were laden with grinning monkeys and figures that hung on the end of ropes, and I tried vainly to stop them; but my voice was strangled in my throat, and my feet were rooted to the ground.

12

Next morning a typewritten envelope lay on my plate at breakfast. There was a similar one for Ursula. They were both from Sir Frederick Lawton, and were to let us know that he had decided to come down again that day. I don't know what he said to her; but in his letter to me he said that he hoped I would be there to meet him: he had, after all, decided that he would come back and see how the land lay. He was greatly obliged to me for having given up my time. The note was polite; but it read somewhat like a dismissal, and I was not altogether pleased. Ursula was delighted, and hurried off to make arrangements.

After breakfast, I strolled out into the garden. The sun was shining brilliantly, the birds were singing, and all nature seemed swept and washed clean. I took a path that led away from the dark shrubbery towards some stone steps leading down to the lily-ponds. The wind blew freshly through my hair; and as I looked back at the dark old house, I thought again how dead it looked—only half-inhabited, if at all. If I were wise, I knew I would walk straight to the garages, take out my little car, and hurry away without a backward glance, leaving this strange adventure behind me. But I was caught.

As I went down the stone steps towards the pools, where the goldfish swam beneath the great dark leaves, I saw Evelyn Ross coming along the stone path towards me. She was gazing at the ground, and did not see me; her hair was tossed by the wind.

My heart gave a great leap: suddenly I knew that Hugo had been right: it was she who was keeping me here. It was not transferred interest: it was love. It had not been moral indignation, but jealousy, just as he said, which had moved me to wait for them both the evening before, to speak to him as I had done, and to lay myself open to his mockery. I remembered then, in a flash, how he had told me that one either loves at once or not at all; and I knew that of all the people in that apparently crowded drawing-room two nights ago, when I had blundered in as an intruder, the one who had really made the deepest impression on me was the one who had said nothing, who had watched in the background.

She came on. She might have been reading her future destiny in the square mossy flag-stones of the path, so absorbed was she. When she came so close to me that my shadow fell under her eyes, she looked up with a start, and I saw with dismay that her first reaction to me was fear. One of her hands fluttered to her throat, and her breath came faster.

'Oh!' she gasped, 'I'm so sorry! I thought I was alone.'

I gave a rather forced laugh: 'Anyone would think you were planning some deep-laid scheme,' I said facetiously. 'Even so, you needn't be afraid of me. I won't give you away.'

She managed to smile. I could see that she wished me to go and leave her alone with her thoughts; but I could not bring myself to do so. I stood there in her path, blocking the way, wondering what it was about her that had captivated us all, first Jim's father, then Jim, then Hugo, and now me. I did not think her beautiful, and I had no reason to think her intelligent either, since I had heard her speak only a few commonplace words. Nevertheless, as she faced me and waited patiently for me to move out of her way, I felt shaken to the depths by a sensation new to me, and—yes, very disagreeable. Before, my passing fancies had been light and easy to deal with. This, I recognized, was going to give me trouble. Still, I had sufficient sense left to realize that she must not be allowed to know how she was affecting me. I didn't believe that one should let people know they had power over one: nobody, man or woman, could be trusted so far. I therefore wiped the expression off my face, and gave myself up to retrieving my position. I hoped that she had noticed nothing. There had, actually, been almost nothing to see; but from the outset I gave Evelyn credit for preternatural powers of perception.

I looked at my wrist-watch, which is always a good move when one is embarrassed. 'I wonder when Sir Frederick will arrive,' I said casually. 'He is coming down again to-day after all. I expect you know.'

A look of slight worry crossed her brow. 'Yes, so Ursula told me,' she said in that low voice which so unaccountably stirred me. 'I'm glad.'

'Why?' I asked her, rather more eagerly than I had intended; but I could not keep the interest wholly out of my voice.

'Oh, I don't know,' she said, looking down. 'I suppose——'— she spoke with a slight hesitation between the words which made one hang on her lips—'it's because he gives one confidence.'

'Yes, doesn't he?' I said. I was as delighted with this quite ordinary remark as if the Sibyl of Cumæ had uttered it from the depths of her cave. 'He's a wonderful man.'

'You didn't know him before?' she said, with a smile at my enthusiasm.

'No, but my brother knows him and has worked under him. My brother says he's more than a great surgeon—he's a great man. He has a unique interest in people. Well, his present behaviour shows that, doesn't it?' I rattled on. 'He doesn't know Hugo Ullstone, but he's taking an interest in him just to fulfil a promise to a dead man.'

Evelyn gazed past me, beyond the low walls of the sunken garden to the blue hills just visible in the distance between the trees. There was an expression in her eyes that made me wish I hadn't spoken so cheerfully and so directly. I had forgotten for the moment that Hugo's father might have meant a good deal to her for a time. I laid a hand on her arm. It gave me an electric thrill in my finger-tips to touch her, but my manner was perfect.

'Look,' I said, 'come and sit down here on this seat and tell me what's bothering you. I can see you've got something on your mind.' My tone was avuncular, and she let me lead her to the moss-grown stone seat in the wall facing one of the pools. I took a newspaper out of my pocket, I remember, and spread it out for her to sit on, thinking that the seat was rather hard and cold, and that she wouldn't like to sit on the moss and perhaps stain her frock.

'Now, come on,' I said, turning to look at her. 'Tell me what's worrying you. I'm a stranger—an onlooker—here to-day and gone to-morrow. You can talk to me.'

She turned and stared at me for a long time, so long that I had time to study carefully and at close quarters the way her dark wavy hair grew in a peak off her forehead, and, finally, to look into her dark blue eyes. At last she said:

'There's nothing you can do about it.'

'How do you know,' I said, 'unless you tell me?'

It was her turn to lay a hand on my arm. 'Surely *you* don't need to be told,' she said. 'You can see.'

'You mean,' I said, flattered by her belief in my perception, 'there's trouble brewing between Hugo and Jim.'

She nodded, biting her lip. Suddenly her words came fast and breathlessly: 'You think it's my fault, no doubt. But I don't do anything. I don't *do* anything. Things just happen to me. It's always the same. My life may seem to be going smoothly—I keep out of the way—I float along with the current, content if I can avoid being seen; and then, all of a sudden, I find myself caught up in a whirlpool once again.' Her smooth pale forehead became creased horizontally in lines of anxiety and bewilderment: 'If only I could escape! If only I could escape!'

I looked at her, my heart beating furiously. I longed above all things to say, "*I* can give you escape. Come with me and we'll get married and I'll look after you for the rest of my life.' And for a moment I nearly did say it. What restrained me was not the knowledge that if I said those words I wrecked my career—I gave up all hopes of the profession I had chosen and hitherto had desired beyond everything in the world, disappointed my family and my friends, and probably prepared for myself a life of uncongenial work and a disillusioned old age; no, what restrained me was the conviction that that was not what she wanted me to say, that I should merely be inviting an astonished and chilling rebuff. After all, vanity is sometimes stronger even than love, whatever we may like to believe. So I grasped a lump of my hair in my hand, and pulled it so hard that it hurt, and said instead:

'Well, go on: tell me about it.'

She brooded for a while in silence, her eyes fixed on the green pointed buds of the water-lilies. 'Yes,' she said. 'I need someone to talk to. You're right. It should be Ursula—but Ursula hates me. Whatever I do or say, she misunderstands. And you know'— she turned back to me with one of those confiding movements that I found so endearing—'I can't live in an atmosphere of misunderstanding.'

'Then why don't you leave?' I said gently. 'Surely there's no reason why you should be subjected to—well, what amounts almost to persecution, if one's sensitive. Mind you, I think you take Ursula too seriously. She strikes me as capricious and flippant and full of wild-cat ideas—but not a hater. Still, I've only been here a couple of days, so perhaps I shouldn't attempt to judge.'

'I don't take her too seriously,' she said sombrely. 'But I can't leave, because she won't let me.'

'Won't let you?' I said, astonished. 'But you just said she hated you! And how could she keep you, anyway, if you really wanted to go?'

Evelyn gave a little laugh. 'How simple you are!' she said, but without scorn. 'It was Ursula who brought me here to nurse her father, because she didn't want the trouble—didn't want to have to bother with *his* caprices and demands. Well, I came and did my best, as I always do wherever I'm placed. I've been brought up to do as I was asked, without question or complaint. In the end, you know, one gets that one doesn't mind. But you're a man. You could never understand that.'

'No,' said I with a shudder.

'Then,' went on Evelyn with a subdued bitterness that grew more intense with every word, 'when I had done all they asked, and he had come to depend on me—as might have been expected—they decided that this would never do, either. Or rather it was Ursula who decided, and she talked Jim into it. One can talk Jim into anything—except decency and commonsense. So there I was, in the whirlpool again, with their father beseeching me to marry him, and Jim and Ursula working away at their little plot. As if I didn't see through it from the first! As if I weren't driven almost mad myself by——' She buried her face in her hands.

'Poor girl!' I murmured. I longed to stroke her smooth dark hair, but I dared not. Her weakness lasted for a moment only. She looked up, paler than before, but calm and resolute.

'James Ullstone told me all his secrets,' she said. 'He laid bare his whole life to me. I listened. I knew about the existence of Hugo. I knew the danger Ursula and Jim were running by treating their father as they did. I knew that Ursula in particular was incurring his furious anger by her behaviour with Dr. Parmoor, which she flaunted in his face. I tried to warn her. All I succeeded in doing was to bring suspicion on myself. She accused *me* of influencing her father against her. Actually I tried to influence him the other way—Oh, what's the use of trying to explain?' She crushed her long white fingers together, and pressed her hands to her breast. 'Nobody will ever understand.'

She got up, and went to the edge of the lily-pond, where she stood looking down into the shallow green water; the stout goldfish came to the surface, expecting to be fed, but she saw nothing of what was before her eyes, of that I was sure. I too got up, and, following her, put my arm round her shoulders; this, I knew, she could not mind, since it was done solely out of sympathy and the desire to console. She looked up at me, her eyes swimming with tears:

'You see,' she said in low broken tones, 'James Ullstone saw through their scheme, too—Ursula's and Jim's, I mean. I did my best to prevent him from seeing—but he was too quick. He saw that Jim was beginning to—take notice of me. And he was furious. Everything affected him that way. He flew into violent rages about nothing, and when there was something real, he became murderous. We realized afterwards that it was his illness, but we didn't know this at the time. And so when I, in all innocence, went on trying to reason with him, to plead with him not to disinherit them in favour of Hugo, he just thought that I was in the plot too. He thought I cared about the legacy because —because I wanted to marry Jim.'

She turned, and pressed her forehead against my breast-pocket; and I remember thinking at the time, as I gazed across the pond to the distant hills, that she might find the hard things— pens and so on—in the pocket rather uncomfortable. One does think such absurd things at such moments. But I did not dare to move. I said:

'And didn't you?'

She looked up at me: 'Oh no! I never wanted to marry Jim. I was—I am—very fond of him. I think he needs someone to look after him, to restrain him. But I was never in love with him. What happened was—something quite different from what he and Ursula planned. *He* fell in love with *me*.'

My thoughts whirled. I could not remember exactly what I had been told by the others, though I knew that the general impression was that Evelyn was devoted to Jim, whereas he wanted her only when somebody else did. Still, doubtless that was merely Ursula's version and could be discounted. What I did remember clearly was what Hugo had told me the previous evening: "she regards herself as still pledged to Jim." Was he too just talking to put me off the scent? Or had Evelyn herself told him this, in self-defence? Or was it true? I longed to ask her, but I didn't want to let her know that Hugo and I had been discussing her. So I said cautiously:

'That's the sort of thing that often happens. You're not bound to bother your head about that.'

She moved away, out of reach of my encircling arm. 'You don't understand,' she said unhappily. 'What *I* feel doesn't come into it. What Jim wants, he thinks he must have. And he thinks he has a claim on me. He accuses me of having led him to believe that I cared about him. He says that if I desert him, he doesn't care what happens to him.'

'Oh, rot!' I began angrily. 'Naturally he says that to you. He knows he can play on your feelings. It's a well-known gambit, that. You needn't pay any heed to it. He'll go to the dogs, anyway, with or without you, in my opinion.'

She interrupted me quietly. 'Perhaps you're right. But that's not what concerns me now. You don't know Jim. I do. And it's not his threats against himself that are worrying me now: it's his threats against—other people.'

'Hugo?' I said sharply.

She nodded. 'He—Jim—came to my room last night. I had been out to dinner with Hugo. Jim was lying in wait for me when I came home. He threatens that unless Hugo leaves this house within a few days, he will—I don't know what, but I'm afraid, terribly afraid. Jim is like his father in many ways: he's subject to the most uncontrollable rages, and if he and Hugo met when things were like that with him, I'm afraid—I'm afraid, as much *for* Jim as *of* him.' She looked up at me, her eyes wide with fear. Somehow I found myself at her side again, my arm round her. I patted her gently, while she went on:

'To-night, while I was with Hugo, I talked to him about things here. He asked me to, you understand: he asked me my opinion. He was most gentle and sweet. I told him frankly that I thought he oughtn't to stay. He agreed. And I think he was rather relieved to be able to agree. I think now he would go—will go, unless something happens to make him change his mind.'

'You mean,' I said, 'if he meets Jim, and Jim makes it impossible for him to go by ordering him to, or something equally offensive?'

'By threats,' said Evelyn. 'Hugo will certainly not go if anyone threatens. And oh, he should, for the sake of his own happiness—this peace of mind he's always talking about!'

Again, I wanted to ask, 'And will you go with him?' but I did not dare. A hope was beginning to spring up in my mind that perhaps she was no more in love with Hugo than with Jim: that she had gone with Hugo out of sympathy and a desire to help. After all, it was he who had made a dead set at her; she had said and done nothing except agree, and what else could she have done without being unkind?

'Well,' I said to her, 'the thing is to keep them apart as far as possible, and hope for the best. I'll certainly do my best to persuade Hugo to go, now that I know the true situation; and what's more, I'll try to get Sir Frederick to use his influence that way. But Hugo's a very tricky customer. If he thinks we're all trying to move him one way, he'll certainly dig his heels in. In fact, the best thing would be if we could bring ourselves to persuade him to stay. But I'm no good at acting—are you?'

She shook her head. A tear fell on my coat, but she was smiling now.

'Ursula wants him to stay,' she said. 'Perhaps we can leave that part of it to her,'

Slowly we walked back to the house together: Evelyn said she had things to attend to indoors. We mounted the five shallow stone steps from the lily-ponds, and crossed the lawn still sparkling with dew. As we walked, I became aware, with a thrill of sus-prise, that Evelyn had laid her hand in the crook of my arm. We must have looked as if we were still deep in intimate con-versation, though neither of us said another word.

I left her at one of the side doors, and walked towards the garages, which were part of the stables. I was still thinking of Evelyn and what she had told me as I crossed the flagged court-yard, and I did not become aware that I was being watched until I heard a scuffle of horse's hooves behind me. I turned to see Jim, mounted on the tall bay mare which was his favourite.

He had a good seat on horseback, as one might expect since he had spent most of his life there; but I thought, not for the first time, that the rider looked inferior to the animal he rode. I walked on, ignoring him, towards the garage where my little car was housed; and I was greatly surprised when I heard his horse's hooves coming up close behind me. He passed me, and drew up in front of me, using unnecessary strength on the reins, and causing the good-tempered animal to swerve and buck a little. Jim himself was red in the face with fury; his voice was so thick that I could not at first make out what he was saying. Painfully I came out of my dream to realize that I was being violently attacked and insulted. I gathered that I was a cad and a vagrant, and that the sooner I removed myself, the better for me: if I didn't, he would call the police. Further, if he saw me so much as address a word to Miss Evelyn Ross in future, he would flay the skin off my back.

All this left me not so much angry as amazed: amazed that a fellow of the same age as myself, speaking the same language and belonging to the same race, could behave in such a way—in a way impossible to me and therefore almost beyond my compre-hension. He did not seem to see how absurd he was: that was what occurred to me as I watched him perched up there on his fine mare, looking so arrogant and small, wanting, without the smallest justification, to have his own way in everything. I really couldn't think of anything to say in answer; and while I stood staring at him and marvelling, he did a thing of which I wouldn't have thought even him capable: he leaned across the neck of his mount, and with a back-handed movement dealt me a stinging blow across the face with his riding-crop. Before I had recovered my balance, or even fully felt the pain, he had given his mare a smart kick in the ribs and had dashed away, with a clatter of hooves, through the gateway of the courtyard.

I went on thoughtfully to the garage, fingering the weal that had risen immediately on my cheeks and the bridge of my nose. When I was able to examine it in the driving-mirror, I was gratified to see that it was a fine angry colour, red on the cheekbones and purple on the nose.

'This,' I thought, 'will take some explaining away,' and I wondered what Evelyn Ross would have to say about it; for however hard I tried to deceive her and the others, I knew that she at any rate would guess what had happened, and why.

14

Sir Frederick arrived that afternoon.

I didn't see him on his arrival, because I had taken my car out into the country for a long run. Away from the atmosphere of that great house, which seemed cut off from the world by its miles of encircling wall, I began to recover my balance a little and to see things in perspective. I might even have forgotten the intrusive affairs of this family I hardly knew, if I had not been reminded of them by the painful weal across my face. Again I thought, it might be better if I never returned; but honour— whatever that may mean—insisted that I should not run away now that I had been struck a physical blow, and also I felt that I could not let Evelyn down. I could not bear to think of her counting on me, however little, and waiting for me, and realizing at last that I had deserted her. So I enjoyed my drive through the country lanes, under the great overarching elm trees, past meadows of buttercup and sorrel, across close-cropped moorland along an open undulating road; but in the end, when my speedometer had ticked off fifty miles or so, I turned the nose of my little car, back to the drive gates with the monkeys on the gate-posts. As I passed through, I had the sensation of something's closing in behind me; and it would not have surprised me if I had turned to see those two groups of stone monkeys grinning at me behind my back.

By now it was early evening; and there was just time for me to get ready for dinner, so that I went straight up to my room, and saw nobody. I didn't know whom Sir Frederick had seen or talked to before my arrival; but over dinner he seemed his usual bland, serene self, untroubled by any problems. Of course, to a man of his standing, such problems hardly counted: he had much more important things to think about, I thought, as I watched him blandly eyeing the dessert nuts through his eye-glass and selecting the best. I wondered how his first encounter with Hugo had gone off; it was not possible to tell, since Hugo had seated himself beside Evelyn and they were absorbed in conversation, to the exclusion of the rest of us. Sir Frederick talked to Ursula, to Hilary, even to Biddolph and Aunt Susan, and ignored Hugo, Evelyn and me. Jim was not there.

After dinner, Sir Frederick, as I had expected he would, took me by the elbow and led me away to the library as before. When he had sat down and crossed his legs and folded his hands and smiled at me, he said:

'That's a nasty mark you have on your face. How did you come by that?'

Nobody so far had asked me this; but I had my story ready.

'A branch hit me in the face while I was driving through one of the lanes,' I said. 'It's nothing.'

Sir Frederick accepted that with a nod. 'Well, be more careful in future,' he said. 'You might get it in a more vital spot next time.' But his tone was bantering, and I could not tell whether he knew the truth or not, though I suspected that he did. 'And now'—he leaned forward and gave me a quizzical look from under his grey eyebrows—'I have a piece of information for you which will surprise you. But first I must have from you your word of honour that you won't reveal it to anyone until I say you may.'

I gave my word. I was proud that he thought fit to trust me.

66

'It is this,' he went on, speaking softly though distinctly. 'The young man who arrived here yesterday is no more Hugo Ullstone than you are.'

'Good God!' I said; and as the conventional exclamation of surprise crossed my lips, I realized that I was not nearly as surprised as I might have been expected to be: 'Who is he, then?'

'He's a young man, half-English, half-French, with a liking for adventure—or at least, for practical joking—and a very pretty gift for acting. His parents are rich and fashionable. They think he is here on a visit, to improve his English. If they find out the truth, there will be a big row: I gather his father is a very unaccommodating man, and his temper has been sorely tried already by the escapades of——' He hesitated, and I asked eagerly:

'What is his name? I can't imagine a name that would fit him better than Hugo.'

'His name is Marcel—Marcel de Souvigny. But you must go on calling him Hugo, of course. He'll answer to it: he has thought himself so thoroughly into the part that he'll find it hard to get back into his own skin again. As a matter of fact, one of the things that annoyed his father was that he was far too much interested in the stage—not as an onlooker, nor as a connoisseur of actresses—that's allowed—but as an artist, a performer. He actually deputised for someone on the stage in one of Paris's more experimental theatres, and did very well until his father got wind of it and forbade him to go near the place on pain of six months' exile in the family château. So you see, he's a lad of parts, and his passion for acting has found another outlet.'

Sir Frederick threw back his head and laughed quietly, dangling his monocle on its black ribbon and watching the effect of all this on me. I did not know whether to be shocked or amused; really, I was rather shocked, I suppose; but I wanted to be convinced that it was all right, and Sir Frederick's manner was reassuring. I looked at him in growing wonder and admiration.

'How on earth did you find out all this?' I said.

Sir Frederick brushed an invisible speck off his knee. 'Well,' he drawled, 'when I realized what I'd let myself in for by my promise to poor Ullstone, it occurred to me that I ought to inform myself a little more precisely on the subject of my promise. So, as I had friends in Paris, I asked them to find out what they could for me about the young man, his activities, his companions, and so on. No news had come through when I left home to be here to meet Hugo. Then, on the evening of your arrival, I got a telephone call from my secretary to say that the dossier had come, and she thought I ought to see it at once. Her tone was so odd—and she's a sensible girl, not given to hysterics—that I thought I had better do as she suggested. She plainly didn't want to send it on here. I must confess I was curious. Then I had the excellent notion of asking you to take up the post of observer while I was away. You very kindly agreed.'

He smiled benevolently at me, and I thought, what would I have said if I had known he was going back merely to open a letter, not to perform a brilliant and life-saving operation? And I knew that, confronted with the same smile, I would have "very kindly agreed."

'Thanks to you,' he went on, 'I was able to leave that evening. I read the documents sent to me by my friends in Paris. They had gone further than I had intended—they had employed a private detective.' His look of deprecation was a pleasure to witness. 'The result—these people are very conscientious: they really do earn their livings, the best of them—the result was a thesis, not only on Hugo but on everything and everyone connected with him. There was two hours' solid reading for me, and when I'd finished, I knew about his flat, his clothes, his car, his employees, his hobbies, his exact physical appearance and his friends. There were photographs of Hugo himself and others of those mentioned; among them, one of Marcel. There was also Marcel's biography. I took particular interest in this because my informant said that Hugo had left Paris for England in the company of this Marcel, who was described as his greatest friend. Of course, I had no suspicion—I could not possibly know—that the two had decided to change rôles. Still, I thought it best to come back and see for myself how things were going, as well as relieve you. I arrived here this afternoon—and I was confronted, not with Hugo Ullstone, but with his friend Marcel, who acted his part with the greatest aplomb and had obviously been accepted by everybody. Now I ask myself'—he pointed his eyeglass at me—'what can be the meaning of all this? Is it just a joke, arranged between the two of them, or is it something more? I must confess, I don't yet see any plausible answer. But an answer is certainly called for; and I propose to stay here for a few days and see if I can work it out for myself without disturbing anybody too much. A pity there should be a scandal in such a pleasant family—and I don't want to make things too unpleasant for this young man Marcel, either, unless it's unavoidable. I liked him, didn't you?'

'Yes, I did, very much,' said I. But I was cast down and chagrined at the knowledge that I had been deceived, just like the others. I needed time to sort out my impressions, to reconsider my feelings for Hugo—for Marcel, that is—in the light of this revelation. To think that I had imagined he needed my protection! One hates to have one's chivalry—the best that is in one—taken advantage of, because one knows one won't be so chivalrous next time.

I began to remember some of the things he had said to me. I could hear him saying, the evening before, 'I'm afraid I have deceived you. It is a harmless deception. You will understand it all quite soon, if you care to.' I had thought that odd at the time, but my head had been too full of him and Evelyn to take in any special significance of his words. Evelyn! I sat up abruptly. Sir Frederick was watching me—dangling his monocle, and smiling.

'So *our* Hugo—Marcel, that is—isn't of mixed blood after all?' I said.

'No.'

'And he's not related to any of these people?'

'Not in the least.'

'Good heavens!' I said, really staggered this time at the thought of his duplicity. 'You should have seen the act he put on, of devotion to his father!—of hostility to *you*, Sir Frederick, because the operation hadn't been successful. I had to defend the whole profession against what I thought were his oriental ideas. And to think it meant nothing at all!'

Sir Frederick shook his head. 'I wouldn't go so far as that,' he said gravely. 'Our young friend was acting—but he was acting *a part,* you know—a character not invented by himself. You may be pretty sure that what you witnessed was a faithful representation of the true Hugo's feelings and opinions.'

'Yes,' I said, relaxing. 'I suppose so. But—he went a good deal beyond his part in some respects.' I was thinking of him walking away with Evelyn Ross towards the shrubbery—the way he had commandeered her at the outset. That was Marcel, not Hugo: Marcel would always make a bee-line for any presentable woman. And of course, it had to be Evelyn, not Ursula, though Ursula was, one could not deny it, the more obviously attractive: for wasn't Ursula supposed to be his half-sister? Naturally he wouldn't dare to look at her, even. My thoughts ran on:

'Where is the real Hugo now, sir?'

'In London, I presume,' said Sir Frederick. 'Naturally I lost track of him as soon as he set foot on the Channel boat. My friends' instructions to their private detective ended there, and I had made no arrangements for this side. I take it that he will wait quietly there till Marcel joins him, and reports. Then he will decide what to do. Oh,' said Sir Frederick, crossing and recrossing his long legs, 'I don't suspect either of the young men of any criminal intent. I imagine that Hugo Ullstone was chary of putting his own head into the family den, and so he just sent his friend instead. It's a joke in very questionable taste. Still, one sees his point of view. And Marcel too—no doubt he's merely doing it to please Hugo, and from a sense of adventure. One can't see what he stands to gain by it.'

'He can do a good deal of mischief while it lasts,' I grumbled; but Sir Frederick did not seem to hear. He got up:

'Well! We must join the others. Just keep your eyes and ears open, and say nothing.'

'Like the three monkeys,' I said with a grin.

'Like *one* of the monkeys,' corrected Sir Frederick. 'The other two were deaf and blind. I think you and I should be on the alert until we are sure there's no foul play intended. Probably it will all solve itself quite naturally. Marcel will leave after a few days, and rejoin Hugo. Hugo will realize that he can never make his home here. They will both return to Paris—and no one will ever be the wiser.'

He spoke soothingly, almost as if I were an anxious patient, and he were laying my well-founded fears to rest. Somehow I could not believe that it would happen as he said; and I did not think that he believed it either. I noticed that there was no question of his sending me off as if I had accomplished the task set and could go free now that he was there. He obviously counted on my staying.

I followed him across the thick-carpeted floor. I too was anxious to get back to the drawing-room, to the others—to Marcel, and Evelyn. Sir Frederick pulled open the heavy door with its great curtain, and at once the silence was broken for us: from the drawing-room came sounds of a piano, and singing, and talk and laughter.

15

I shall never forget the evening that followed. There are such evenings—days—even weeks—in one's life that have this special quality; and they give one a sort of confidence in the universe, that it is not a mockery based on despair, but that somewhere behind the curtain of habit and routine, boredom and disappointment and frustration and falsity, there is happiness. I know I thought, as I looked on, as I took part, "Why can't one always live like this?" and yet I would have found it hard to say what "like this" meant, even at the time; and now I only know that it was so—I can't say why or how.

When Sir Frederick and I walked into the room, we saw Marcel sitting at the grand piano. He was singing *Sur le Pont d'Avignon*, in the manner of Jean Sablon, and he had his head thrown back, and he seemed to laugh as he sang. There was a light, laughing quality in his voice that completely carried his audience away: even Aunt Susan had relaxed and was smiling and tapping with her foot, and Uncle Biddolph was looking perfectly fatuous with enjoyment, leaning over the back of her chair and stroking his moustache, like an Edwardian buck at the music-hall. Ursula was standing beside Marcel with her hand on his shoulder, and she too had utterly forgotten everything but the moment: legacies, parents, unwanted half-brothers, marriage-prospects, everything but the picture Marcel was conjuring up before her, of grave little girls and grave little boys who *font comme ça,* on the bridge of Avignon. . . . In another moment, I thought, she will break into song and dance herself.

I glanced at Hilary to see how he was taking it. He was leaning against the mantelpiece smoking a cigar, and looking on quite perceptively but with indulgence. The only two who were not joining in were Jim and Evelyn. They were both sitting on the settee, but far apart, one in each corner. He was looking at her, miserably and angrily, and she was ignoring him; but I could see that his nearness and his concentration on her embarrassed her. She looked pale, and when I came in, she raised her eyes to mine with a glance which I interpreted as supplicatory. But I could do nothing just then: if I had tried to interfere, there would have been another scene, and I couldn't bear to introduce such a discord into the harmony. I felt a warm satisfaction, though, at the knowledge that it was to me she looked for help, already.

Marcel, seated at the piano, had his back to her and could see nothing. He had, in fact, temporarily forgotten her. Ursula had gone round to the other side of the piano now, and they were laughing across at each other, quite absorbed. In fact, Ursula was singing with him now: '*Les messieurs font comme—ça*'; and off they went again in the refrain: '*Sur le pont d'Avignon, l'on y danse, l'on y danse.*' . . . They finished in a burst of laughter, and with many runs and chords on the piano from Marcel; and there was applause, led by Sir Frederick, and cries of '*encore!*' Marcel played the opening bars of *Au Clair de la Lune*, and instantly our mood changed.

He sang it through, by himself this time, with intense feeling. Ursula watched him, but she did not attempt to join in. From where I was standing, I could see both of them; and as his clear, insistent, pleading tenor voice uttered those so-well-known words, I saw the change in Ursula's expression go deeper, from seriousness to tenderness, to pity. He was addressing himself to her, and she could not do other than respond. "What woman could?" I thought. "Marcel is irresistible when he chooses; and he's no longer bothering to keep to his rôle. What's going to happen now? Ursula thinks he's her half-brother; but he isn't, and he knows it. He no longer cares to pretend. Yesterday evening was the pretence—his paying court to Evelyn Ross. Or does he just pass from one conquest to another?" I wondered, ought I to suggest to Sir Frederick that Ursula should be let into the secret quite soon? Or would it perhaps be better and wiser to leave her in ignorance?—"*Ouvre-moi ta porte, pour l'amour de Dieu.*" It sounded heartrending; he had the whole room hushed to a holy silence—the young humbug, I thought.

At the end, he looked down for a moment at the keyboard, and then, as if anxious to dispel the emotions he had invoked, he broke into a dance-tune. Ursula clapped her hands: 'Oh, let's dance!' she cried. 'Hilary darling, roll back the carpet!' In a few minutes, the floor was cleared. 'Oh, but,' said Ursula, standing in the centre of the polished floor, 'we *must* have Hugo. He can't be the pianist! Can anybody else play?' She looked doubtfully at me. I shook my head.

'You can,' said Jim spitefully to her from his corner.

'Yes, dear, but I'm not going to. Hilary! Open up the gramophone and get out some records. You can attend to the music, can't you, darling?'

Hilary, grunting but amiable, did as he was told. Ursula turned and looked at Marcel, and he obediently left his piano-stool and came towards her. In a moment they were circling round the room together, to the tune of one of those older, better dance-tunes: *Time on my Hands*, I think it was.

I looked towards the settee. I saw Jim make a movement towards Evelyn, and I saw her turn a frightened look on him and shake her head. I fancied she drew away from him, further into her corner. Jim looked down at the floor between his feet; then he jerked himself up and made for the door, narrowly missing a collision with Marcel and Ursula. Nobody bothered about his going. I crossed the floor to Evelyn: she looked up timidly, with a smile; and soon we too were circling round. I held her close; she didn't seem to mind. I wasn't a very good dancer; but I avoided any complicated movements, and Evelyn was so small and light and so responsive that I managed much better than usual. I wondered if Evelyn minded that it was I and not "Hugo" who was her partner; but if she did, she gave no sign.

Hilary changed the record for a slow waltz; at that, even Aunt Susan and Biddolph gave way and joined us in their own

73

more stately measure. We others made no attempt to change partners: nobody wanted to, and this was an evening, apparently, when one could do as one wanted and get away with it. I said to Evelyn, 'Are you happy?'

She nodded, and raising her dark-blue eyes—those eyes with the look of fear somewhere in their depths—she said in a whisper, 'Jim did that to you, didn't he?'

'Did what?' I said. I had forgotten the weal on my face. It had ceased to smart unless one touched it, and I had forgotten how conspicuous it must be.

'Your face—he struck you,' she said, her brow creased horizontally with worry.

'Oh, it was nothing,' I said, gratified by her concern and only too anxious to display my magnanimity. 'I don't suppose he meant to spoil my beauty. I ought to have got out of the way.'

Evelyn shook her head: 'He is so violent—so uncontrolled! He frightens me. I hate violence.'

I looked down at her, amazed at the vehemence of her tones. 'How did you know?' I said.

'I saw it all. After I left you, I passed him, and I turned back, thinking he might do something violent and perhaps I might be able to stop him. But I was too late. He had struck and gone before I could reach you. So I went away.'

'Tell me,' I said, 'do you still regard yourself as in any way bound to him?'

She looked down. 'Not now.'

'Because you hate violence?'

'Because I won't be forced. He has gone too far this time.'

'You mean,' I said incredulously, 'in hitting me?'

'That,' she said, 'and other things.'

I braced myself for another act of courage. 'Tell me another thing,' I said—and the effort of asking caused me to stop propelling her round the floor, so that we stood still, facing each other and holding hands: 'Are you interested in—Hugo?'

She stared at me in an amazement that I thought exaggerated; but she did not look angry. She looked—the word forced itself on me again—scared. 'What makes you think so?' she countered.

'Oh, I don't know: your going off with him last night—and some of the things you said this morning.'

74

'I'm interested in his safety. I would be in anyone's.' We were still standing in the same spot, and I became aware that we were getting in the way of the other dancers. I guided Evelyn to the settee.

'In mine?' I said, as I took my place beside her.

'Of course,' Her response was instant, but I was aware that I had taken the wrong line in asking that. She wasn't interested. Her mind had been running on quite other lines. Or was it that she wasn't yet prepared to be appropriated by anyone else, including me?

'Well,' I said, somewhat chagrined by this discovery, when I had thought I was getting on so well, 'at any rate, Jim can't object to Hugo's dancing with his own half-sister.' And I cast her a sharp sidelong look to see how she took this; but she answered gloomily:

'Jim objects to everything. He objects to Hugo's very existence.'

With that, the conversation somehow came to a dead end. I sat there with her on the settee for a while; but the *tête-à-tête* was definitely over. "Strange little creature!" I thought. "Her attention has now left me completely. I wonder why. Have I said something to offend her?" But she didn't look offended: she just looked preoccupied.

Presently, when one of the records ended, Sir Frederick crossed the room purposefully and claimed Ursula; Marcel, left alone, came towards the settee. He looked quite serene and not at all conscious of having neglected Evelyn; I expected her to accede at once to his request that she would dance with him. But she did not. She excused herself on the ground that she must go and see about something to do with the house; and then she went away. Marcel and I were left alone on the settee.

He did not seem to want to talk; and I felt too much burdened with my new knowledge about him to begin any ordinary conversation; so after a minute or two, I went over and joined Hilary Parmoor at the gramophone. It was evidently the moment he had been waiting for: very soon I found myself taking over from him while he went off to get a glass of whisky. . . . Record followed record. Half an hour later, I was still there. Sir Frederick, now, was dancing with Evelyn, who had returned; and Ursula and Marcel were together again. It seemed to me that I was trapped in this corner for the rest of the evening. It was rather hard. True, I was not the world's best dancer; but I ventured to think that Evelyn would be better off in my arms than in Sir Frederick's. . . . However, there was no help for it. I went on, playing record after record at random from the pile. At last I found myself watching Evelyn telling Sir Frederick that she would not dance again: she felt tired, and would say good night. . . . Sir Frederick opened the door for her, and bowed. Hilary was standing in the doorway, glass in hand.

'Excuse me,' I said hastily to the company, and went after Evelyn.

16

Evelyn had moved so quickly up the stairs and along the corridor that she had almost reached the turning to her own room when I caught up with her. When she heard me running, she turned, and the look she gave me was so alarmed as to be almost angry. Her hand went up to her throat. Her brow was furrowed, and in her throat I could see the carotid pulse beating.

'I'm awfully sorry, Evelyn,' I began; but before I could apologize further, her expression changed—melted; and she smiled.

'It's all right, Jake,' she said, still a little breathless. I could not remember having heard her use my name before, and I was delighted. 'I didn't know it was you. What's the matter? Have I left something behind?'

I realized what had scared her: she must have thought that it was Jim who was pursuing her. 'Not some*thing*,' I said playfully, 'some*body*. You forgot to say good night to *me*.'

This time I did not get the feeling that I had made a mistake in referring to myself. On the contrary, her next step surprised me. She came forward, put her two hands on the lapels of my coat, and looked up at me. Startled, I leaned down and gave her the kiss she seemed to be granting me. I did not make a good job of it. I forgot even to put my arms round her, and the result was more a peck than the kind of kiss one dreams of oneself as giving—the kind that sweeps away all doubts and hesitations and so forth.

76

'Good night, Jake,' she said, completely in control of herself; and I gasped out, 'Good night, Evelyn,' and turned and ran away, back to my own room. I could not face the others again yet. I had to think. Mingled with my elation were a number of queries, such as: "What do I do now? Is that equivalent to a proposal?" and I seemed to hear my father's voice saying, "Will she make a good doctor's wife, my boy? You can't run a profitable practice with the wrong wife, you know." I had always thought him a callous old brute for thinking of marriage in those terms, though my brother said he was right; but now, I found myself, in spite of myself, measuring Evelyn up against that standard. The answer to the question was, yes, I thought she would. A still more pertinent question was perhaps, would she wait another three years for me to qualify, and another three before I could afford to keep her? Would we both feel the same by then?

With my mind in such a turmoil, though I found it hard to go back to the drawing-room, I found it harder still to stay alone in my room. I wished I could have a talk with Marcel: I felt he understood much better than I did about all these things, and would advise me.

But when at last I did go down—when I opened the drawing-room door—instead of music and laughter, there was silence. The gramophone was closed, the piano too. Everyone had gone—or so I thought at first—although the carpet was still rolled back and the furniture still stood against the walls. Where had they all gone to? Aunt Susan and Uncle Biddolph to bed, no doubt, after their unaccustomed exercise; Sir Frederick to the library for a smoke and a read. And Ursula and Marcel? Oh, that was easy: they had gone for a walk—to admire the moonlight. Well, there was nothing against it, I supposed. . . .

And then I saw that the only member of the party left behind was Hilary. He sat in one of the deep chairs with his eyes shut and his feet stretched out and his glass on the floor beside him; his hands were gripped tightly across his broad chest. I did not know whether he was really asleep or not; but evidently he wished me to think so, for as I stood there he breathed out a long sigh as of somnolent content.

I closed the door softly, and went away.

PART TWO

I

THE body of Hugo Ullstone—the real Hugo—was found lying in the shrubbery next morning.

It was I who found him. After a restless night, in which terror at my commitment with Evelyn—if it was a commitment—was mingled with a determination to go through with it, I got up and dressed as soon as it was light, and tiptoed along the corridor, and down the stairs, and out into the open air. I was not ordinarily an early riser at that time—eight o'clock and morning tea was my idea of how to begin the day—and now, at half-past five, the world seemed strange to me, strange and exciting, though a little forbidding. There was nobody about the house, and I had to undo the chain on the heavy front door to get out. The lawns were white with dew that looked like hoar frost, but the air was mild. The birds, with their incredible morning uproar, had the place to themselves.

I walked along, bareheaded and feeling like an intruder, but pleased with myself for having made the effort. I looked back at the house. With its blinds drawn, it looked uninhabited: like Maud's lover, I "knew that the death-white curtain meant but sleep. Yet I shuddered and thought like a fool of the sleep of death." I had no special purpose; I did not consciously choose my direction. I shall never know what made me take the path towards the shrubbery, rather than that to the lily-pond, or that to the road. By the time I reached the shrubbery, the noisier birds had changed their excitable chatterings for rarer and quieter converse, but the blackbird was fluting loudly above them all. The huge rhododendrons that flanked the wide path closed in over my head. I had not known that they could grow to so great a height.

It was under one of the rhododendrons that I found him, beside and just off the main path. I saw the soles of a man's shoes sticking out from underneath the bush, and I thought for a moment that it must be a tramp or a poacher; but the shoes were patent leather, and the legs were clothed in trousers of an excellent dark material, well-creased and neither worn nor muddy so far as could be seen.

I drew near cautiously and parted the long branches. He was lying on his face, with the right hand gripping a handful of leaves in the death-agony, and the left arm doubled up under his face, so that the forehead rested on the back of his wrist. I saw the back of a clean white soft collar, and I noticed the stud, and the way the coat-collar revealed it because of the position in which he had fallen and because the coat was buttoned up in front. I saw the rounded, rather dusky yellow cheek, and the thick black straight hair. I touched the temple with my finger-tip, but I knew already that this man was dead, and had been dead for hours. I waited no longer, but hurried back to the house, pushed open the outer door which I had left ajar, and the inner door, and ran up the stairs to Sir Frederick's room, which was next but one to Marcel's.

He came at once when I tapped. I stepped inside. He still looked dignified, I was glad to see, even in pyjamas; his hair was a little ruffled, but less than other people's, and he had already slipped on a dressing-gown and picked up his eyeglass.

'There's a dead man in the shrubbery,' I said. I was somewhat breathless through running, but quite calm now that there was a prospect of something to do.

'Who is it?' said Sir Frederick, perfectly wide awake.

'I don't know,' I said. 'Nobody in this house.'

Sir Frederick gave a nod, presumably of relief.

'But I have a hunch,' I went on, 'that it may be somebody who—well, sir, would you mind getting dressed and coming along? It's absolutely essential that you should have a look at him first.'

'*I* can't do anything for him now, my boy,' said Sir Frederick. 'He's beyond our ministrations, lucky fellow, if your observation is correct.' He gave me a sharp look, and saw that I was not in any doubt. 'Right! Just wait outside, and I'll be with you in three minutes.'

It can't have been many seconds longer than three minutes when he joined me, looking completely dressed except for the white silk muffler round his throat in place of collar and tie. I was waiting for him in the hall, on tenterhooks lest the household should wake before we got away. But nothing stirred. I let him out through the doors, and we set off together in the direction I indicated. He asked me no more questions as we walked along. It was getting lighter, and the birds were almost silent; even the blackbird had ceased to call.

We came to the place, and Sir Frederick stooped over the body. I was going to do the same, but he motioned me away. 'Don't disturb the ground too much,' he said. 'Keep on the path till I tell you, and then step where I've stepped.'

He passed his hands lightly over the head and back. I saw his finger stop over a small hole in the coat, just beneath the right shoulder-blade.

'Shot,' he said, 'shot in the back, but not at very close quarters, I think—though that will be for the police to say. Now, Seaborne, I'm going to move this body so as to get a good look at the face. There's no danger, really: the *rigor* is such that we can easily replace him in the same position exactly. But all the same, it's against the text-book, and you'd better forget you saw me do this, unless I tell you otherwise.'

I nodded. I had now taken in a good deal more about the body than on my first hasty inspection. I had confirmed my first impression that it was the body of a young man, rather short— about five feet six, I would say—and very well rounded; the head rather large, the hands and feet small; the clothes neat, dark, expensive, but with a continental cut; a ring on each hand, one of them a ruby solitaire that looked valuable: evidently robbery wasn't the motive, unless the hands were too plump to enable the killer to get the rings off easily. My eyes came back to the feet: the patent leather shoes, the black silk socks with maroon-coloured clocks. . . . And now Sir Frederick was carefully levering the stiffened cadaver over on to its side. It was a strange sight, not to be lightly witnessed even by those accustomed to the handling of corpses, and to a layman it would have been quite horrifying. . . . For a moment, he studied the face; then he gently let the body sink back into its former position, face downwards.

'Yes,' he said, getting up and brushing his knees, to which a few damp leaves still clung. 'There's no doubt about it: it's Hugo Ullstone. Poor fellow! How right his father was to be worried about him! What on earth is he doing here? You knew it was he?'

'I guessed it,' I said. 'I'd never seen him, nor even his photo. You know him from his photo, sir, I suppose?'

Sir Frederick drew out a wallet from his inner breast pocket, and took out a typewritten card on which a small photograph was pasted. I preferred looking at this to looking at the face now pressed once again on to the damp ground. It was the same face, though—of that there could be no doubt. It was a round, rather large face with big solemn dark eyes, and cheeks so fat that they hung down a little and gave him a sulky, cherubic air; it was the face of someone temperamental, spoilt, and with a grievance—but fundamentally likeable and pathetic. What he needed most in the world was affection, kindness, one would say; and the world is a very hard place, even for the most fortunate. . . . I handed the photograph back, and Sir Frederick restored it carefully to its place.

'Well,' he said, 'the next thing is to notify the police; and then we must break it quickly to the family, before the police arrive.'

We turned away together, and I was glad when in a moment or two we emerged from that gloomy little wood on to the open pathway across the lawns. The sun was now well above the horizon, casting its pale beams into our eyes.

'He looks younger than his age, doesn't he, sir?' I ventured as we walked towards the house. 'Your card says he was twenty-four last February; and yet, looking at him, one would take him to be younger than Jim and Ursula.'

'Yes,' agreed Sir Frederick. 'That lad hadn't come to maturity. Perhaps he never would have done so.' He echoed something of what I had been thinking: 'The world was too hard a place for such as he. Perhaps he's better out of it.'

'Even with all that money?' I said.

'Perhaps because of all that money,' said Sir Frederick grimly. 'Do you realize just how many people stand to gain by his—removal?'

I glanced at him, startled; but there was something in his expression that warned me not to ask any more. We reached the steps leading up to the porch. He paused, with one foot on the bottom step, and looked down at me, while I waited like an obedient student for my instructions.

'Leave the police to me,' he said, 'and when they come, answer their questions promptly and directly, but don't volunteer more than they ask and don't offer your own conjectures or opinions. Tell the exact truth about your own reason for being here: say you stayed here to oblige me. I shall confirm everything.'

I nodded.

'While I am telephoning the police,' he said, 'you must go and break the news to the others. You had better begin with Marcel among the men. As for the women, Ursula must be told as soon as possible. She will take it well, I'm sure: no need to be afraid of hysterics in *her*.'

'Oh, but—sir——' I protested agonizedly, 'I hardly know her! How can I go and knock her up in her room with a piece of news like that?'

'Well then,' said Sir Frederick impatiently, 'get one of the other women—the housekeeper, perhaps—or what about Miss Ross? You seemed to be getting on very well with *her* last night. She's not closely related to the deceased. Get hold of her, and get her to break it to her cousin—they are some sort of cousins, I understand. I'm sure she'll do everything that's required of her. Now hurry, hurry! The sooner we get this thing out of our hands and into the hands of the authorities, the better.' He looked at his watch: 'Half-past six: you know what time you found the body?'

I nodded again: 'Five-forty.'

'He has been dead since before midnight, that's certain,' said Sir Frederick. 'What time was it when our party broke up last night? Did you notice?'

I reflected: 'Not long after half-past ten, I think—that is to say, when Miss Ross left, and—and I followed her. I came back to the drawing-room just before eleven, and everybody had gone except Dr. Parmoor.'

'Yes,' said Sir Frederick, 'yes. Her going seemed to start a general movement towards bed, or elsewhere. I myself was left with that whisky-soaking doctor-fellow, I remember, and I went off to the library, leaving him there. Well, we shall all have to account for our movements between then and midnight.' He fixed his grey eyes piercingly on me for a moment: 'You are about to gain some experience in medico-legal jurisprudence,' he said, 'most useful.'

His tone implied that I was very fortunate to have got caught up in this murder, and that I owed it all to him. He went off purposefully up the steps to his task, leaving me to mine.

2

As I went along the corridor, not quite so quickly this time, I was thinking of the difference between Marcel and Hugo: evidently personal resemblance had nothing to do with this impersonation-plan. I passed Marcel's door, and hesitated, wondering if I ought to tell him first, as he was the most nearly concerned; but I decided that the women—Ursula, that was— had first claim to consideration, and the way to Ursula lay through Evelyn.

I tapped at Evelyn's door.

She was evidently a light sleeper. Almost at once I heard the electric switch snapped on, and various other sounds; in a few moments she opened the door. She looked as neat and tidy as in the daytime; her dark hair was smooth, and she held a bright green silk wrap closely round her. She appeared neither pleased nor displeased to see me—just puzzled and anxious.

'Evelyn,' I said, 'can you come with me? There's been a— discovery. It doesn't concern you—not particularly.' Then, seeing her look of growing alarm and bewilderment, I blurted out: 'Hugo Ullstone—the real Hugo—has been murdered. I found his body in the shrubbery.'

She stepped back a pace and leaned against the door-jamb, and closed her eyes. I thought wildly of smelling-salts; then I realized my mistake: of course, she didn't know about the real Hugo.

'Not Marcel!' I said, shaking her. 'The fellow you—we all— thought was Hugo isn't Hugo at all. He's alive and well. I've got to break this news to him in a minute. This Hugo is someone you've never seen. But he's the real Hugo all right. I've seen his photo.' I babbled on, giving her time. With a great effort, obviously, she pulled herself together. She opened her eyes, and gave me a faint look of recognition and—well, friendliness, perhaps affection, I thought and hoped. She stretched out a hand and laid it on my arm.

'How awful!' she said. 'Poor Jake, how awful for you!'

I pressed her hand gently against my sleeve. 'I want your help, Evelyn,' I said, coming closer to her. 'Evelyn, we've got to break the news to Ursula. I came to you first, thinking you'd help me. Will *you* do it for me?'

At that, her eyes opened wider. 'Oh no, Jake, I couldn't!' she said, greatly distressed. 'Ursula can't bear me, as you know. She wouldn't take it at all well from me.'

'But you're the only other woman here,' I urged. 'One can't count Aunt Susan: she might have a stroke. Surely at such a time Ursula will forget her own petty little feelings and see you as you are—see you like a sister. Come on!' I begged her, seeing that she was wavering. 'There's no time to lose. The police will be here at any moment. Sir Frederick is 'phoning them now.'

'All right,' she said. 'I'll come with you. I won't actually break it to her, but I'll be there. Wait a minute,' and she ran back, presumably to powder her nose.

3

The interview with Ursula was short and sharp. She too came quite quickly, and she looked soignée. She had taken time, I noticed, to light a cigarette before she came, and she was already made up as in the daytime, with powder and lipstick, and her hair was brushed and set in its usual waves. When she saw us, her look of annoyance was not flattering.

'What's the matter?' she said. 'Why are you two babes in the wood wandering about in the small hours? Is it an elopement? If so, don't bother: nobody cares. But you'd better stay and have some breakfast. Well, what are you waiting for? You have my blessing, children——'

I interrupted her: she was about to close her door. 'Ursula,' I said, 'please be serious. Something very serious has happened. First of all'—I remembered my mistake with Evelyn—'the man you think is your half-brother Hugo is not Hugo at all. He's called Marcel, and he's here in Hugo's place, as Hugo's friend——'

It was her turn to interrupt me. 'Well, really!' she said. 'You two are impossible! Is that what you're running round the house and waking people up to tell them? My dear Jake, my dear Evelyn'—and she cast us both, especially Evelyn, a very scornful look indeed—'my dear precious pair of prigs, I know all about Marcel and Hugo. Marcel told me himself last night. The dear boy is a wonderful actor, but he can't keep a secret. I should have thought he would have told everybody by now: certainly I'm surprised he hasn't told you two, even before he told me. Or has he?' And now she cast looks of sharp suspicion from one to the other of us.

'No, Ursula,' I said, as sharply as she. 'He hasn't told us anything. I knew because Sir Frederick told me—that's all. And that's not what I've come to tell you.' I could not be bothered to spare her any longer: 'The real Hugo—your half-brother—has been murdered—shot in the back—and his body's in the shrubbery. The police will be on their way by now.'

This time, to do her justice, Ursula reacted as violently as I could have wished. She didn't look as if she were going to faint; but her whole expression, bantering and sarcastic, changed so suddenly that it shocked me in its turn. I don't know if she changed colour—the light was dim and at her back, and she was wearing too much make-up—but the sudden substitution of one expression for another was as remarkable as if I had dealt her a physical blow. I once saw something similar, when a man, a fellow-student, talking to another man and telling stories, went off into what looked like helpless laughter; and the man to whom he was talking said to him rather roughly, 'Control yourself, man! You're hysterical!' Instantly the man who was laughing stopped, so suddenly that one was afraid for him; and for his laughter there was substituted an expression of resentment so violent that the other speaker recoiled, not through fear but through shock—shock at the suddenness of the change, so he told me afterwards. So it was with Ursula. I had thought that she was callous and careless. I had dealt with her roughly on that assumption; and the result shocked and surprised me.

85

She got a hold on herself immediately.

'How did he get there?' she said.

'I don't know,' I said. 'I found the body there soon after half-past five this morning.'

She did not ask who did it; she did not even ask how I came to be there at such an early hour. 'I'll come at once,' she said, in a brave attempt at business-like tones; but her voice was trembling a little. She held her burnt-out cigarette to her lips: 'Give me a light, please, Jake.'

I gave her a light from my lighter, and I noticed how her hand too trembled. She glanced at Evelyn.

'Have you told Jim?' she said.

'No, not yet,' said Evelyn. 'Would you like me to, Ursula?' Evelyn spoke gently and considerately, though she did not attempt any ministrations.

Ursula reflected: 'No. I'd better tell him. And Jake—you'll tell Marcel? I'll deal with Aunt and Uncle, too, Evelyn, if you'll tell the rest of the household.'

She did not mention Hilary: presumably she took him for granted, and anyhow he wouldn't wake till much later. He had not been down to breakfast yet since I had been here. Ursula, now quite in control of herself, went on:

'Where is Sir Frederick? Tell him I shall be down immediately. Breakfast had better go on as usual.'

She went in and shut her door; the perfume she used, and the smell of cigarette-smoke, lingered after her. Evelyn and I gazed at each other in some dismay.

'And now—I've got to tackle Marcel,' I said, glancing fearfully along the corridor towards his room. 'What a business! To think that it doesn't really concern me at all! Still——'—I looked down at her, so pale and anxious-looking, and added, 'if I can be of any help to—anybody, I don't mind.'

She pressed my sleeve in answer. 'I do wish,' she said anxiously, 'she had let *me* break the news to Jim. I understand him better than she does, strange as it may seem. I can always handle him. She rubs him up the wrong way.'

'Well, why don't you?' I said. 'She can't really want to do it, you know. Probably she just thinks it's her duty. If you think you can do it better, go along and do it. You can get him to pretend to Ursula that he hasn't heard. Don't forget to tell him first that Marcel isn't Hugo.'

She nodded. I gave her a hasty peck on the forehead, and braced myself for what was to come. As I stood by Marcel's dark door and began the first of a series of knockings, I watched her small figure toddling off down the long corridor, and I thought what resolution often resides in puny frames and in spirits by nature timid and shy.

4

Marcel did not look soigné. His dark hair was rumpled, and his eyes were heavy with sleep. But his negligé became him more than the best efforts at smartness of most of us. As he pulled the girdle of his maroon-coloured dressing-gown, I thought, "How well he does everything!" Just as if he were on the stage, his gestures and movements had an unconscious grace and timing. But he was not acting now.

'Oh, really, Jake!' he said when he saw me. 'Was it necessary to waken me so early? I wish you would not be so—so very hearty.'

'Listen,' I said to him, pushing him to one side and going into the room. I closed the door behind us. 'Listen: do you know anything about Hugo?—the real Hugo, I mean, because I know you're not he——'

Hugo—or rather Marcel: it was still hard not to think of him as Hugo—Marcel did not look put out; he merely looked puzzled and irritated. 'Well, all right,' he said, 'what of it? I would have told you myself if I'd had a chance. I suppose Ursula has told you, or Evelyn: you can trust a woman not to keep a secret.'

I stopped him: 'You haven't answered my question. Do you know anything about Hugo?'

Marcel rubbed the back of his head, and yawned: 'All I know is, he was supposed to meet me last night, and he didn't. I shall take the car and go after him this morning.'

'Where was he staying?' I said cautiously.

Marcel stopped rubbing his head, and stared: 'In the town, of course. I thought you knew everything!' He had walked towards the window, and had taken a cigarette from the large silver box on the table. As he looked up after lighting it, he caught my expression at last. 'I say!' he exclaimed in changed tones, 'is there anything wrong? You look troubled.' Then, as I didn't answer, he gave a short laugh: 'You didn't suppose I intended to stay here for the rest of my life impersonating Hugo, did you? I merely came to break the ice for him—or rather, to give him a chance of deciding whether he wished to know his dear relatives or not. I began with the girls, naturally: Evelyn the night before, last night Ursula. It was arranged that I should trot them out for him to look at.'

'You mean, he was waiting in the shrubbery?' I said. 'He couldn't have seen much of them in the dark.'

'No, no,' said Marcel impatiently. 'I took Evelyn out to dinner in the town, as you know, to the inn where Hugo was staying. I was able to spend some time with him there. He agreed with me that she was a charming girl. He was not afraid of her—but then she isn't really related to him. He said he wished she were his sister.' Marcel was warming up to the plot: he had forgotten to observe me, forgotten the look on my face that had startled him; and he was pacing up and down, emphasizing his points with an occasional sweeping gesture. 'Hugo sees all women as possible sisters—or not—because he is vowed to celibacy. Poor fellow! I pity him, profoundly. Personally, I would rather not have been born. He will end in a monastery, of course—but I ask myself, of what sort?' He paced across the room again, towards the plaster fireplace: 'Last night, I promised him he should see his sister. I wanted him to come along and look in through the drawing-room windows after dark, since he refuses to show himself yet; but he wouldn't. He was afraid. Poor Hugo! He is afraid of everything. So I suggested he should wait in the shrubbery, and I would take her for a walk in the moonlight. It was a very romantic idea. Of course, my poor Jake, you with your Anglo-Saxon stolidity and fear of catching cold wouldn't understand. But I thought that Ursula would look loveliest by moonlight, with her yellow hair, in that yellow frock of hers—like a goddess, absolutely, you know!' He kissed his finger-tips at the vision he had conjured up, and then rounded on me with a quizzical look: 'Of course, if it rained or was too cloudy, all was to have been cancelled. But it didn't rain. The moon was brilliant. Yet he never came.'

'How do you know?' I said.

'Know? I did just as I had arranged: I paraded Ursula there for his inspection. Then I escorted her back to the house, and I went back to the shrubbery myself, as I had promised, to have a word with him. But there was no sign of him. Either he didn't come, or he came and left without waiting for me. I was furious! I ran back to the house—and Ursula was still there, in the drawing-room. Afterwards, when all had gone to bed, we had a long talk—alone. Ah!' He smiled at the pleasant recollection. 'She is a marvellous girl! I'm glad she is not *my* sister. It was then that I told her that she and I were not related. I had to, naturally. I think I don't flatter myself if I say that she was as much pleased as I.'

'Did you tell her about Hugo?'

Marcel stared: 'I told her some things, of course.'

'Did you tell her he had arranged to come to the shrubbery?'

'No, no, of course not! It wouldn't have been tactful. She might have been offended. We forgot all about Hugo, after I had explained to her who I was. We spoke of him no more. We spoke of each other.'

'She didn't know that he was staying near here—in the town?'

Marcel shook his head impatiently. 'Of course not!' he said again. 'She would be bound to be curious. She would feel obliged to see him at once—to ask him to come here. And perhaps I'm not yet quite ready to leave. Another couple of days here—I'm entitled to that—then I go, and Hugo can come and take my place or not, as he pleases. But what business is it of yours? You have the most confounded habit of asking questions! One would think that you were a member of this family!'

'One more question,' I said, 'just one, and I've finished: what name did Hugo give at the hotel? A false one, presumably?'

'Yes, yes—Hugo Smith, or Hugo Brown. I forget. The name Ullstone was too well known.'

'But he kept to Hugo? It's just possible that someone may have suspected him, and made inquiries, and let the family know? Hugo is not a common name, and he was not an ordinary-looking fellow—was he?'

Marcel shrugged his shoulders: 'How should I know what

inquiries were made? What does it matter, anyway? He's not doing anything criminal, and neither am I.'

He leaned against the fireplace, looking down.

I went up to him and laid a hand on his arm. 'Look here,' I said, 'I don't want to break this news too violently, but you'd better prepare yourself for a shock.'

He looked up at me, startled again as my tone and my expression went home.

'Hugo *was* in the shrubbery last night,' I said, 'but—somebody dealt with him in such a way that he never left it. I mean,' I hurried on, seeing his eyes widen in alarm, 'he was murdered—shot in the back. I found his body there this morning. For God's sake, man,' I said, as he swayed towards me, 'pull yourself together! The police will be here any minute. Think of the time you were there—with Ursula—without her. Think if you heard anything—saw anything suspicious.' I seized him by both arms. 'You didn't do it, did you? If you didn't, you have nothing to fear.'

Marcel passed his hand over his forehead, and looked round rather dazedly.

'Don't drink anything,' I said, 'until after you've seen the police. Black coffee if you like, but no whisky or even brandy till afterwards.'

Marcel leaned his arm on the mantelpiece, and pressed his forehead against his arm. 'How horrible!' he whispered. 'How horrible! And yet—there was no place for him in this world—no place at all.'

5

The police came. In the first car was the Superintendent from Chode, a man named Mallett, who seemed to know the Ullstones quite well. He was tall and bulky and red-faced, in appearance exactly like what one expects a police superintendent to be; but his manner was considerate and friendly, and a trace of Scots accent made one feel at home with him—too much so perhaps. That accent of his must have been a great asset. With him was the doctor, whose name was Fitzbrown. He too was tall, but thin and raw-boned and dark, with curly black hair and a black moustache. One liked him immediately and without reserve, though he was not at all forthcoming. He too seemed to know the Ullstones very well indeed, and to be familiar with all their problems, yet he took no great notice of them, but went about his job.

These two, after a brief consultation with Sir Frederick in the hall, went off immediately with him to the shrubbery; and shortly afterwards a second car arrived, bringing a photographer, two uniformed policemen, and a plain-clothes man who took measurements. Lastly, the ambulance came, and poor Hugo's body was carried from the shrubbery on a stretcher, and taken away.

6

It was interesting to see how, from the moment the police set foot in the place, our relationships changed. The Superintendent, to begin with, very naturally pounced on Marcel; and he was the first to be summoned into the library, where the doctor and Mallett were installed. He emerged, looking very white and shaken, an hour later; and he was received by us with every sympathy, as if he were a hero. Ursula was waiting for him, with Evelyn and me, in the hall; and by common consent we all went upstairs to his room, collecting the others, I don't know quite how, on the way.

There, in the great room with the plaster fireplace, we gathered round Marcel like conspirators holding a council of war: yes, he was decidedly the hero of the occasion. He had put on his maroon-coloured dressing-gown again, and he sat in one of the big chairs, leaning forward and sometimes stroking back his dark hair from his worried brow. Ursula sat on the arm of the chair and encouraged him: he was now "darling," I noticed. But still, most people were "darling" to Ursula.

'But darling!' she cried, 'they can't possibly suspect you? Why, what do *you* stand to gain by Hugo's death?' She looked round triumphantly, from Jim to Hilary, from the Biddolphs to Evelyn and me. 'Why, practically all of us stood to gain by it more than you did!'

Marcel clasped his head more firmly in his hands.

'Huh!' said Jim, 'Hugo may have left him something in his will.'

Marcel looked up agonizedly, as if someone had switched on the wireless at the wrong station and too loudly: 'I don't imagine,' he said, 'that poor Hugo has had time to make a will. He had not made one when I left him last.'

'How do you know?' said Uncle Biddolph with sudden interest. Then, realizing that he had spoken to someone without being first spoken to, he turned to Aunt Susan and said: 'How does he know?'

Aunt Susan bridled, showing that she had heard the question, had accepted it, and passed it for immediate consideration. Marcel answered, frowning:

'Because he was asking me how he ought to set about it. Hugo was always obsessed with the thought of death. But until his father died, he had no property of his own. Everything he had was paid for, handsomely; but apart from an allowance—pocket-money, he called it—he had nothing. And so, when he suddenly found himself the heir to all this fortune, he felt he must do something about it. He felt it a great responsibility, you see. Hugo was not like other people. He took life very seriously—too seriously.' There was a suggestion of tears in Marcel's voice, and I did not think that he was acting when he again clasped his head in his hands and hid his face from us.

There was a respectful silence for a moment, and I saw Ursula's hand hover near his head, and then withdraw. Dr. Parmoor spoke next, quite coolly and impersonally:

'Have you any idea what depositions he would have made, if he had made them?' he said.

Marcel answered quite simply and mildly, looking up at him: 'No—not exactly, that is. But I am sure Hugo would have done the right thing. I think he would have made a few bequests to people who had been kind to him, or had served him well; but he would have bequeathed the rest back to his half-brother and half-sister, if they had given him a chance—if they had shown any friendly feeling towards him.' He turned to Jim: 'He would not have bequeathed anything to me! He knew I did not need it, and I would have dissuaded him. You are unable to believe that, I suppose.' His tone of wounded dignity was magnificent, and Jim shifted uneasily and said nothing. Ursula broke in:

'Of course we believe you, darling! We believe everything you say—don't we?' She looked round at us, and nobody dared to contradict her. 'You know that Marcel told *me* all about himself last night, before this happened? That's sufficient proof of his sincerity, I hope!'

'Nobody's questioning it,' I put in from my corner. I was standing beside the fireplace, leaning against it, and Evelyn was beside me. I took the opportunity of slipping my arm round her waist, and when she did not resist, of drawing her towards me; and so henceforward she leaned slightly against me, but whether this was because she was so much absorbed in the scene that she did not notice, I didn't know and didn't very much care. The feeling that I was supporting her gave me a new confidence, and I went on rather recklessly: 'The only thing is, he left it for the police to find out for themselves, and they may get nasty about it.' It was funny how, now that he was no longer Hugo, I found myself slightly opposed to Marcel.

Marcel looked up resentfully: 'Don't worry: you will have to explain yourself, also,' he said.

'Oh,' I said jauntily, 'Sir Frederick Lawton knows all about *me.*'

'Yes,' said Marcel spitefully, 'but who knows anything about Sir Frederick Lawton? He killed Hugo's father and got well paid for it, it seems. Who knows but what he may have had something to gain by getting rid of Hugo?'

'Don't be ridiculous!' I was beginning angrily, when, without ceremony, the door opened and Sir Frederick himself walked in.

'Well, well!' he said, stopping short at the sight of us and fixing his eyeglass, 'what a lugubrious scene! Come, come, you mustn't take it all so hardly.' He went over to Marcel and patted his shoulder: 'Cheer up, my friend! You passed through your ordeal very well, and I think I may say that the police are quite satisfied with your story—so far.' He beamed round at us all: 'Fortunately I had taken the precaution of having this young man's *bona fides* gone into before he arrived, and so, most unexpectedly, I was able to confirm his account of himself.'

There was an uncomfortable pause, while everybody thought along Marcel's lines: "Yes: but who can confirm yours?" At last, to break the silence, I put in somewhat officiously:

93

'I wonder, sir, can you tell us what is the legal position?—I mean, if Hugo has died intestate?'

They all looked at me, and I felt embarrassed. I may even have blushed. Sir Frederick looked too, with a rather curious smile.

'Well,' he said, and his eyeglass dropped with a tinkle against a waistcoat button, 'well, of course, the property would go to his next-of-kin.'

'And who are his next-of-kin?' interrupted Ursula brightly. 'We are, aren't we?'

'So far as I know, yes,' said Sir Frederick, twirling the eyeglass between finger and thumb. 'He was not married, it seems, and he has no full brothers and sisters, and his parents are dead. He may have cousins in India, and perhaps they'd have some claim if they cared to make it, but——' He stopped, and seemed to come to a decision: 'I don't know, really, if I'm right in telling you young people this; perhaps I should leave it to the police. But the matter will soon be public property, and I don't see why it should be kept from you any longer than necessary.' He placed one foot on a chair in front of him and leaned forward, elbow on knee: 'The fact is, Hugo did not die intestate. He left a will—a rather rough-and-ready one, but the Superintendent thinks it's valid.'

'Good heavens!' exploded Jim. 'Where was it found?'

'It was found,' said Sir Frederick with solemn relish as we craned our necks towards him, 'it was found on the body. It was written on a piece of hotel paper, and it was correctly signed and witnessed by the hotel proprietor and his wife.' He paused again, with diabolical knowledge of human weakness.

'And——?' urged Ursula, not troubling to hide her impatience. 'Don't tell me you don't know what's in it!'

'Oh, yes,' said Sir Frederick gravely, 'I know what's in it. I'm afraid you won't like it. He left all his property to his friend, Marcel de Souvigny.'

At that, Marcel looked up as if he had had a tooth drawn, and let out a positive howl of anguish. 'Oh, no, no!' he moaned, 'he can't have done that to me!' I wish I could reproduce the despair in his tones. 'It's a trap! They want to make me look guilty of this murder!' He jumped up, and his eyes fell on Jim Ullstone, lounging against the chimney-breast opposite me: 'It is you—*you* have planned it! I knew you were my enemy, from the start!' And he made a rush at Jim, who, to do him justice, did not stir.

Ursula bounded after Marcel and clutched his arm:

'Don't be absurd, darling!' she cried. 'Jim didn't know who you were. He thought you were Hugo!' And she dragged him back to his chair, while he protested; but soon, realizing the justice of her remark, he allowed himself to be soothed.

'I shall not touch a penny of it!' he went on protesting, while Ursula stroked the back of his head and murmured things that sounded like "There, there!" in motherly tones. 'Not a penny! I shall give it all away!'

Sir Frederick sighed, as if something difficult had been accomplished safely, and took his foot off the chair.

'But what I really came for,' he said, 'was to tell you that the Superintendent wants to see Jim.'

We all looked at Jim, who flushed angrily: 'What, me!' he said. 'Oh, good God, that's preposterous! What does he want me for? I'm not going.'

Sir Frederick restored his eyeglass to his waistcoat pocket. 'Please yourself, young man,' he said, 'but I think your obstructionist tactics are misplaced. The police probably want to ask you merely about the contents of your gunroom.' And calm, dignified, and as indifferent as a god, he walked to the door.

Jim, disconcerted, cast angry looks round at all of us.

'I think you'd better go, dear,' said Ursula with unusual gentleness.

'I suppose I had,' he muttered, and followed Sir Frederick.

I whispered in Evelyn's ear, 'Let's clear out.' Half to my surprise, she consented. There was a general movement towards the door; it seemed to me that we all realized we had better leave Marcel and Ursula alone.

7

We walked out through the front door, past the policeman on guard, into the sunshine, and stood for a moment on the top step, between the stone urns, admiring the view. It was so peaceful and pleasant and well-ordered, with its well-cut lawns and flower-beds, and the park-land stretching away into the distance, that it irresistibly invited one to forget the presence of such disagreeable things as greed for gain, and violent death, and retribution hovering near. By common consent, we turned away from the path leading towards the shrubbery, and made for the little sunken garden where we had talked the day before. The grey walls were bright with arabis and aubretia. We sat down on the stone seat in the recess, and watched the dark pool.

'Well?' I said at last.

She looked up at me, with that look of alarm in her eyes which was what had appealed to me from the first. She said nothing.

'What do you think of it all?' I said.

She looked away, again without answering.

'Do you think it was somebody here who killed him?' I pressed her. 'Or was it an accident—some tramp or poacher?'

She shook her head: 'What's the use of pretending, Jake? We know it wasn't an accident—don't we?'

'I suppose we do,' I said glumly. 'Poachers don't carry revolvers, they carry shot-guns; and they certainly don't use them on human beings if they can help it. No, it's certain that poor Hugo was decoyed there and shot—or else somebody found out that he was coming there, and lay in wait for him.' A wave of indignation rose up in me. 'Good heavens!' I said, 'what a foul trick!'

There was a pause, while we both stared at the dark pool with its flat lily-leaves and pointed buds sticking out of the water. 'You were there when the body was found, weren't you?' said Evelyn.

'It was I who found him,' I said, not without a certain irrational pride, which I noticed in myself and deplored as I spoke.

'How dreadful!' she said with a shudder. 'But then, of course, you are used to such things.'

'Not quite so used as that,' I said with a laugh. 'Still, perhaps it was better I should find him than that you should, for instance.'

At that, she turned and rested her forehead against my shoulder. 'I am so frightened!' I heard her breathe; and again I put my arm round her protectingly.

'Why?'

'Frightened—lest they find out—something——' Her words came out slowly, and I bent my head to listen.

'What?' I urged her, as her words ended in a sigh.

'Something we shan't like,' she ended; and then, to my dismay, she buried her face against my sleeve and burst into tears: 'Oh, Jake, it *can't* have been Jim—surely it can't have been Jim!'

At once I was on the alert. 'What makes you think so?' I said, almost sharply. She drew away from me, and wiped her eyes.

'I didn't say that. I didn't say I thought so,' she said tearfully. 'But, Jake, you know how threatening he has been. He was violent to you. He has threatened Marcel. In those violent moods of his, he could do anything. And now'—she sobbed again for a moment, and then checked herself—'he's with the police, and he'll make such a bad impression on them! He will bluster and be truculent and refuse to answer their questions, and they'll think he's guilty. I know they will!'

'Well,' I said unsympathetically, 'perhaps he is. We don't know yet, do we? And if he is, he'll deserve all he gets. But Evelyn—aren't you forgetting, as Ursula said just now, that he didn't know about Hugo, the real Hugo, I mean? He thought Marcel was Hugo, as we all did.'

'Oh, but,' said Evelyn, bursting afresh into tears, 'he did—he did know! I told him!'

'*You* told him?' I said, startled beyond measure. 'Look here: was everybody in this secret except me?'

'I don't know,' sobbed Evelyn. 'But it was Marcel—he couldn't keep it a secret. He told Ursula last night—and he told me the night before. He thought it a great lark. He told me all about himself and Hugo; and then he said, "Would you like to *see* Hugo? I'm going to meet him now." So we went off to Chode, to the hotel where Hugo was staying; and we dined there. And we saw Hugo, but he and Marcel pretended not to know each other for a while. Then, in the end, Marcel got up and went to Hugo's table and brought him over and introduced him to me. I thought him very nice, but very sad.' Her tears flowed again. 'Marcel explained to him that I wasn't really a relative, and he said he was sure they could trust me—though why he was so sure, I don't know——'

'Perhaps he thought it was what you'd best like to hear,' I said grudgingly. 'Marcel is an adept in the art of pleasing.'

She did not hear my unkindnesses. Her thoughts were running on, almost too fast for expression, as the picture grew always clearer. I could almost see it myself as I watched her: the slender, debonair, vivacious Marcel, and his stout, rather solemn friend, bowing before this representative of the house that he was afraid to enter, although it was his property.

'He sat down with us at our table and we talked for a while,' she said. 'He was very nervous at first, but he soon saw that there was nothing to fear from *me*. I think he quite liked me, and Marcel seemed very pleased at the way things were going. He tried to persuade Hugo to come next day to the house and say who he was, Marcel didn't in the least mind being shown up: in fact, he seemed to enjoy the prospect, and he gave Hugo a description of all the people. It was very amusing, the way he did it: he mimicked Aunt Susan and Uncle Biddolph, and Dr. Parmoor, and Sir Frederick Lawton——'

'And me?' I said.

'No, not you. I don't think he mentioned you. I too tried to persuade Hugo to come to the house and announce himself. I assured him that he had nothing whatever to fear, except perhaps a little unpleasantness from Jim, and perhaps from Ursula. But nothing would persuade him. He just sat there shaking his head and looking solemn and sad, and nothing that Marcel or I could say would move him. It seemed to be Ursula he was most afraid of meeting, I don't know why. The more Marcel described her and said how attractive she was and how vivacious and gay, the more stubborn Hugo seemed to get about not coming. He had some terrible inferiority-complex where white women were concerned.'

'Can you wonder?' I said.

'No, I suppose not. Well, in the end, Marcel had what he called the brilliant idea of letting Hugo see Ursula without being seen.'

'It was Marcel's idea, then?' I said.

'Yes.'

'But why at night? Was that his idea too?'

'Yes—but not until he had tried to persuade Hugo to come by

day. I don't think he was altogether serious when he proposed it at first, but Hugo seemed to like the idea, and Marcel got carried away. He said it was so romantic: *au clair de la lune*.'

'Now I know,' I said, 'why he sang that song—and sang it so feelingly.'

Evelyn nodded. '*I* knew at the time. I wondered if Hugo were outside and could hear. But I don't suppose he came out of the shrubbery.'

'Tell me,' I said, 'what exact arrangement did they make?'

'Marcel said he would take Ursula for a walk some time after dinner, when the moon would be high. Hugo was to be in the shrubbery and watch them pass. I told them I thought it was a ridiculous idea, but Marcel wouldn't listen, and Hugo seemed quite glad to agree.'

'And you knew all this, and you didn't tell me!' I said reproachfully.

Evelyn gazed at me. 'I never thought of it!' she said, with such earnestness that I felt I had displayed an unworthy curiosity; and yet it was not that. But when she looked at me with that anxious, searching scrutiny, I could no longer remember why I thought she should have told me. 'And then too,' she went on, 'I thought they'd rather nobody knew. They didn't say so— Marcel didn't ask me to keep it to myself—but I felt that Hugo preferred nobody to know.'

I laughed. 'Naturally,' I said. 'He must have realized that it was all rather silly.'

'No.' Evelyn remained quite serious. 'I don't think he did. It didn't sound silly then, as Marcel put it to him. I think Hugo liked the idea of coming at night, secretly. I believe he would have liked to do everything by night, and vanish during the day. He was so terribly unhappy—one could see that. He could never have faced us openly. And yet he didn't want to go without having seen his brother and sister—especially her. So if you think of it from his queer point of view, it's not so unreasonable after all.'

I put my arm round her waist. '*You*'d make anything sound reasonable,' I said. 'But you haven't told me how you came to tell Jim.'

Again she rested her forehead on my shoulder. 'Can't you

guess?' she said. 'I told you yesterday when I met you in the garden, how troubled I was because of his threats against Hugo. I told you how he came to my room the night before, after I had been out with Marcel. It was then that I told him that Marcel wasn't Hugo—that the real Hugo was waiting, not so very far away—I didn't say where—to find out what we were like; and that Marcel was his only friend. Jim was quite staggered, of course—but it diverted him from Marcel, which was all that mattered at the time.'

'Well, really!' I said, taken aback again at the thought of what I had been missing—of how they had almost all been in the secret except me. 'But you didn't tell him about the moonlight rendezvous, you say?'

'No, no, of course not!' protested Evelyn vehemently. 'I'm sure I never let fall the slightest hint, even. I've searched my mind for anything I could have said, but there's nothing. All I said was that Hugo was "not so very far away." And now I'd give anything not to have said even that, because Jim in his suspicious state of mind was quite capable of finding out all about Hugo, where he was staying and what his movements were. How he could possibly have got to know about the evening meeting, I can't think; but——' she turned away.

'So you *do* think he's guilty?' I pressed her.

'No, no!' Her protest was more vehement than ever. 'It's not that, it's not that! It's just that I can't get these things out of my mind. I keep remembering how he went out of the room yesterday evening just before we started dancing, and how he never came back. I don't want to think such thoughts, but in spite of myself my mind will keep asking, "Why did he go? Was it because he knew something, and wanted to follow Hugo to the shrubbery?" Her dark eyes widened with fear: 'He mightn't have meant to kill him,' she said breathlessly, 'but when he found himself there alone with him, mightn't one of those terrible rages of his have come over him, so that he shot him without thinking of what he was doing? And if he did, it *must* have been my fault, somehow. In my efforts to protect Marcel—to protect Jim from himself—I'm responsible for Hugo's death!'

I waited until this fresh paroxysm of grief was over. Then I said, 'Look here, Evelyn: whoever killed Hugo didn't do it in a sudden spasm of rage. He did it quite deliberately. He took a gun with him and went out to shoot him in cold blood. Is that like Jim?'

She shook her head: 'No, I suppose not.'

'And then again,' I went on with growing conviction, 'when you come to think of it, what would Jim gain? He couldn't know that the property would revert to him and Ursula if Hugo died. He couldn't know whether Hugo had made a will or not. As a matter of fact, Hugo had, as we know. And I'm afraid that the police will find Marcel's movements more interesting than Jim's, therefore, whatever they may pretend now about being satisfied— especially as it was Marcel who arranged the meeting.'

'Oh, but——' Evelyn was beginning, when a shadow fell across the paved walk, and we glanced up to see Dr. Parmoor looking down at us benevolently.

'So there you are!' he said. 'They've been looking for you everywhere. Jake, it's your turn next, I'm afraid, old chap. The police want to question you.'

I got up, feeling unreasonably indignant, as if I were already being accused. Evelyn looked up at me imploringly, as much as to say, "Don't tell them what I've told you!"

I nodded down at her reassuringly, and went off. Parmoor sat down heavily, with a grunt, in the place I had vacated.

8

My interview with the Superintendent passed off much as I had expected. No one else was present except a policeman who took down my answers in shorthand; and I was not allowed to gather the smallest hint of the way the Superintendent's mind was working. After taking me through the circumstances of my own arrival, he questioned me closely about the evening of the murder, and especially about the exact movements of those who were in the drawing-room; but he did not ask me a single question that involved any expression of opinion, or any judgment, on my part: to him I was simply a time-table. Jim Ullstone left the room at about five minutes past nine, and did not return. I stayed until ten-thirty, when I followed Miss Ross and saw her to her room. On my return, the drawing-room was empty except for Dr. Parmoor. Did I myself go out again? No. Did I see or hear anything or anybody? No. The Superintendent seemed quite satisfied with my answers, and did not press me further. Then he took me through my discovery of Hugo's body, and my rousing of Sir Frederick. That was all. It was clear that he had finished with me, and his mind was on the next person.

I ventured to ask whether he wished me to stay on in the house. At this he looked up sharply:

'Yes: you'd better stay till after the inquest. After that, you can go.'

'Shall I have to give evidence?'

He looked at me with not very flattering appraisal: 'Yes. You'll have to depose to having found the body. But it'll be quite formal so far as you're concerned. Sir Frederick will take over the description.'

He turned back to his own notes, and I went away. The bust of Euripides, with its long hair and beard, watched me sourly as I made for the door.

9

Standing on the steps of the porch, I looked out over the lawns and the flower-beds, wondering what I should do now with my day.

It was a delightful morning, warm and sunny; but a great load of depression sat heavily on me. It was not, to be frank, because of poor Hugo that I had this sudden sense of emptiness, of loneliness and futility. After all, I had never known him, and I could feel only a passing regret at his pitiful end. It was, I realized, because this brutal happening had dispelled the romantic atmosphere in which I had been living for the past three days—was it really only so long?—into which I had plunged through the thunderstorm and the blinding rain to the House of the Monkeys. To-morrow or the next day it would end, this curious adventure, in the dusty, matter-of-fact setting of a country law-court. I did not want it to end—not yet, anyway. I wanted to go on, to find out something: no, not, I'm afraid, who it was that had shot Hugo, but some larger question that included the less: what was the mainspring of these people's lives? Who was there among us whose life was lived on such a different plane from mine that to achieve his end he could deliberately take a gun and shoot a fellow-creature in the back? Again and again there came into my mind the scene of my first entry into the drawing-room, into that circle of hostile eyes. The answer lay there, if only one had the wit to discern it. I had been the first, the accidental target of that murderous hatred, then Marcel; and then at last, and correctly, Hugo. Yes, that was the experience I had so strangely undergone, of coming within the sights, as it were, of somebody's will to destroy. But try as I would, I could not tell whence that will to destroy proceeded.

I paced slowly out along the gravel walk, and down to the lily-pond, half-hoping to find Evelyn still there, for I had not been gone more than twenty minutes or so; but neither she nor Parmoor was to be seen. I sat there for a while, watching the goldfish coming to the surface, then diving and shooting with a whisk of their fins and tails beneath the great dark leaves; I sat smoking and thinking and wondering what was happening at the house up there.

I had just ground out my third cigarette-end on the flagged pathway, and was preparing to leave, when I heard a low whistle above me, and I turned to see Marcel looking down at me over the wall and smiling. In a moment he had run down the steps and joined me.

'That's a wonderful place for eavesdropping,' he said, sitting down beside me. He had recovered all his aplomb: there was no trace of his previous agitation as he took out his cigarette-case and passed it to me. I noticed, however, that it was not the gold case with the initials H. U. any more, but a silver one carrying his own monogram. I was not yet prepared to forgo my grudge against him for having deceived me.

'There's been nothing to eavesdrop about,' I said sulkily, 'for the last half hour, anyway.'

'No, but I've been watching your thoughts.' He turned to me with all his old eagerness and laid a hand on my arm. 'My dear fellow, don't be annoyed with me because I talked to the women about myself before I told you. *Tu me plais beaucoup.* I like you very much. But you know how it is: when one is with girls, one does and says anything to please them. You don't? Oh, but you're an Anglo-Saxon——'

'I'm not!' I protested. 'I'm a Celt. Look at my hair!'

'Well, you've imbibed this humid atmosphere. You are all chivalry. It's a mistake. You will agree with me some day. Perhaps you do already, but it's an idea you have, and you won't give it up. Isn't that so?'

One couldn't help liking him. Whatever he did was vivid, alive, and already I was as much cheered as if I had been sitting in shadow and the warm sun had just reached me in my corner. 'You shouldn't have told them,' I admonished him. 'They must have let it out to someone else, and he must have——'

'Don't!' said Marcel, grabbing my arm violently. 'Do you think I have not thought of that? I'm not a fool—and Hugo was my friend. But how could I possibly know that anyone would want to *kill* him? I thought, in this country such things didn't happen.'

'Tell me,' I said, to divert him from the momentary spasm of remorse I had caused, 'What are the police after? Have they any clues?'

At this, he looked up, immediately alert and interested. 'So far as I know, nothing,' he said. 'Personally, I think they're merely marking time until the results of the post-mortem come in. Then they'll look for the weapon. There are a couple of men down in the shrubbery, measuring the ground, the distance from the edge of the trees to where he was found, and so on, and going over the pathway for footprints. But up to the present I don't think they've found anything, to judge from their faces. Of course, they would like to arrest *me*. I am the obvious suspect. I arranged for Hugo to be there, and he has left his money to *me*. Fortunately, I have an alibi.'

'You have?' I said.

'Yes. I spent most of the night in the drawing-room, talking to Ursula. We didn't part till about three o'clock this morning; and the doctors say Hugo was shot some time before that, probably around midnight. Ursula has already corroborated my statement. She's a marvellous girl—she doesn't care a straw for convention. She'll stand up for me against the world.'

The complacency in his tones irritated me, and I said rather spitefully, 'I'm afraid her corroboration won't be enough for the police, you know. They'll assume she's saying it to exonerate you. You'll need a third party as witness—and I don't suppose you have that.'

'Oh, but we have!' said Marcel triumphantly. 'Of course, I could point to the ashtray full of cigarette-ends that we left there—and you can tell Ursula's by the lipstick. No, but what happened was this: I brought Ursula back from our walk some time after eleven, and we found old Parmoor still in the drawing-room, fast asleep. He woke up when we came in, and we had a drink, and then I excused myself and ran back to the shrubbery to see if Hugo was there. I had some idea of fetching him with me if he'd come, and making him meet Ursula. Well, when he didn't appear as arranged, I ran back again to the drawing-room——'

I interrupted him: 'There goes your alibi. The police could say you killed Hugo then.'

'Oh, nonsense!' said Marcel calmly. 'I wasn't away more than ten minutes—and where am I supposed to have got the gun from? Besides, they would have heard the shot.'

'Maybe,' I admitted. 'Well: what did you do them?'

'I ran back, as I say, and found Ursula and Parmoor there in the drawing-room. I thought at the time that they'd been having a few words, possibly about me; and later, Ursula confirmed this. He was a little the worse for drink, but not much—not enough to interfere with his movements. When I came back, he went off at once, without saying a word.' Marcel paused.

'And then?' I pressed him.

'Well, then, my friend, we turned on the wireless and danced for a while, by ourselves. Then, when it was midnight and the wireless stopped, we sat down on the settee and talked. It is very good, talking to Ursula. She told me—but no, there's no reason why I should tell you what she said.' He laughed, with a pleasure that struck me as in very bad taste.

'I should think not!' I said, rather stiffly. And then, after some hesitation, in case he should think me inquisitive, I added: 'If you marry Ursula, it won't matter that Hugo left the property to you.'

Again he laughed, and gave me a resounding slap on the back.

'What a fellow you are!' he said joyfully. 'Of course I shan't marry her! My parents would never allow it, in any case. They have a very nice girl chosen for me already, one of my cousins, whom I like very much and who likes me. Her father, my uncle, is a millionaire. No, no, my dear friend! One does not marry on such a slender acquaintance, if one is wise! And I don't think Ursula would want to marry me, even for the sake of the family fortunes. Why do you ask? Would you be jealous, perhaps?' He turned to look at me, pushing me away with one hand on my shoulder. 'Oh no, of course—it is the other one you fancy, at the moment, anyway.' I blushed, and he shook his head solemnly: 'Be careful!' he admonished me. 'These things are all very well, but you'll be surprised how differently you'll feel in six months' time, or six weeks' even.'

I nodded glumly. 'I daresay you're right,' I said, 'but at the moment I don't see it that way.'

'Ah well, never mind, it doesn't matter,' said Marcel carelessly. 'But look here: I want to talk to you seriously.' And his manner changed, in the engaging way it had, from playfulness and a pretence of cynicism to a deep earnestness that made one feel he regarded one as his dearest friend. He leaned forward, clasping his hands in front of him: 'You know, don't you, that Hugo—poor dear old fellow—left a will in my favour? Well, I've been having a talk with Sir Frederick. He's been speaking to the doctor who came with the police, and this man, who seems quite a decent chap, told Sir Frederick that so far as they can see, the will is perfectly genuine. They've already confirmed the fact that it was signed by the hotel proprietor and his wife. So you see, it's really true: I'm saddled with this property, whether I like it or not. And the next thing is, what am I to do with it?'

He turned his serious dark eyes on me, as if he expected an oracular answer; but, nevertheless, I was somehow aware that he had already made up his mind. However, as he waited for an answer, I said cautiously:

'Hadn't you better put off deciding anything until you can consult your own people—your father, for instance?'

Marcel held up his hands in horror. 'My father!' he said, and then rapidly and violently: 'Do you know what my father would say? I will tell you exactly, word for word. He would say: "This property is legally yours. Do not be foolish. If you act with naive quixotry, you will regret it. You think you will have enough with what I shall leave you: good! But one never has enough for perfect security in these restless times, and it is excellent to have property in another country. You did not seek this windfall; all the more reason why you can accept it with a good conscience. You owe it to your family, your future wife and your children, not to throw it away." ' Marcel tossed back his head and laughed, pleased with what no doubt was his excellent mimicry of his father. 'If he knew about this, he would be quite capable of bringing pressure to bear on me to make me keep it. My father likes bringing pressure to bear on me: he thinks it is not only a right but a duty—it is what sons exist for. So don't tempt me, my friend! In twenty years' time, I shall doubtless be giving the same advice to my own son. But leave me this one opportunity to be myself!'

He seemed to be greatly moved. I laid a hand on his shoulder. 'Well, in that case,' I said, 'it's easy.'

Again he rounded on me violently: 'It's not easy!' he said. 'Don't you know that it's never easy to part with money? Oh no, you've never had any, so you don't understand. But—the more one has, the harder it is. I—even I——'—he struck himself on the chest—'already find it difficult. Already I hear an inner voice saying, "It is yours. Keep it! Give them a present, if you like, but keep the whole. Legally it is yours. Morally—who can say?" And so on, and so on. No, no! Unless I act quickly, I shall find reasons for doing the really easy thing, the thing everybody else would do. You are honest—disinterested——' He grasped me by both arms and stared into my face.

'All right,' I said, a little bewildered but admiring. 'What is it you really want to do?'

He turned away and looked into the distance. 'I want to make a deed of gift,' he said. 'I believe that is what one does. I don't know exactly how, but a lawyer will tell us. Will you come with me and help me, if I can get permission for us to leave here for a few hours?'

'Of course I will,' I said heartily. 'That is, if you really mean it. And——'—I hesitated before saying this, in case he might be offended, but then I thought I would risk it—'you'll be finally giving the lie to any suspicion the police might have that you had anything to do with Hugo's death. They can't say that, if you give back the money.'

Marcel nodded. His approval of himself for this generous act was obvious, but, I thought, justified.

'How are you going to divide it?' I went on. 'Equally between them both, I suppose—though of course this house is a difficulty. Joint ownership isn't much good.' I wondered if I should suggest the inclusion of Evelyn, and then decided that for me in my position, this was impossible. As I talked, I became aware that Marcel was studying me with his head on one side, and a very odd smile on his face. At last, disconcerted at being regarded as amusing when what I was saying was deadly earnest, I stopped and said in some irritation:

'What's the matter? I thought you said you wanted my help.'

'So I did, my poor old fellow,' said Marcel, laughing. 'But only to come with me and see the lawyers. The rest of what you say—pooh!' he snapped his fingers. 'You don't think I'm going to give this legacy back to Jim and Ursula? Not at all! What would happen? Jim would squander it. Ursula would marry that doctor of hers, or maybe someone else, and *he* would have it. No! They both have money enough to live on—she told me that last night. Why should they have more? Their father did not wish it.'

'But,' I said, shocked and bewildered, 'you said, only this morning, that if Hugo had left a will you were sure he would have done "the right thing," as you called it. If it was the right thing then, it's the right thing now!'

'That was before I knew he *had* left a will,' said Marcel calmly. 'I called it "the right thing" because I thought that that was how *he* would feel. I was wrong. He didn't want them to have the money, any more than his father did. He thought it right to follow on the same lines as his father. That being so, I shall do the same. I don't want the money for myself, but I won't give it back to the very people they deprived of it. I won't undo all their work.'

I could think of no immediate answer, though the reasoning exasperated me. For the first time, I found myself completely on the side of Jim and Ursula; but I could think of no way of persuading Marcel.

'Well,' I said at last, seeing from his complacent smile that there was no arguing with him, 'what *do* you intend to do about it, then? It's a pretty cruel thing you're planning, you know—to put a stranger in here over their heads. *You* wouldn't like it. And won't the newcomer be in some danger, like poor Hugo?—not,' I added hastily, 'that I'm suggesting that Jim and Ursula had any hand in his death.'

Marcel swung his foot to and fro. I noticed, as one does when people are talking, the pointed shoe and the black silk sock not unlike those that Hugo had been wearing. The phrase "stepped into his shoes" idly crossed my mind.

'The new owner,' he was saying, 'won't be in any danger, because nobody here would benefit by his death. Nor will he be a *complete* stranger. No, I think my choice is very good. You see, my dear fellow, I have decided to make this property over to *you*.'

It was some moments before the words I had quite distinctly heard arranged themselves into a significant pattern in my brain.

'You're mad!' I shouted, jumping up. 'I wouldn't accept it!'

Marcel merely smiled up at me, unmoved.

'Your consent won't be needed,' he said, 'or so I understand. One day, when it's all settled, you will receive a registered letter—and the deed will be done. If by that time you still feel you can't undertake the responsibility, you can always hand it on: passing the buck, I believe the Americans call it.'

I looked down at him sourly. 'Well,' I said grudgingly, 'I can't stop you, apparently. But I refuse to have anything to do with it. Don't count on *me* for any help in such a wild-cat scheme.' And I walked away, leaving him there to enjoy his joke, if joke it was, and my discomfiture.

10

I don't know how I passed the rest of that day. All round us was an air of intense activity; but what it amounted to we were not allowed to know. The police car came and went, carrying messages with reports to and from the Superintendent. Slowly he was working his way through the rest of the household: Ursula, Evelyn, Dr. Parmoor, Aunt and Uncle Biddolph, the servants indoor and outdoor. Doubtless a mass of shorthand notes were accumulating there in the library; but how they fitted together, or indeed whether they fitted together at all, was at present a complete secret, though wild rumours flew to and fro among us from time to time and vanished, like bats in the shrubbery. Towards dusk, the police left us, and all we knew was that the inquest would take place the morning after next in the courtroom at Chode.

After that, of course, we could think of nothing else. We did not talk much about it, but we were all preoccupied, not so much with poor Hugo any longer, I'm afraid, nor even with his murderer, but with what sort of a figure we would cut in the courtroom. Most of us, I suppose, had never been in a courtroom before, and knew very little about the procedure. I myself had been only once, when I was called upon to give evidence about the speed of a motor cycle in a minor accident. I remembered how nervous I had felt when all eyes were turned upon me as I took the call, and yet rather elated at my sudden importance. I had given my trifling bit of evidence with what I thought was admirable clarity; but the magistrate had not seemed impressed, and had taken me through it all again, with the air of a rather impatient schoolmaster helping a backward child. I retired crushed; but I received three-and-sixpence for my trouble, I remembered, and better still, the motor cyclist, who had been fined ten shillings mostly on the strength of my evidence, met me outside, grasped me warmly by the hand, and thanked me for my fairness. We went off together and had a drink. That, so far, was my only contact with the law; and as Sir Frederick had implied, it was hardly sufficient for someone with my profession in view. But this was a very different matter: here a death was involved, a murder, and every word one said would have to be weighed. Anxiously in my mind I went over that early morning scene: the finding of the body, the attitude in which it lay, how I had acted. There was no fear that I would forget: the picture was stamped for life on my brain, however many more such scenes I might later have to witness.

Dinner that night was a very queer affair. Our preoccupation, each with his or her own thoughts, was so marked that at times there was dead silence except for the sounds that even the best-bred people must sometimes make with a knife and fork. Sir Frederick was not there; we understood that he had gone off to dine with this Dr. Fitzbrown, the police-surgeon. I thought, "He might have taken me, even if I am only a student! After all, if it hadn't been for him, I shouldn't be here," and I felt that in some perhaps not easily definable way, his conduct was contrary to the spirit of the Hippocratic Oath, by which all members of the medical profession are bound to stand by one another. Parmoor was completely silent; evidently he was still feeling aggrieved at Ursula's conduct of the evening before. Aunt Susan and Uncle Biddolph conversed together in undertones, ostentatiously isolating themselves; and judging by their looks, they were not at all pleased with the company in which they found themselves, rubbing shoulders perhaps, or passing the salt to, a murderer. Aunt Susan's mouth was turned down in bitter disapproval, and Uncle Biddolph's long moustaches drooped in perfect agreement and sympathy. I thought I caught them glancing most often at Ursula and Marcel; and I wondered if they knew the nature of Marcel's so-called alibi. It seemed quite likely.

Ursula herself was unaware of their scrutiny. She was looking very thoughtful, and her manner was far quieter than usual. She sat at the head of the table, with Marcel on her right hand, in Sir Frederick's place. Evidently what Marcel was saying engaged only half her attention; she appeared to be listening, but though he was obviously bending all his arts upon her, to charm and amuse her, she did not laugh when he did—she merely smiled, and rather gravely at that. Jim, at the other end of the table, occasionally made a loud remark in aggressive tones; but finding no one willing to listen to him, he left the table long before the rest of us, and went out, as usual slamming the door.

I had managed to sit by Evelyn, and whenever there was a chance, I pressed her knee or her hand under the table. She responded, and once or twice gave me a wan smile; but she was looking pale and tired, as if she had a headache; and as soon as dinner was over she excused herself and went away. This time I did not follow her. The only person I really wanted to talk to was Marcel, and he was clearly engaged for the rest of the evening. I wondered if he had meant it when he said he could not marry Ursula.

The question was, did he really mean anything he ever said?

II

Yes, that was the question. It kept me awake that night for hours, while the moon rose slowly, and her coldly beautiful, always eerie, never-to-be-taken-for-granted light flooded my room. I watched the squares of the window-pane, reflected on my carpet and then on my wall, as they moved with the passing hours; and I thought what different creatures we are by night and by day.

An owl, settled in a tree near by, uttered amazing whoops that sounded like joy, and probably presaged the horrid death of some unwary mouse or vole; she was so close that I went to the window to look for her, but even in that bright light I could not see her. The park looked incredibly lovely; and I shuddered, remembering how, this time last night perhaps, Hugo Ullstone, pacing up and down the path in the shrubbery, had met his sudden death—how one minute he had been, however sad and lonely and however much of a misfit in the world, nevertheless a man, young, rich, able to enjoy many of the good things of life, even if some were denied him; and then, in another minute, a shot had rung out, and he was lying face downward on the damp earth, grasping the dead leaves in his own death-agony.

"A shot rang out." "Yes, of course," I thought—and last night was just such another night as this. If anyone were to fire a revolver-shot now, I imagine I would be bound to hear it. There had been no sound for the past hour, so far as I had noticed, except the fierce clamour of that hunting owl. Had anyone heard the shot? We did not know. Possibly the police, by now, had found somebody who had heard it. The noticeable thing was that none of us had—that is, nobody who was in the drawing-room. Why not? Because, of course, there had been noise: piano-playing, and then the gramophone. So that when Marcel went out with Ursula, Hugo was already dead, lying in the wood under the rhododendron. He never saw that bright vision, his half-sister, served up to him so romantically in the moonlight by his best friend. And Marcel had spoken the truth when he said that he couldn't have shot Hugo in the ten minutes when he ran out again to the rendezvous, because someone—Ursula and Parmoor, if nobody else—would surely have heard the shot.

The next thing, I thought, was to find out whether Evelyn had heard anything: this would narrow the time down again. And then there was Jim, who left still earlier—but Jim might be the murderer; one had to think of that. If he weren't, he might have heard the shot. Presumably, if he had, he had told the police. He had said nothing to us, so far as I knew. One of the rumours, earlier in the day, had been that Jim was arrested; but however much suspicion against him was mounting, the rumour was evidently false: up to the present, Jim was free.

Slowly I came back from the window to my bed, and flung myself upon it. Fortunately it was not my business to solve this mystery, and that police-superintendent and his men looked thoroughly efficient: if I had been the criminal, they would have terrified me almost to the point of confession. No, I need not trouble my head about that: only about my own bit of evidence— to give it clearly and concisely and not sound too eager and anxious to oblige.

And then at last, like a hawk that has been long hovering, my thoughts took a sudden sweep and made a pounce down upon their real objective. What was this mad scheme of Marcel's? Did he really mean it? Was it really feasible? Was it possible that I, Jake Seaborne, medical student, was at the moment the potential owner of this great house, this splendid park, and heaven knew how much accumulated wealth with which to rule over them?

12

I intend to be quite honest.

The thoughts that then came rushing into my mind were not concerned with how, if this property really came into my hands, I could do justice by restoring it to Jim and Ursula. First of all I found myself anxiously wondering, "Did he mean it?" The answer was, I thought, "Yes, at the moment of speaking," though I was not perfectly sure even of that. But what was much more dubious was, would he mean it to-morrow, and the next day, and the next day? Would he ever mean it sufficiently to take the necessary steps—find out the legal position, how you conveyed property by deed of gift from one person to another? Would he have to have my consent, I wondered. I believed not. I did not ask myself, would I give my consent if it were asked or needed; such a decision could easily wait, I thought, until it was called for. Now, I avoided it as if it were a stone in my path.

I knew so little about Marcel! I knew him capable of actions that other people would call fantastic, exaggerated, romantic; but I also knew him for an actor—some might say perhaps, a poseur. Yet was he? Hadn't he an honesty that most of us couldn't boast of? And wasn't he reckless? His coming over here with Hugo showed that. Also, I thought, he had a queer sense of humour that might enjoy bestowing this enormous gift on an obscure student to whom he happened to have taken a fancy— who had befriended him, with no idea of gaining anything thereby. It would amuse him to cause consternation in the bosom of, say, Aunt Susan and her like; and he was quite malicious enough to enjoy humiliating Jim. As for Ursula, he could console her, if necessary, and if he thought fit, very easily. . . . Yes, there was a possibility, not only that he meant it, but that he could remain sufficiently interested to carry it through.

My next thoughts were concerned with the technicalities of the business. The lawyers would make difficulties, of that there could be no doubt, and they would do their best to dissuade Marcel from any course so unusual. Still, that might only make him more obstinate; and since he appeared to have plenty of money, he would probably get his way. But surely, in any event, it would take a very long time. There were first of all the wills. First there was the will of James Ullstone, so unexpected and unorthodox: presumably that was already more or less settled, though nothing seemed to have been done yet about assessing death duties and so on, and doubtless this murder would hold up everything in connection with that too. Then, presuming that the will of James Ullstone was valid, there was this hastily-concocted will of Hugo: that too would have to pass the test of validity before Marcel's intentions could be regarded as anything other than an agreeable fantasy. Was the will written on hotel paper, signed by the hotel proprietor and his wife, a solid affair, as potent as the lawyer's parchment beginning in Gothic characters: "This is the last Will and Testament," and maundering on in its comma-less legal jargon about the Said So-and-So? Those who had mentioned it so far seemed to think it was. One could only hope that they were right, and that these two hurdles were safely over.

And so one came back to Marcel: wouldn't he have to wait until both these wills were safely proved and stamped and all the rest of it, whatever it was, before he could put his own idea into practice? And how long would that take, with a big estate like this? A month, two months, six—a year? And by that time, would the mercurial Marcel remember even the name of Jake Seaborne? It was not likely. His parents, his friends, his fiancée, would see to that. And yet—and yet—Marcel was no ordinary person. If he really meant it, he might fix something up provisionally, perhaps?

Outside, the owl, after a period of profound silence—digestive, probably—suddenly rent the air again with her barbaric yelpings. I rolled round and pulled the bedclothes over my head. It was no use: I could not shut out the vision of the moonlit park, the long façade of the house, the drives, the gates, even the monkeys—and myself as the master of it all. "I shall be a great benefactor," I thought, as sleep at last assailed me. "I won't give up medicine, of course; but as I shan't have to work for money——'

I fell asleep.

13

Next morning, I awoke with a feeling of strangeness on me, as if something very important had happened, about which I was both elated and alarmed. It took me some minutes to remember what this was. I dressed more carefully than usual, smoothing down as best I could my rather unruly hair, anxiously counting the number of clean collars still left to me, and wishing I had brought another suit. Hitherto I had not bothered to let my people know where I was; now, I thought, I must get in touch with them and ask them to send me a parcel of clothes.

Usually, I was punctual in my habits. This morning, having not only overslept but taken longer to dress, I found myself one of the last to reach the breakfast table. Ursula was there, soignée and fresh-looking as always, already smoking her after-breakfast cigarette, and apparently absorbed in a household account book. I said "Hullo!" to her as I sat down; but instead of her customary cheery answer, I received only an abstracted "Good morning," and the momentary look she gave me was unsmiling. Then, having poured me out a cup of coffee, she returned to her accounts without another word.

Slowly I became aware of an intense silence; yet I had heard them talking before I entered the room. I looked round: they were all, except Ursula, staring at me in a most peculiar manner. Opposite me, Aunt Susan and Uncle Biddolph had suspended all activity in order to concentrate on me a stare of dislike and disapproval, so powerful that for a moment I could not take my eyes off them. Of course I knew they disapproved of my presence in the house: they disapproved of almost everybody and everything, and a stranger was fair game; but the two faces side by side, one round and red, the other long, pale and lugubrious, had not so far bothered to register such open animosity. Compared with this dual barrage, the contemptuous glance which Jim threw at me over his shoulder, from the sideboard where he was helping himself to bacon and grilled kidneys, seemed quite familiar and normal. But what surprised me most was the stare of Dr. Parmoor. He had, at this time in the morning, heavy rings under his eyes and a generally derelict appearance; but he usually managed to look, if not amiable, at least easy-going and nonchalant. Now, as he turned to me from his place beside Ursula, I was surprised to see in his dark red-rimmed eyes with the yellow sclerotics, a spark of active interest such as one might expect from a bull in the arena as he charges towards the toreador. He looked, in short, as if he had some design on me, something that afforded him satisfaction, even amusement. I could not withstand his gaze; I shrank back, surprised and disconcerted, and buried my face in my coffee-cup.

Marcel was not there. Usually he stayed in bed to breakfast; but this morning, I had reason to believe, this was not the reason for his absence. It must have been he of whom they had been speaking when I entered the room and put a stop to the conversation: someone, they were saying, had caught the 8.20 a.m. train up to town and wouldn't be back till evening. I had overheard the words "legal advice," and had assumed that they referred to Hugo's death and to-morrow's inquest; but now, with a rush of blood to the face and a racing of the heart, I realized that not only did they mean Marcel, but that the legal advice he was seeking concerned *me* and his idea of yesterday. Then they all knew about it! That would account for this overpoweringly hostile atmosphere. "Surely," I thought, "he hasn't been so utterly crazy as to tell them!" And then I remembered one of Marcel's outstanding characteristics: he couldn't keep a secret. He had betrayed the secret of his identity on the very night of his arrival; he had revealed himself first to Evelyn, then to Ursula next day. He had given away his plan for a rendevzous with Hugo. And now, he had told one of them—Ursula, no doubt—about his projected deed of gift of their ancestral home to me. Was it any wonder that I was the cynosure of murderously hostile eyes?

I shuddered, remembering—impossible though it now seemed, over the prosaic breakfast-table—that one of these people might actually be guilty of murder; but Marcel's words, that there was no danger unless one's death would automatically confer a benefit on someone, recurred to me, and I took heart. I returned Parmoor's curious stare with one equally ambiguous and, I hoped, equally bold. I glowered across the table back at Aunt Susan and Uncle Biddolph, and managed to make the latter lower his gaze to his plate. I directed a proud and injured look towards Ursula's blonde head, but it passed over her, as she was not looking at me. Then I got up and went to the sideboard, and boldly helped myself to the remaining bacon and kidneys, elbowing Jim in the process; but, nevertheless, these manifestations cost me something. I felt that this change of front towards me was unjust and undeserved, and the sense of injustice boiled up in me and made my throat dry and my knees shaky. It was a great relief to me when the door opened and Evelyn came in.

She had already breakfasted, of course: Evelyn was always punctual, earlier than the others, for everything. She had come merely to say something to Ursula, apparently about household matters, and she went straight to her and conferred with her for a minute or two. As she stood leaning over Ursula, her hand on the back of Ursula's chair, and they both scanned the account-book, Evelyn's dark head was very close to Ursula's fair one; they might have been sisters, or at any rate bosom friends. It was hard to realize that apparently they detested each other. What had gone wrong, I wondered, to fill them with mutual suspicion and dislike? Each accused the other of being a mercenary schemer, an *intrigante*; which of them, if either, was at all justified? Or were they both seeing each other through utterly distorted spectacles—distorted by feminine jealousy, perhaps, or whatever one is to call such a deep-seated natural antipathy? I wished it were not so. I liked Ursula. I was in love with Evelyn. I wished that they would somehow meet across me and be friends. . . .

At that moment, when I was giving them what must have been my most sentimental look, Evelyn happened to glance up and intercept it. She smiled. It was the first real smile I had received that morning, and I welcomed it hungrily. Had she not yet heard of Marcel's scheme, or had she heard and didn't she care? I hoped—I was sure—it was the latter. I felt I must see her at the earliest possible moment and talk to her, find out what she thought.

She left the room, and I jumped up and followed her. At the door, I glanced back. Nobody had stirred. They sat in stony silence, looking down at their plates now, as if I and my move-ments did not exist. Yet I knew that the minute the door was closed behind me, they would burst into animated conversation, at my expense. I slammed the door and raced after Evelyn.

14

She was making for the kitchens, jingling a bunch of keys as she walked. She looked so neat and self-possessed and competent, glancing to right and left, taking everything in as she passed, noticing things that needed doing, planning the order of the day, that I held back for a moment in order not to catch her up too soon and spoil the picture. I thought, "What a strange thing it would be if, through me, this little creature should become legally what she is in fact, the mistress of this house!" There was no one, of that I was certain, better qualified to fill the post. Ursula? Ursula wasn't really interested, as she would surely be the first to admit if she were honest—and she usually was honest, I was forced to own, so far as I could see. She had not wanted to undertake the burden of nursing her father; so, too, running this great house was not really her line—not the practical side of it, anyway, though she made an excellent figurehead. If Fate so decreed, she might yet, I thought, have to yield place to the better woman.

I ran the last few yards, and caught Evelyn up, taking her by the arm. She turned at once, smiling up at me when she saw who it was. Her smile had a new quality in it, I thought, and there was a look in her dark blue eyes, a sort of tenderness, that made my heart leap up in joyous expectation.

'I want to talk to you,' I said breathlessly. 'When can I see you?'

'You're seeing me now,' she said. Then, seeing that I was too desperately in earnest to be withheld by banter, she added gently, 'I'm free this morning, as soon as you like. Just let me give the cook her orders. You can wait for me outside, in the rose-garden if you wish.'

'No, no,' I said. 'I want to take you off somewhere in the car. Nobody can object. We can leave a message saying we'll be back by dinner-time. The police don't seem to be bothering much about us to-day. Marcel has gone up to town, it seems, so why shouldn't we have the day off, too?'

Evelyn considered for a moment. 'All right,' she said.

'Meet me in the courtyard,' I said, overjoyed. 'You aren't afraid of—anybody, now?'

She shook her head, smiling. 'And you?' she said.

I drew my hand across the place where yesterday Jim's riding-crop had fallen. 'It's gone,' I said. 'It's forgotten. It can't happen again.' I took her hand. 'I'm not afraid of anything or anybody, either.'

'Good!' she said, giving my hand a shake and a squeeze. 'That's the spirit! Keep it up, remember. I'll be with you again in ten minutes or so.'

She went off, as before, intent on her duty, leaving me stupefied with delight. As soon as I had watched her out of view and had recovered my balance, I tore madly back again along passages, barging my way through doors until I reached the cobbled courtyard, now bright in the morning sunshine, where the well-groomed pigeons were strutting and cooing and keeping a sharp lookout for possible admirers bringing food. Already I was their friend, and even to-day I had not forgotten to bring some crumbs in my pockets from the breakfast-table; but I could not spare time for them, beyond tossing the crumbs on to the ground and leaving them; normally I would have expected a much better show for my money, a perching on hand and arm and shoulder. But now, Evelyn was on her way towards me. I rolled back the heavy doors, disclosing my small but oh! how useful sports car; and I had time just to reverse her out into the yard and run a duster over the seats and the windscreen, when Evelyn appeared. In a moment we were away, leaving the dark house behind us, and past those lodge gates with the exasperatingly wise monkeys, on to the open road again.

I could not believe my good fortune.

15

No, I could not believe it. Here we were, rushing through the air together. Beside me was the girl whom, two days ago, I had believed entirely devoted to Jim; and then there had been that brief scare when she had gone off with Marcel and I had thought they were completely taken up with each other. Now all that was over. She was by my side, leaning close to me to get what shelter there was from my small windscreen, or perhaps to let me know that she was there, and happy to be with me like this, really alone and away from everybody for the first time. It was exhilarating and intoxicating, and for a long while I did not need anything else. I drove on happily without talking, content to savour the moment, knowing that we had the whole day before us and no one could interrupt.

We had lunch at an inn I knew of; and afterwards we climbed up the hillside behind the inn, by a winding and not too steep path to the summit. The afternoon was warm and sunny; the deep blue sky was edged with huge cumulus clouds piled up on the horizon, and the gentle breeze that played around us was scented with gorse. Nobody was in sight. Sheep grazed on the short grass near us as we lay looking down at the village and the river, the church and barns; and scraps of poetry learnt in school and almost forgotten came floating back into my mind.

'How quiet it is!' I said. 'Sometimes I think I'd like to live and die in a place like that; but of course one wouldn't be able to stand it for long, really.' I turned to her impulsively: 'I wish we hadn't to go back and face to-morrow, don't you?'

There was a world of anxiety and worry in her answering look. 'I wish we need never go back at all!' she said in a low passionate tone.

'Do you really?' I said eagerly; and yet, given this obvious opening, I found myself overcome by an absurd shyness, which prevented me from saying the appropriate thing. Instead, I hurried on, looking down at the village in pretended interest: 'Of course, I don't suppose one could earn one's living there.'

Evelyn gave me a sidelong look. 'If what I hear is true,' she said, 'you won't need to.'

Although I had already assured myself that she, like the others, knew of Marcel's project, nevertheless I was startled at thus being brought into the open. I had not had time to think about what line to take: whether to scoff at the whole thing as a joke, or whether to let it be discussed sufficiently seriously for me to discover what they all thought of it. My somewhat stammering answer was a mixture of both:

'Oh, I don't suppose anything will come of it,' I said doubtfully. 'You know what Marcel's like. For one thing, he talks too much. That accounts for all the black looks I got at breakfast this morning. I thought so.'

Evelyn laid a hand on my sleeve: 'Are you so very surprised?'

I was touched by the sympathy and sadness in her voice: it was as if she said, "I have suffered from their hostility, too," and it drew me towards her. I laid my hand on hers.

'You at any rate will believe,' I said, 'that I've done nothing whatever to provoke this action—if it is action and not just talk—on the part of Marcel. It's entirely his own idea—a caprice if you like—and it surprised me as much as it surprised the rest of you. The question is, if he goes through with it, what am I to do?'

'You mean——?' said Evelyn. I could see from the anxiety in her face that she was bending all her mind on to my problem, and I was grateful. I gave her hand a squeeze.

'I mean,' I said, 'where do I stand ethically? Legally I suppose I couldn't refuse: that is to say, I can't prevent Marcel from carrying out his idea on paper, any more than I can prevent him from making a will in my favour, because he can do it without my knowledge. But—if ever it came about, what would be my position? Wouldn't I be morally bound to hand the whole thing back to Jim and Ursula?'

Evelyn reflected, looking into the blue distance. As we lay silent, the sheep came cropping closer and closer to us. A lark rose from the ground and in a few moments was high above us, trilling and moving its wings with the same amazing verve.

'Well,' she said at last, 'that would be for you to decide, of course. But since you ask me my opinion—and I wouldn't give it unless you did ask me—I really see no reason why you should.'

'You don't?' I said, in a voice as carefully non-committal as I could make it.

'It's very difficult,' she said, withdrawing her hand gently from under mine, and clasping her arms round her knees. 'At first sight, I know, somebody honest and generous and—simple, like you, would naturally think he ought to return it to those he'd call, I suppose, the rightful heirs.' Her voice was kind, but there was a hint of irony in the last words. 'Yet after all, Jake dear, who *are* the rightful heirs? You can't decide, quite on your own, that Jim and Ursula are, when their own father—who made a fortune, you know: the estate would have had to have been sold long ago if he hadn't—when he left it away from them? He knew them better than you do.'

'Tell me, Evelyn,' I said, 'why do you really think he did it? Was it a brain-storm? Or do *you* think he had good reason?'

'I think he thought,' said Evelyn, again after a pause, 'that whatever he left to Jim would be squandered—that any large fortune put into Jim's hands would be the ruin of him, more quickly than anything. And as for Ursula, he thought she'd spend it on Dr. Parmoor; and James Ullstone didn't like Dr. Parmoor. He called him a waster.' She gave a rueful laugh.

'One of the things I used to get into trouble with James for was my trying to put Dr. Parmoor's point of view. It was silly of me, but I never could help trying to make James see other people's points of view, and all I got for it was that I drew his anger on to myself.'

'I expect he appreciated what you did at its right value, at any rate in his saner moments,' I said. 'What I can't understand is why he never left *you* anything. That seems rather mean, after all you'd done for him.'

'Yes, but,' said Evelyn, 'you see, he thought I might be going to marry Jim, and in that way Jim would have got my share after all. I don't blame him. I know how he felt. And he was not himself at the last. One must never forget that.'

I put my arm round her: 'Still seeing other people's points of view!' I said. 'Listen, Evelyn: if anything comes of this, would you—do you think you could bring yourself to share it with me?' My heart thumped, and my breath came fast, but I added as lightly as I could: 'If you think I must take on the responsibility, the least you can do is to help me.'

Evelyn drew away from me a little and turned aside. 'We'll see, Jake dear,' she said in subdued tones. 'The time hasn't come to think about things like that.'

'But you don't altogether turn the idea down?' I pressed her, driven on by an inner compulsion that both exhilarated and terrified me.

'No,' she said, quietly but decisively. 'I wouldn't be here with you otherwise.'

I would have kissed her, but she put up a hand between us and held me back:

'Ask me again some time—not now—not yet.'

'But why?' I said, goaded on by her reluctance. 'You know I'm in love with you; and you like me, or you seem to—though at first I thought it was Jim, and then again Marcel. Why can't we have it all settled between each other, and let nobody else know?'

Evelyn shook her head: 'They *would* know. We wouldn't tell them, but—do you think you could hide it for five minutes, my poor dear? If I agreed wholly to your—your suggestion, then that would mean we were engaged, wouldn't it? And do you imagine that it wouldn't show on your face as soon as we got back? Ursula would see it at once, and so would Marcel, I think: he's not stupid, however indiscreet he may be. And then—and then——'

She clasped her hands together, and the lines of worry that I had come to know so well deepened on her forehead.

'What is it, darling?' I said. 'What are you afraid of now?'

'It's always the same thing,' she said forlornly, 'always the same. The moment they know, they'll work to destroy us—to eliminate *you*. Jim—well, you know how violent he was when you just talked to me. He has sworn that nobody else shall have me. Do you think he'll take it tamely if he knows you plan not only to get his property but me as well? Ursula will go about it more subtly: she'll fill your mind with poisonous stories about me——'

I interrupted. 'I can't believe it!' I said. 'She wouldn't be so wicked!' I was thinking of my sentimental picture of them both, Evelyn and Ursula, at the breakfast-table this morning. 'And if she were,' I added violently, 'it wouldn't be any use. She couldn't influence me in the slightest!'

Evelyn was not heartened. 'You think so now,' she said, 'but you don't know the power of lies, especially if they're constantly repeated. You'd begin by disbelieving, but gradually you'd wonder if perhaps there mightn't be something in them. Then you'd find yourself watching me, trying to trap me; and in the end you'd twist everything I said and did until it fitted in with what you'd been told. You'd succeed. One always does—that's the sad part of it. So——' She turned to me with a smile, though there were tears in her eyes, 'shall we say no more about it now? and then, if you still feel the same in six months' time——'

Six months' time! The words awakened an echo in my mind. It was Marcel who had said to me only the previous day, "In six months' time you'll feel differently." It seemed, in one way, an eternity; and yet I was prepared to swear fidelity for all eternity. Perhaps it was easier to swear eternal constancy than to envisage exactly what would happen in six months' time. Nevertheless, I said valiantly:

'Well, I shall regard it as settled, so far as I'm concerned.' But somehow she had succeeded in robbing the occasion of any sense of joy or triumph. Again a silence fell between us; and soon afterwards we left.

The sun was still shining, and the sky was just as blue, when I drove her home; but the day seemed colder and darker to me, and a load lay on my spirits. I tried to talk, to sound cheerful; but everything I started seemed wrong. How could I ask her to envisage a happy future after what she had just told me? Wasn't my proposal rather an addition to her troubles than a help? *What* was it that was troubling her so deeply? It could not be simply Ursula's hostility, real or fancied: she had had to put up with that for a year now, and she seemed to have been able to do so fairly easily; at any rate, it had not driven her away. What was it that she knew, and could not disclose even to me?

The answer that sprang to the mind seemed too glaringly obvious to be believed; and yet, was it? Didn't all that she said come back to the same thing—her fear of, or for, Jim? Was it possible that she knew for certain what all of us probably suspected: that it was Jim who had slipped out when we were dancing, and gone to the rendezvous, about which she, Evelyn, had told him; and there, seeing in the flesh the youth whom he regarded as the potential author of all misfortune, had yielded to his own violent temperament and shot him as he stood in the pathway looking out, silhouetted against the moonlit garden? Such knowledge would be enough to break the spirit of someone less delicately made than Evelyn, I thought: imagine her feelings as she watched Jim, wondering if he would betray himself, and watched the police, wondering whether they had already found, or were on the point of finding, a decisive clue?

I glanced sideways at her from time to time. No, I could not talk about her and me: her present trouble, whatever it was, made her incapable of envisaging anything beyond to-day. But if she would only have confided in me, how I could have eased it for her! We could have talked then, without restraint, and together we could have discovered what was best to do. It was no use my asking her: she would only have denied it. The time for confidences had not yet come. Perhaps it would come, I said to myself, after my declaration of to-day. I would have liked to ask her, "Does he know you know?" I believed he did, and that that was perhaps the heaviest burden of all: for if he did, would he not be watching her, to see if she would betray him? That would account for her reluctance to let me come into the open and announce our engagement: Jim would assume, naturally, that she had confided in me, and that again would mean I was in danger. She had warned me as best she could: she had spoken of his jealousy. What she had not been able to say was that there is an even more powerful motive for murder than the desire to eliminate your rival in love, and that is the silencing of someone who knows your secret. He would trust her only in so far as he believed her to be still free, or perhaps devoted to him. And then with a shock I realised that if once his suspicions were aroused, she too would be in danger as much as I. And so it behoved me to do as she wished, not only for my own sake but for hers.

All this reasoning took me to the lodge gates. I felt much the happier for it, and as we drove up through the great avenue, I was able to say to her:

'Don't worry—I understand. You can count on me. I won't show any sign in front of the others; but I'm there if you want me.'

She smiled up at me for the first time since I had made my declaration on the hillside, and pressed my hand. What I did not tell her was that from now on I was going to make it my business to watch Jim's every movement, while not appearing to, and to try to find out what the police really knew.

16

Sir Frederick Lawton was with us again at dinner that night. This evening, we were not quiet: there was a good deal of talking, even of hilarity, which revealed the underlying tension. We were all thinking of to-morrow's inquest, wondering how we would acquit ourselves and what would be the outcome. Sir Frederick was the only one of us who remained his usual self, pleasant, imperturbable, far above it all. How I envied him, and wondered by what method one attained to such a god-like manner!

I felt profoundly uneasy, even guilty, as I looked at him; and when, not altogether to my surprise, he fastened upon me after dinner and marched me off to the library for one of his talks, my heart beat fast and my knees shook. I would have given much to get away from him; but he was inexorable. He placed me in the chair he wished me to sit in, and leaned back, and crossed his legs, and folded his hands, and surveyed me with his bland and apparently benevolent smile. This time he did not offer me a drink, not even a small one; nor did he take one himself.

'Well, Seaborne,' he began—and I knew at once from his voice that I was in for an even more uncomfortable time than I had expected—'you *have* been busy since yesterday, haven't you?'

I gave him an obstinate look, as if I didn't understand; but I understood perfectly, and the tips of my ears burned.

'I must say,' he went on, 'I little thought, when I asked you to stay here and act as my locum, that I should soon find you installed as the possible master of this house. I must confess I never saw anything done so quickly. If you become as skilful at your job, you'll be an asset to the profession—provided you remain in it, of course.'

I wish I could convey the cutting contempt he managed to put into these words, without altering his pleasant tone, his easy attitude, his benevolent smile. I blurted out:

'It's nothing to do with me. It's not my fault that Hugo was killed. And this idea isn't mine—it's Marcel's.'

Sir Frederick inclined his head in politest agreement: 'Of course. I accept those statements, though I've no proof of either. But I accept them. I like to think I'm dealing with men of honour.'

I glanced up sharply to see if his look was openly jeering; but no, it was as before, only less smiling. I found myself embarking on a hasty self-defence; but even to my ears it sounded unconvincing and confused. I was trying to remember the arguments with which Evelyn had bolstered me up; and this effort not only was unsuccessful but also prevented me from thinking of any arguments of my own. I managed, however, to say that I thought that Marcel had the right to do as he pleased in the matter.

Sir Frederick listened patiently to the end. Then he said:

'What you mean is, he *can* do as he pleases, and neither you nor anyone else can prevent him except by persuasion. But if he does as he pleases, and it pleases him to hand this property over to you, and the law allows it, as it may for all I know'—the contemptuous note predominated again—'that still leaves *you* with your own choice of action. What are *you* going to do?'

He waited for an answer; but as I said nothing, he went on:

'I hope you're going to give it back to the people who've always lived here—whose home it is—Jim and Ursula Ullstone.'

I opened my mouth to say something rude about Jim; but Sir Frederick held up his hand:

'Whether they're worthy of it or not doesn't concern either you or me, you know. You're not, I hope, going to be hypocritical enough to pretend that you'd be accepting the gift because you felt you owed a duty to society! Yes, I see you were. Well, well!'

He shook his head over me as if I had given some foolish answer in an examination, or had bungled some bit of minor surgery. As he studied me, he swung his monocle to and fro like a pendulum:

'The point is, Seaborne,' he said, 'if you accept this gift, you will be doing yourself a grave injury. You don't believe it. The idea of owning this house and land has gone to your head, as well it might at your age. But if you act upon your very natural immediate inclination, you will be snatching at something that isn't really yours. Whose it really is by now is a question that you aren't called upon to answer. But what is quite certain is that it isn't yours. You can't call the sudden caprice of this young man, an outsider who has acquired this power by an accident—his friend's violent death—you can't call that a valid title. No, no: if you accept it, it will be pure robbery, and not all the false reasoning in the world will alter the fact.'

I got up, trembling, this time with anger:

'Sir,' I said in tones so shaky that I could hardly articulate my words, and my throat felt hot and dry, 'you can't say that to me. That's an insult, and I won't stand it. I have the right to make my own decisions without any direction from you or anybody—though,' I added, and it was true, 'I have the greatest respect for you, as you know. But I don't think you ought to presume on it to dictate to me about my own affairs.'

Sir Frederick watched me, interested, as I stumbled through

this long speech. The black ribbon of his monocle ran through his long fingers as he sought for the glass and applied it to his eye.

'O-oh!' he said, 'so it's got as far as that into your blood, has it? By Jove, what a remarkable thing!' He bent forward a little, peering at me as being evidently a more interesting specimen than he had realized, and added: 'You'll have to look out, my boy. By the way, has someone been talking to you? You sound to me as if you were putting forward a point of view not entirely your own. However, that's your affair.' He suddenly dropped his easy manner, and sat upright: 'Sit down, Seaborne.'

I obeyed at once, to my own surprise.

'What I have to say to you is entirely in your own interest,' he went on, incisively. 'You may choose to ignore it, but I am bound to say it, since I am responsible for your being here. *Don't have anything to do with this proposed gift.* Don't listen to anybody who advises you to accept it. If this foolish young man means what he says, and you find yourself in the fantastic position you covet at the moment, repudiate it at once, and let everybody know here and now that that is your intention. That would put a stop to the whole business, and to heaven knows how much trouble besides.'

He paused, but I said nothing. My head swam with the conflict between my desires, which included Evelyn, and his devastating words. With the utmost seriousness he went on:

'We do not know who killed Hugo Ullstone; but we do know what a disturbance was caused by his coming here, and we know that it cost him his life. It seems very likely that somebody got rid of him because he seemed about to step into possession here. And he had good reason to regard himself as the rightful heir, morally as well as legally. Now you are proposing to step into the same invidious position. Don't you realize what you're doing?'

I still attempted resistance. 'If you're trying to frighten me——' I began.

'I am,' said Sir Frederick decisively. 'You will have every reason to be frightened, in my opinion.'

'But,' I said, remembering an argument of Marcel's, 'what would anybody gain by eliminating *me?* The property would then pass to my heirs, wouldn't it, and so right away from here?'

'Yes, if the deed of gift became a fact,' said Sir Frederick. 'But what's to prevent anyone from eliminating you before it is carried into execution? Marcel is safe, because Hugo's will may be valid; but you are not—unless somebody expects to gain by making you the cat's-paw: then you are safe during the interval—probably a long one—before the deed is executed. But otherwise——' He dismissed me into eternity with a wave of the hand.

I had not thought of that. Nevertheless, I could not take it seriously. It seemed to me that in my case everything would be different. If that was all—— But apparently it was not. He leaned back again, and his tone changed:

'However, that wasn't really what I wanted to say to you. All I ask you to observe is this: firstly, that a murder has been committed here in our midst, and the motive is almost certainly concerned chiefly with this property. Secondly, you yourself, actuated by greed—the desire to possess this same property—have altered your whole outlook and your aim in life. You have become a different person. You are prepared to rationalize, to lie to yourself, to give up a useful career, to throw in your lot with a set of people you don't really understand or approve of, and who won't really accept you. In short, you are arranging for yourself a life of sheer misery, full of cares and conflicts and all manner of unpleasantness, and without any adequate compensation, so far as I can see.'

'It probably won't come to anything,' I said sullenly.

'I agree,' said Sir Frederick with annoying promptitude. 'It probably won't, luckily for you. But that is all the more reason why you should return to a sane point of view about it. If it does materialize, in my opinion you are lost. If it doesn't, you are going to be disappointed and embittered for the rest of your life. You will go about seeing yourself as a landowner *manqué*, and boring all your acquaintances with the story of what might have been, like the people—and they are legion—who claim to have been cheated out of a legacy. Pull yourself together—and remember who you are, as the Red Queen said.'

He got up and walked to the door

17

I stayed where I was. I could not answer. I was choking with annoyance, like a child robbed of a new toy; but I knew in my heart that he was perfectly right, and this increased my annoyance to strangulation-point. At the door he turned:

'By the way,' he said, 'the police think that Hugo was shot down at the edge of the shrubbery, as he stood there looking out. They think he was shot by someone standing inside, on the path or behind a tree. They saw—what you and I didn't notice—that there was moss on the points of his shoes, and two lines on the path where the toes had dragged. Some of the leaves in his right hand came from the beeches which fringe the wood. The police can therefore trace exactly what happened: where he stood, where the murderer stood, how Hugo was dragged while still alive towards and under the rhododendron bush where we found him.'

I was sufficiently roused by this to shake off the chagrin that gagged me, and ask:

'Have they found the weapon?'

'Yes,' said Sir Frederick. 'It was a Colt revolver, and it appears that the bullet used was American. They found it embedded in a tree. They know the calibre, of course, but I'm afraid my knowledge of these things is small. The revolver came from this house, so Jim says: it was in the gunroom, and anybody could have taken it. It had belonged to his father. He denied having ever used it himself except for a little target-practice in the gallery here, and said his shooting was confined to recreation. He said he knew nothing about the ammunition. He made a very bad impression on the police, and they are spoiling for a chance to catch him.'

'How soon will they bring it off, sir, do you think?' said I. I was beginning to feel better, and my annoyance with Sir Frederick was evaporating, leaving behind it an awkward sense of shame.

'Ah!' said Sir Frederick, returning a pace or two into the room, 'that's another matter! Here they have all these bits of information, collected with the greatest diligence and care; and no doubt many others too. I daresay that in the end they will be able to piece them together into a connected whole. But until that happens, they don't know what's relevant and what's not, don't you see?—any more than you or I do. Anybody with determination could have shot poor Hugo as he stood on the edge of the shrubbery, from a distance of six or seven feet, which they say was the fact. Anybody of average strength could have dragged him the short distance into the wood.'

'You say he wasn't dead, sir?' I asked. I had risen, and we were now standing near the fireplace, our difference of opinion forgotten. 'How was he shot, then?'

'The bullet entered the body just *here*'—he turned me round and dug his finger into a spot in my back—'and came out *here*'—he turned me round again and stabbed a very tender place just below my sixth rib. 'He doubtless collapsed where he stood, and was dragged in a dying condition to the place where we found him. He does not appear to have struggled. But there was a death-spasm: his position and attitude show that. The person who shot him was aiming at the heart, but he just missed. The bullet passed below.'

I considered this for a while. Then, remembering something he had said earlier, I asked: 'You say the revolver came from this place. Where did they find it?'

'They found it quite easily,' said Sir Frederick. 'It was in the lily-pond.'

'Good heavens!' I said, remembering how Evelyn and I had sat there, and thinking of the revolver lying near by in the mud all the time, under the lily-leaves—at least, so I supposed. 'What a queer place to put it!'

'Why?' said Sir Frederick, leaning his elbow on the mantel-piece, and dangling his monocle towards me like the carrot towards the donkey. 'Isn't it the place you'd choose yourself, perhaps?'

I looked up sharply, but he was smiling.

'It's too obvious, for one thing,' I began; and then, catching his expression, 'unless, of course, the person hiding it wanted it to be found.'

'Exactly!' nodded Sir Frederick, like an examiner who, having given every help to a rather slow candidate, has at last extracted a correct answer.

'And therefore,' I went on slowly, 'the owner of the revolver must be known, and the intention must be to incriminate him.'

Sir Frederick nodded again: 'As the owner was Jim's father, the person who was most likely to have inherited it was——?'

'Jim!' I exclaimed, struck with the way in which every avenue seemed to lead back to him.

'And though he denies having ever learnt to use it with any skill, nevertheless he admits to having used it a few times at this indoor target upstairs.'

'He admitted that?' I said.

'Not at first,' said Sir Frederick. 'When they suggested he might have, he denied it. Then he said it was possible he had at some time or other: he had forgotten, being interested only in the shot-guns and the sporting rifles. That's how he went on, and that's what I meant when I said he had made a bad impression on the police.'

'Did he make a bad impression on you, sir?' I said.

Sir Frederick reflected. 'That's a good question,' he said, 'though rather difficult to answer. I think I would say rather that he gave me a sensation of discomfort because I knew what a bad show he was putting up. But whether it was guilt or *gaucherie*, I'm not so sure.'

'You spoke of American ammunition,' I said. 'Is anything known about that?'

Sir Frederick shook his head. 'Not so far as I've heard,' he said. 'The rest has not yet been found, and Jim says he knows nothing about it. The police are trying to trace it, of course. The trouble is, most of the people here have travelled. Nearly all of them, it appears, have visited America—Jim, Ursula, the uncle and aunt, Parmoor, everybody except Miss Ross, in fact. Not that it matters: the ammunition may not have been fetched by the person who used it. It appears that in some calibres either British or American ammunition can be used.'

'It must have been acquired some while ago,' I said, 'otherwise the murderer would hardly have dared to use it for fear of it's being traced. I wonder what he got it for. It can't have been to shoot Hugo with.'

'Oh, perhaps he wanted to shoot somebody else,' said Sir Frederick, 'or blow his own brains out. One never knows.'

I thought again. 'About putting the revolver in the lily-pool,' I said. 'Surely that was a dangerous thing to do. Imagine shooting a man in the shrubbery and then crossing the open lawn in the bright moonlight—possibly leaving footprints in the grass—in full view of anyone who might come out of the house. Marcel did leave the house. We know he went to look for Hugo. If he went out by the front entrance, he could easily have seen anyone crossing from the shrubbery to the pond. In fact, I don't see how he could have missed. And even if he didn't leave at the same time, how could anyone take such a risk?'

'Perhaps he didn't,' said Sir Frederick. 'Perhaps he dropped it there later—next day, for instance.'

'Wouldn't that be a greater risk, with the police about?'

'Not necessarily. They couldn't watch all of us all the time. One could count on their leaving the search for the weapon until after they had examined the site of the murder and asked us all a few questions. They would naturally assume that the last thing the murderer would do would be to carry the weapon on his person. You would yourself, wouldn't you? Yes, so would I. Therefore, if you or I were the murderer, we would—if we were cool enough and clever enough—play just that trick. One could easily have walked through the front door past the policeman, carrying the revolver concealed on one's person, and then have dropped it into the pool at a suitable moment when no one was near. If anybody saw one from a distance, he would think one was stooping down to admire the goldfish. I'm only guessing, of course.'

'Of course,' I said.

'You spent some time down by the pool yourself on the morning of the discovery, didn't you?' said Sir Frederick.

I started, and blushed. 'Yes, I did,' I said defiantly, annoyed to find myself at once on the defensive. 'I was talking to Miss Ross the whole time. She'll tell you I didn't drop anything into the pool.'

Sir Frederick laughed. 'You see how easy it is to sound guilty, Seaborne?' he said. 'My question was quite innocent, however: I merely wondered whether you noticed anything odd about the pool—any disturbance of the surface-foliage, for instance. I believe the surface was almost covered with lily-leaves—though

134

I imagine they would close together even after being disturbed. Still, one might have noticed a broken stem or something of that kind.'

'What use would it be now even if I had?' I said, having searched my recollection and found nothing. 'The police have the revolver.'

'We might be able to say that it had been put there before you arrived,' pointed out Sir Frederick, 'and that might be a help, when the time-table of everybody's movements comes to be collated. Still, I'm only an onlooker. My guess is as good as another's, but it's only a guess. Good night, Seaborne.'

. He went off, without another word about the deed of gift; he seemed already to have forgotten it. That was, I thought, because he knew he had conquered.

I sat there in the library for a long time after he had gone, sadly accustoming myself to the bursting of my bubble, my dream of worldly position and wealth acquired without work, of power and endless leisure—power to benefit others, leisure to live the good life. . . . It was no use: such things were not for me. He was right: people like me could never escape from their consciences and live happily on the backs of others, whatever benefits we thought we might be able to confer in return. No, I must go through with it—three more years of toil without pay, then fifty years of toil with pay: the life of the general practitioner. Would Evelyn wait for me? I wondered. She was young, too, and she seemed serious. Was it fair to ask her? Well, I could try. The first thing now was to see Marcel and persuade him to give up his idea of endowing me. I must convince him that he was wasting his time, as I would merely pass back his gift to—to whom? Well, to Ursula at any rate, if it were too much to ask of myself that I should include Jim.

I sighed and rose, stretching myself and yawning. I had sat there for so long that my limbs were stiff and the knees of my trousers were more baggy than ever. The decision was taken, and finally. Duty would be done. I was rather disappointed to find that it gave me no sense of exaltation.

18

When I make a decision, great or small, I can't rest until I have acted upon it. This has always been true of me, especially if the required action is disagreeable, like deciding to have a tooth out. Two things now confronted me, that had to be done: the first, perhaps the easier, was to see Marcel and tell him that I couldn't accept his gift in any circumstances, and that if he persisted, I should transfer it to the family again. The second was to tell Evelyn.

I did not know why, but I shrank from this far more than from the other. I felt that Evelyn—perhaps out of her affection for me: I hoped so, at any rate—would not be able to take an impartial view of the affair, and that she would see my action, not as noble or self-sacrificing, but merely as foolish and perhaps cowardly. Still, it was no use conjecturing: I must seek them out, and let come what come might.

I went first to the drawing-room; but nobody was there except Aunt Susan and Uncle Biddolph, who both looked at me in such a forbidding manner that I was glad to flee without doing more than put my head round the door. Not quite knowing where to look next, I strolled out into the hall and through the open doors on to the porch.

It was a warm evening, and the moon was still bright. The scents of newly-cut grass and some sweet-smelling flower like narcissus came floating up towards me. The porch was as large as some people's houses in area, and was bounded by a stone balustrade over which one looked beyond the terrace to the lawns and flower-beds. I walked across and leaned my forearms on the rough stone, enjoying in a melancholy way the superb scene with its strange bluish-greenish light and great dark shadows. I could see two people, a man and a woman, walking across the lawn in the distance, but they were too far away for me to be able to distinguish them. I had just lit a cigarette, and was absorbed in my thoughts, when a low voice behind me startled me:

'Have you a cigarette to spare, Jake? I'm feeling that way, too.'

I turned sharply. It was Ursula. She had been sitting in the shadow of one of the columns, in a deck-chair; and now she came towards me and leaned her arms on the balustrade beside me. I gave her a cigarette, and as I held out my lighter, I noticed how the flame lit up her profile and her fair hair. She was actually very beautiful, especially now, in this queer light and because her mood was quiet and her features were composed; but still I wished she were Evelyn.

'Who are they?' I said in a voice as low as hers, I knew that she was watching those two figures, and by now, I knew with a pang what she was going to say:

'Marcel and Evelyn.'

I said nothing, and for a while we smoked in silence. At last she said:

'It's all right to drop somebody oneself, isn't it? It seems quite natural, and one thinks they're selfish if they stand in one's way. But to *be* dropped—that seems quite different.'

'I don't know,' I said. 'I've never tried.'

She laid a hand on my arm and patted me: 'You're a good sort, Jake dear. I've known you only two or three days, but I know you through and through, really. Well, I've always been the one to do the dropping, before, and believe me, the sensation of being dropped is one of the queerest I've ever experienced. One just doesn't know what to do about it, if one's a perfect lady. If one isn't, there are various ways of exteriorizing one's feelings, as Marcel would say.'

I did not know quite how to take her: her voice was pleasant and even gay, but it had an undertone that was almost menacing. I said nothing. She clasped her two hands round my forearm:

'I hope you've forgiven us for being so rude to you this morning,' she said. 'But you know, we're all in a terribly keyed-up state, because of this inquest and all the suspicion and uncertainty. We're apt to behave in an abnormal way—to react violently to every stimulus. I quote Hilary this time.'

'Oh, it's all right,' I said awkwardly. 'I realize how you must have been feeling. It was Marcel's fault, not yours. He shouldn't talk so much. I can understand how you all felt at the idea of me—the intruder—as the master of all this.' I turned to her impulsively: 'You can imagine that to someone in my position, the prize was—well, pretty tempting. But—I've decided that in any case I couldn't accept it, so you needn't be at all afraid of me. I was looking for Marcel to tell him so.'

Ursula withdrew her hands from my arm, and for a moment or two there was silence. I was surprised, and rather disappointed; for irrationally enough, I had expected her to be grateful to me for relinquishing my predatory designs upon her property. Presently she said:

'Jake dear, I don't think I should bother to say anything to Marcel if I were you.'

'Why not?' I said, turning to her in astonishment.

'Because, my dear, Marcel is never the same two days running.' She made a slight gesture towards the moonlit lawn, from which the two figures had now vanished. 'Yesterday, you see, he felt magnanimous towards *you*. He was going to endow you for life—at our expense.' She laughed. 'But this evening, probably he has forgotten all about you.'

'Oh, nonsense!' I said, somewhat taken aback, but determined not to believe her.

'Well, have it your own way,' she said with a shrug, 'if it makes you happy. Myself, I believe nothing and nobody these days.'

'Oh, come!' I said. It was a state of mind which I understood and felt sorry for, but with which I could not sympathize. She was jealous, of course. She had been bored before Marcel came, and *faute de mieux* had allowed herself to enter into some unsuitable engagement with Parmoor. Marcel had very naturally blown all that sky-high, with his youth and his good looks and his winning ways—his moods as changeable as the spring weather. He was not serious, with anybody here. When he left, Ursula would get over him; but she would have been freed from Hilary, and what an excellent thing that would be!

'Shall *we* go and walk there in the moonlight, too?' said Ursula, putting her hand in the crook of my arm and drawing me towards the steps. 'Come on! Oh, come on, Jake, do!'

I hesitated: 'Won't it rather look as if we were——?'

She broke in: 'Spying on them? Of course not! Surely I've a perfect right to walk across my own lawn—at least, it *was* mine till the other day—with my own guest? Come on!'

What really troubled me was that I didn't want to be seen by

Evelyn walking arm in arm with Ursula; but I couldn't tell her that, so, still rather reluctantly, I agreed. I knew that her object was merely to annoy Marcel, or even make him jealous if possible, and that she had no thought of me or of my point of view, nor even any awareness that I had one. However, it was easier to agree. We went slowly down the stone steps together, and towards the lily-ponds. Our shadows were black before us on the silvery grass, and now that we were walking across the open expanse of moonlit lawn, neither of us had anything to say to each other. We were both intently watching for the reappearance of the other two.

Presently they came into sight, round the dark right-angle of a tall yew-hedge. They were not arm-in-arm. They were walking a little apart, and curiously enough—at least, it was curious where Marcel was concerned—they did not appear to be talking. In fact, when Marcel caught sight of us, he came forward a pace or two in advance of Evelyn, almost as if he were hurrying to meet us, and he greeted us in tones of enthusiasm that sounded hearty, though of course they might be faked, I remembered, for the benefit of Ursula.

'Oh, hullo!' he cried. 'What are *you* doing here?' He fastened eagerly upon Ursula, separating her from me without ceremony, and walking her away. He had no lack of words now. Ursula responded rather coldly at first, but I could see that she wouldn't be able to resist him for long—his gaiety, his inability to believe that he could possibly have offended. Before they had gone many yards, I heard her laugh. I said to Evelyn:

'They're all right. Let's leave them to go on ahead, shall we?'

We were near the top of the steps leading down to the lily-ponds. Evelyn hesitated.

'Let's go down here for a few minutes and sit,' I urged her. 'The pools must look lovely by moonlight.'

I was still a little ruffled at having found her with Marcel, but I took good care not to let a hint of this appear in my tone, for I knew that she had considerable pride, and would resent pressure from someone whose claim on her was of so very recent origin. Nevertheless, though I tried to infuse into my voice the tenderness of the afternoon, I was aware in myself of a certain harshness of feeling, due to my own slight hurt and injured pride.

Evelyn's response sounded tired. 'Oh, do you think we should?' she said doubtfully. 'Hadn't we better keep with the others?'

I laughed, not at all pleased. '*They* probably don't think so,' I said rather brutally. 'It seems to me that they're quite glad to get rid of us.' And then, unable to help it, I added: 'What were you and Marcel doing out here so late? Was he telling you his latest story?'

Evelyn didn't answer, and I knew I was being unwise; but I went on perversely, in the way jealous people do: 'If you could spare the time and energy to walk about here with him, I don't see why you can't spend a few more minutes sitting by the lily-pool with me.'

'All right,' sighed Evelyn, and though I felt contrite at the weariness in her tone, I could not yet relax. I began going down the shallow steps ahead of her, trying to master my unreasonable annoyance.

'Come on!' I said to her over my shoulder. 'Look, it's simply marvellous in the moonlight, as I told you.'

And in fact the pool did look marvellous with its dark waters and brilliant reflections. The police in their searches had not done much damage. At each corner of the walls, there was a small statue of Cupid, four curly-headed infants in skittish attitudes aiming their bows towards the centre of the pool, as if to transfix the lilies or perhaps the fish. But now, in the moonlight, one could not see the roguish smiles—only a distortion. With my hands in my pockets, I went on down the steps, humming a tune. Evelyn followed.

There was now no sound, except the familiar whooing of the owl in the distance. Ursula and Marcel were too far away to be heard any longer. What made me stand here looking round? Why did I feel disinclined to go further? I supposed that it was because Evelyn was obviously so reluctant to join me, and that killed romance. Somehow, too, the place, in spite of its beauty, looked cold and forbidding. Discouraged, I was about to give way and turn back, when something caught my attention: in one corner, in the angle made by the wall, there seemed to be a darker shadow; and when I concentrated on it, I fancied I could make out a shape: somebody seated, leaning back with one leg thrust out. The moonlight caught the tip of a polished shoe.

My hair bristled. I felt it rise on the nape of my neck like a dog's.

'What's the matter?' I heard Evelyn say; and then, when I didn't answer, 'Jake! What's the matter?' She came up close behind me and gripped my arm. 'Can you see something?'

'Yes, I think I can,' I said coolly. I felt quite cool as I moved forward, down the last two steps and along the flagged path beside the pool. There was no doubt about the foot and leg now. In another second or two I had turned the corner of the pool, and was there, looking down on the dark figure lying back in the corner. The face was turned aside. One hand hung down limply over the stone seat, the other arm rested on the balustrade of another flight of steps. I knew before I lifted the head by the chin and looked, whom I should see. It was Hilary Parmoor. His eyes and mouth were open. He was dead, but he had not been dead for long. The face where I touched it was still warm. On the white shirt-front I could see, now that I was so near, a black mark that smelt of burnt powder; and at my feet there glinted a revolver, which seemed to have dropped from the right hand.

'Good God!' I said, 'he has shot himself! Then it must have been he who——'

But before I could finish the sentence or even turn round, there was a heavy thud behind me. Evelyn had fainted. I was alone.

19

I was in a dilemma. Decency forbade that I should leave Evelyn lying there on the stones—and in the presence of a corpse, too—and yet I wanted above all things to get away, to dissociate myself, to let people know as quickly as possible and so to shift the responsibility. It was too far to the house for me to carry her. Frantic, and conscious of the corpse, as if it were watching me, I scooped up water from the pool and dashed it over her face, shaking her and calling 'Evelyn! Evelyn!' But what I felt was not tenderness nor even concern; it was exasperation.

As she made no movement, and I was looking round and thinking that after all I had no choice but to leave her, I heard voices: Marcel and Ursula. They appeared, Marcel first, at the top of the steps, and through my confusion of thoughts his voice broke comfortingly:

'Hullo! What's the matter? Is anything wrong? Oh!' He turned back and spoke over his shoulder to Ursula: 'It's Evelyn. What's wrong? Has she fainted?' he said to me, coming down and stooping over her.

I made frantic signs to him to keep Ursula away; but of course he did not understand. He had not seen the dark figure leaning back in the angle of the wall, with its shoe visible in the moonlight—for already the moonbeam had moved so as to bring not only the toe but the whole foot into its light. Ursula came slowly, inexorably down.

'Have you loosened her clothes?' she said, making no attempt to help. 'I thought that was the first thing one did.' And at that moment she looked across Evelyn and saw.

She took in at once who it was and what had happened. I heard her draw in her breath sharply, and I myself stood up, ready to catch her if she too fainted. But although she swayed a little, she did not fall.

'Hilary!' she said in a whisper; and then to me: 'You found him here. Is that why she——?'

I nodded, steadying her with a hand under her elbow. Marcel, too, looked up, and said, 'My God!' And so we all three stood there staring at Hilary across Evelyn's body. None of us made a move towards him; and for a minute there was a most profound silence. I broke it by saying:

'I *must* ring the police. Will you look after her? She'll come round in a minute or two. Can we carry her away from here?'

Together Marcel and I carried her up the stone steps and laid her down on the topmost one. She was heavier than I had thought. She had always looked so fragile to me, but as I helped to carry her, it struck me that her appearance belied her. As we laid her down, she moved a little and moaned. I hastened to say to Marcel:

'There you are: she's coming round. You stay here with her and see that no one else goes down there. Ursula had better come back with me.'

Ursula was still standing exactly where we had left her,

beside the lily-pool, and still staring in the direction of Hilary. The moonbeam crept slowly along, revealing his ankle and the edge of his trousers. When I touched her arm, she came obediently.

As we began to cross the lawn, I put my arm through hers, to hurry her; and I was quite startled to hear her say in her usual conversational voice:

'That was my fault, you know.'

'Oh, no!' I said conventionally, though actually I thought it probably was; but then, that was all the more reason why she must be consoled by being assured that it wasn't.

'Oh, yes!' she said. 'Hilary has shot himself out of despair—one of the seven deadly sins, isn't it? He was often very near to it— that's why he drank, you know—but knowing me just kept him on the right side of it. When he found out he'd lost me, there was no reason why he should wait any longer.'

'And had he lost you?' I said.

'Oh, yes!' she said, still in her strangely inappropriate conversational voice. 'I'm in love with Marcel now. You know that. Nobody would look at Hilary when Marcel was around. Hilary knew it too.'

'It's a passing fancy,' I assured her. 'You think you're in love with Marcel because of the circumstances—because everything about him is exotic and strange. But you can no more pin Marcel down than a moonbeam.'

Ursula sighed, and the sigh ended in a little laugh.

'How right you are!' she said. 'That's what we all like about him. We know he'll never turn into something reliable and familiar and everyday.'

We walked on in silence. As we neared the bottom of the steps leading to the porch, I said to her:

'Look here, Ursula, you realize that there may have been another reason for his shooting himself?'

'No,' she said blankly, and I could tell that no such thought had penetrated into her mind, preoccupied and absorbed in its own conviction of liability. 'No.'

I stood on the bottom step and looked down at her, and she looked up at me questioningly, her fair hair gleaming in the moonlight, her lips parted.

'Don't you think,' I said gently, 'that it may have had something to do with Hugo's murder?'

'You mean he——? Oh no, oh no!' she said, pressing her hand to her mouth.

'The only thing is,' I mused, 'he had no motive—or had he? I mean, could he have done it to get Hugo's fortune back again for you?'

'Oh, Jake,' said Ursula, and her voice trembled and faltered as I had never heard it do before, 'don't say such terrible things! I thought—what I had to bear was—bad enough; but don't make me think I made a criminal of him as well as—a coward; for it *is* cowardly, isn't it, to commit suicide? Or don't you think so?'

I put aside her question for the moment.

'I'm not suggesting,' I said, still as gently as I could, 'that you were to blame. I only meant, don't you think he may have thought that that was what you wanted, and gone and done it, and then shot himself? He may have imagined, seeing you with Marcel, that everything was going well with you, and he'd be better out of the way.'

Ursula broke out violently: 'He'd have been better off if he'd never set eyes on me!' and almost pushing me aside, she ran past me, up the steps and into the house.

I followed her slowly. I was inclined to agree with her. I found myself, to my surprise, sincerely regretting Hilary Parmoor. I could never have brought myself to despise him, much less dislike him. He was, I thought, one of those men who compel one, not to condemn, but to ask, "What was it that went wrong with him?"

A few minutes later, I was speaking to Superintendent Mallett on the 'phone. He said he'd come at once. He asked if Sir Frederick Lawton was there, and I said I'd see. As I came out from the dark corner of the hall where the telephone stood on a table, I saw Marcel and Evelyn coming in through the front door. He was supporting her with his arm round her waist, and she was leaning against his shoulder. At the foot of the staircase, they paused and looked tenderly at each other, he down at her protectively, she trustingly up at him. Then they went slowly on their way, up the stairs and round the bend at the first landing. There they passed Sir Frederick coming down.

'Hullo!' said he, screwing in his eyeglass at them and looking quizzical, as if there were something funny in being ill. 'Not feeling well, eh? Anything wrong?'

'Something terrible has happened,' said Marcel irritably, drawing Evelyn past Sir Frederick. 'Jake is downstairs somewhere. He'll tell you.'

They went on. Sir Frederick, after giving them a puzzled glance, came on downstairs, humming a tune. I stepped out of the shadows and confronted him. He gave a start.

'Good heavens, Seaborne!' he said amiably. 'Well, what's this I hear? Another tragedy? Who was it this time? Not you, evidently. Not Marcel or Miss Ross; and Ursula has just passed me on the stairs, higher up, going like the wind. That leaves—let me see——'

'It's Dr. Parmoor, sir,' I broke out urgently. 'He has shot himself—at least, I suppose he has. He's dead, anyway, and it looks like suicide. I've 'phoned the police, and they'll be here as soon as they can.'

'Tut, tut!' said Sir Frederick. 'Where is he?'

I told him. 'Do you want to see him, sir?' I said eagerly, for now that I had got Evelyn and Ursula off my hands, I was ready for business.

Sir Frederick shook his head with a smile. 'Not this time, Seaborne,' he said. 'We'll let the police do their own work this time. There's no question of resuscitation, I gather? No?—and no question of identification. We'll go into the drawing-room and wait there till the police come. We can pass the time breaking the news to Mr. and Mrs. Biddolph. Well, well, poor Parmoor! He will be no great loss, I fancy; a good man gone wrong—but how wrong!'

And he moved on, across the hall to the drawing-room door, with his usual long easy stride, and again humming a tune. I admired, though I was a little shocked by, his imperturbability. I followed him, curious to see how the two shell-backs, as I called them to myself, would take the news.

20

In the drawing-room, which seemed rather dimly-lighted, I saw at first only Aunt Susan and Uncle Biddolph, who were sitting opposite each other at a small baize table playing bézique, she looking sour, he mournful. Then I heard a familiar sound, a dull click behind me, and I turned to see Jim. He had, curiously enough, brought a darts-board in here and had hung it on the wall near the piano where there was a light. He took no notice whatever of our entry, but went on throwing his darts, with his other hand in his pocket. I wished he had not been so hostile to me; after all the emotions of the day, I would have liked to join him.

Sir Frederick had more efficient control than myself. He took no more notice of Jim than Jim was taking of him, and he did not start or alter his leisured tone whenever there was the click of an arriving dart behind him. Aunt Susan looked up from the cards with her lower teeth bared; they were small and yellow. She regarded the great Sir Frederick as being in a big way what I was in a small one: an intruder, whose presence was barely to be tolerated. Uncle Biddolph, too, obviously thought it a sad, bad business.

'I think you people should know of what has happened,' said Sir Frederick in his calm, measured, quite irresistible tones. 'There has been another death. This time, someone from our midst has been removed.' He cleared his throat, though his voice was in no need of any such aid, and added with unction: 'He *appears* to have died by his own hand.' And then he paused, smiling and swinging his monocle at them.

Aunt Susan had folded together her hand of cards at the word "death," and she now rapped sharply with the edges of the stack on the table.

'Who is it?' she said. 'Who is it?' I felt that she would have added, "Speak up, my man!" if she had dared. 'Good God, who is it?' echoed Biddolph, but in a tone of melancholy, and looking not at Sir Frederick but at Aunt Susan.

Sir Frederick paused a while before he replied.

'This time,' he said, 'the victim is—Dr. Parmoor.'

There was another click behind us as another of Jim's darts struck the board; but in a moment he was confronting us.

'Do you mean to say Parmoor has shot himself?' he said furiously, as if we were to blame for these uncomfortable happenings, since our arrival seemed to have heralded them.

'It appears so,' said Sir Frederick, with the same slight emphasis.

'He would!' said Jim, shrugging his shoulders. 'All things considered, it was the best thing he could do. Where is he? In the house? Are you sure he's dead? Have you sent for the police?'

'What could you expect,' said Aunt Susan, nodding her head at Biddolph, 'of a man who lived as he did, drinking, sponging on others, doing no useful work?' She fanned out the cards again in her small white hands: 'A very good riddance, I should say!'

'Oh, come, madam!' said Sir Frederick. 'Few of us are in any position to say that of any of our fellow-creatures.'

Jim sneered: 'He was a jolly bad doctor, anyway! He practically lived here, yet he never diagnosed my father's disease.' He cast an insolent look at Sir Frederick: 'Any more than you could——' But for all his bluster, he was unable to finish the sentence. His eye seemed captured, then held, by Sir Frederick's swinging monocle.

'Any more than I could cure it, you wish to say?' said Sir Frederick. 'Yes, I must own: in my profession, our skill is not always a match for Nature's malignancy—or man's.' And tucking his eyeglass away, he turned on his heel and left.

I followed. As we crossed the hall, he slowed down to let me catch up with him, and laid a hand familiarly on my shoulder.

'Well, Seaborne,' he said, 'this is going to mean more trouble: more police-questioning, another inquest, and so on. Fortunately for me, I don't come into this second case; but you do, as you again discovered the body. Upon my soul, you seem to have quite a flair for 'em!' And he tapped my shoulder quite jocularly.

'Too true,' I murmured.

'But still,' he said, 'it doesn't matter to you, as you're on holiday—and I notice, too, that you have already developed strong attachments here.' His tone was positively waggish. 'So you don't mind staying. As for me, I must be off again to-morrow immediately after the inquest on Hugo Ullstone: work is piling up, you know! Luckily this new event will probably reduce tomorrow's inquest to almost a formality. The police will undoubtedly want to connect the two things, and they'll have to have time for their inquiries. I hope to be able to catch the noon train. I'm sure I can rely on you to do all you can for these unfortunate people—especially Ursula Ullstone. Ah yes, I know Miss Evelyn Ross is your special interest, but don't forget that this last happening is bound to hit Ursula very hard.'

'I think,' I said, 'Marcel can be trusted to look after *her*.' My tone was grudging, perhaps even sulky, not because I didn't want to stay—I did, very much—but because he would assume that I was doing it to please him.

'Ah!' he said, shaking his head at me, 'can Marcel be trusted to look after anyone except himself?' And he went off up the stairs, leaving me standing there staring after him. A moment or two later, I likewise shook my head and followed him, but much more slowly, up the stairs.

21

The police came: Superintendent Mallett and the doctor and a sergeant in one car, then the ambulance and two or three constables. Once again they seemed to fill the hall with their size and their voices and their importance; and once again we, the inhabitants, were made to feel that we were all rather guilty, if not of the actual death, at any rate of something or other—some gross carelessness or neglect at least. I accompanied them to the lily-pond, and stood by while they took several flashlight photographs of the body from various angles, and then transported it on a stretcher to the ambulance. They could do no more until morning; and so, after some more questioning, to our great relief they went away, leaving a man on guard at the pool.

It was after midnight when we went back to our rooms. The women had not been called upon: Sir Frederick suggested that no good purpose would be served by disturbing them, upset as they were; and even Mallett agreed that it was better to leave them till morning. I went slowly up the stairs with Marcel. He was silent, brooding; and as for me, it was so long—or it seemed so long—since I had talked to him that I no longer knew what to say. But the very fact of my embarrassment drove me into volubility.

'Well,' I said, 'what do you think of this? He can't have been dead long when we passed there, you know. By the way, where had you come from? It was a wonder you didn't hear the shot.'

'Oh, but I did!' said Marcel.

'You what?' I said, stopping short on the half-way landing where the stairs divided.

'I heard a shot,' said Marcel sombrely. He walked on up the stairs, not waiting for me, and I was obliged to catch him up. 'That was my very bad luck. But I'm not sure yet if I shall mention it to anybody,' he added carelessly. I noticed that he had already, according to his custom, mentioned it to me; and he had not asked me to keep it to myself, even! My heart beat fast as I asked him:

'Where were you when you heard it—and were you alone?'

He did not answer. Instead, he went on uttering his own thoughts: 'I am very much afraid,' he said, 'that that poor girl must have been the last to see him alive. If so, the police——'

'What poor girl?' I cried in exasperation. 'Which of them are you talking about now? One never knows, with you, which is first favourite from one hour to the next!' Against my better judgment, I went on hotly: 'I think your behaviour is most unfair. You hurt Ursula's feelings very much by going off with Evelyn this evening; and you must know—or at any rate, if you don't, I'm telling you—Evelyn is engaged to *me!*'

'Ursula's feelings? Bah!' said Marcel. 'What feelings has she got, I ask you? Isn't she responsible for driving that wretched man to his grave? As for Evelyn, my poor friend——'—the pity in his voice was quite maddening—'she is not faintly interested in you, let me tell you! She agrees to what you say only because you pester her; but she would leave here to-morrow with me, if I asked her!'

I gasped. I wanted to laugh him to scorn. But without my willing it, a cooler feeling intervened, blocking my first impulse and introducing reason: the most unwelcome thought, "Can he be right?"

'You haven't answered my question,' I said with dignity. 'Where were you when you heard the shot?'

This time he answered without hesitation: 'Over by the

shrubbery. Evelyn and I were together when we heard it. I thought then that she seemed nervous and alarmed, but I assured her that this time it must be a poacher or a gamekeeper or something. I really thought it was, you see.' He mused: 'I wonder what Parmoor was saying to her when he—but we can ask her in the morning. She's in no state to be bothered now.'

'You saw them together?' I asked, amazed, for I had never noticed any special exchanges between Parmoor and Evelyn. It seemed to me that Parmoor was interested in no one except Ursula, and even his interest in her had a quality of resignation about it, as if he knew he might have to relinquish that tie, too, at any time.

'Oh, yes,' said Marcel. 'They went off together after dinner—didn't you see them?—and it was later, when I was walking up and down on the terrace by myself, that I met her coming back alone. I believe she had left him down by the lily-pool. She seemed unwilling to go in just then, and so we walked off together: the moonlight was so beautiful! It was not long after that when we heard the shot. I think she must have feared, or even guessed, what it was. She is very sensitive. Poor girl!'

Again I gasped, but this time inwardly. 'You're as changeable as a weathercock,' I said in a tone which I tried to keep light. 'One never knows where one is with you. Tell me——'—we had now reached his door, and he had his hand on the knob, as if anxious to get away from me—'have you forgotten all you said to me yesterday?'

Marcel regarded me from under bent brows: 'You are not going to take advantage of a generous gesture?' he said, sadly and reprovingly. 'I hope not. It would not be worthy of you, my friend. I have taken some advice since then, and I am told that I should do nothing until I have had time to reflect and consult with my parents.'

I laughed shortly. 'What a memory you have!' I said. 'So you don't even remember that it was I who first gave you that advice, and you who protested against it? Well, never mind: I wouldn't have accepted it if you had stuck to your intention. So Ursula was right! She said you didn't mean it!'

Marcel ground his teeth with rage, and I saw him stiffen as if he had been flicked with a whip.

'Ursula!' he said. 'Wherever she is, there is trouble.'

'You liked her well enough just now,' I said.

'Oh!' He made a gesture of repudiation. 'That was before I knew of this tragedy. It is revolting that a woman should be so careless of the feelings of a man who loves her. I could not respect a woman who had a man's life on her hands.'

Again he made as if to open his door and go; but I stood there so determinedly that he was forced to stay.

'And what makes you so sure,' I said, 'that she was responsible? Wasn't it rather his own character? And don't you think, if *she* was in any way to blame for tipping the balance of his mind towards suicide, *you* were too?'

'I?' Marcel's outraged innocence would have been comic if it had not been so exasperating. 'What had I to do with it? I never suggested to Ursula—never even hinted—that she should abandon her old lover for me. In fact, I made it clear——'

'Yes,' I said, squaring up to him, 'you made it clear, once you had awakened her interest in you, that you had nothing to give her in return. And now you desert her in her moment of greatest need—you turn against her and condemn her. Marcel, you are a god-dam' prig!'

His face was now a mask of fury, white and pinched at the nostrils; but I was in full cry, and I could not stop even if I had wished.

'And now, I suppose,' I said, 'you'll do the same to Evelyn: you'll lead her to think, for a day or two, that she is all in all to you—as you did on the night of your arrival—and then, when she has dropped me for you, you'll turn round and tell her she is a foolish girl, and you're awfully sorry but you have commitments at home! As for this wretched property: if it turns out to be legally yours, I know exactly what you'll do, in spite of all your "generous gestures" and your protestations: you'll stick to it, as most people would, on the ground that you owe first consideration to your family or your future bride or something. By the way, how many people *have* you promised it to besides me? Ursula, perhaps? And now Evelyn?'

Marcel still gripped the door-knob, and his knuckles were white. I thought, impersonally, how handsome he was with his dark hair and his cream-coloured face and his fine features and scornful expression.

'I may as well tell you here and now,' he said through his teeth, 'that I intend to remove Evelyn from this household. She is the only one here who is deserving of my help. As for you, you are a vulgar lout, and I am glad I saw through you in good time.'

He turned to the door; but before he could open it, I pulled him back by the shoulder.

'Do you mean you are going to marry her?' I shouted furiously. 'I thought you said you were already engaged!'

He checked me superciliously: 'Don't worry, my good friend. Everything will be arranged according to your idea of the proprieties. There is no question of marriage between Evelyn and myself: I have already told you, I am not free to choose a wife; nor does she expect it. But what I do propose is to take her under the protection of my own family, into a household where her qualities and services will be appreciated—away from here, where she meets with nothing but hostility and persecution, and where her very health is endangered!'

'And you mean to say,' I gasped, hoarse with indignation, 'she is fool enough to entrust her future to *you?* Well, in that case I give up. But let me tell you, *you* are responsible for all the trouble in this house, beginning with your ridiculous idea of impersonating Hugo. I don't believe it was he who suggested it—I believe it was you: not out of any fixed plan, I grant you that, but out of idleness and irresponsibility. And *you* are responsible, if anyone is apart from the actual murderer, for his death. A fine one you are to accuse Ursula, with that on your conscience!'

Marcel made a noise like 'Tchah!' This time, when he broke away from me, I did not stop him.

As I turned away from the rudely-slammed door, I felt rather depressed; for in spite of everything, I really liked Marcel, and it seemed a pity that whenever we met we should arrive at some misunderstanding. I did not entirely mean all the things I had said: he was fickle and incalculable, but not malevolent; and what right had one to expect dependability in somebody so entertaining and mercurial? It is all due to this abominable habit of passing moral judgments, I thought.

But what of Evelyn? Was it true, what he had said? Did she really regard me just as a nuisance, a pesterer? That was a very humiliating thought. I reached my own room, and switched on the light. Standing in the middle of the carpet, I brooded. Why, if she felt that way, hadn't she told me? Had I mistaken completely her attitude to me? True, at first I had thought her rather unenthusiastic about my approaches; but then, she had been preoccupied with other matters, and she had not known whether my own intentions were serious or not. She had, after all, confided in me, and then, in her quiet way, responded to my advances. I had thought that her quietness proceeded from a quiet and serious nature, and that it meant more than raptures coming from others. Was I wrong? If so, what could have been her motive for deceiving me?

And then, as I stood there, seeing nothing except an enormous yellow and red medallion in the carpet at my feet, another and more sinister thought intruded: could it possibly be that Evelyn was—well, not quite balanced? There had sometimes been on her face an expression of anxiety, bewilderment, even fear, that seemed to me to have no sufficient reason: a look that reminded me of something seen elsewhere. Hitherto I had suppressed in my own mind the recollection of *where* I had already seen that queer look of worry, of suffering: the creased brow, the watchful eyes, the fluttering movements of the hands. But I knew, all right.

It was less than a month ago, when we students were being taken round the wards of a mental hospital, and I had stopped to speak to a girl who, I had been told, was a voluntary patient, suffering from some mild temporary neurosis. She was, of course, perfectly coherent, and to all appearances quite sane: a good-looking girl, dark like Evelyn, with a creamy complexion and blue eyes; a girl who looked after her dress, face and hair; refined in manner and in speech. As I talked to her, that same look of worry began to show itself, and the nervous movements of the hands became more rapid. Suddenly, before I could prepare myself, she opened her mouth and uttered the most ear-splitting series of screams, followed by a spate of abusive language. Then she returned to apparent normality. 'Oh, she's getting on all right,' the doctor in charge said later when I asked a question about her. 'She was pretty bad when she came in—the result of wrong home conditions and general maladjustment—but she's improving under treatment. She'll be out in a fortnight or so.'

I shook myself: what a horrible idea, to compare Evelyn with this unfortunate girl! "Everybody takes to Evelyn," I thought: "in fact, men don't seem able to resist her. First there was Ursula's father, then Jim, then Marcel, then myself—and possibly Parmoor as well: who knows? Why else should she be walking with him after dinner, perhaps sitting with him down by the lily-pool? Why else should he choose her as the last person he wished to see and to talk to before he left this planet?" And I remembered how once before I had seen him join her there. "Yes, everybody falls for Evelyn," I thought; "and why? Isn't her appeal for us all just that she looks so worried, and one longs to take her under one's protection and make her happy? Whereas Ursula looks bright and gay and self-reliant. That's why, though she is outwardly so much more attractive than Evelyn, one just doesn't fall for her. But Parmoor did—or didn't he? He didn't seem very keen on that divorce, now I come to think of it. Suppose my idea is right, and that with him too it was Evelyn, not Ursula: what difference does that make? Well, for one thing it accounts still better for Ursula's dislike of Evelyn—for whatever we men may think of Evelyn, Ursula can't stand her. And"—I realized with a start—"it means that Parmoor didn't shoot himself because of Ursula, whatever his reason may have been. Well then, was it because of something that Evelyn said to him in those last few minutes by the lily-pool? Was it then that she told him of her intention to leave here, either with me or with Marcel, and was that the last straw?"

Possibly. But still, I felt that someone of Parmoor's maturity would have some deeper reason than mere jealousy or disappointed love. He was, as Sir Frederick had said, a *good* man gone wrong.

22

It was certainly an odd fate that brought Jim Ullstone, Marcel and myself together in the same car next morning, on the short journey into Chode, to attend the inquest on the body of Hugo Ullstone. Sir Frederick had preceded us: it appeared that by the Coroner's wish he had been requested to accompany the police-surgeon, Dr. Fitzbrown, and the jury, when they inspected the body. I could well imagine him smiling benevolently and swinging his eyeglass at them while he pointed out the interesting features. Under his guidance, I was sure that it would all seem just a phenomenon to be inspected. He would have made a journey through the gates of hell seem the most natural thing in the world, nothing to be alarmed at. As for us three, we sat as stiff as pokers, and as silent, I next to the chauffeur, the other two withdrawn as far as possible into their corners behind.

When we arrived at the Law Court, a small crowd had gathered; and for the first time in my life I experienced the discomfort of being frankly stared at and openly commented upon by irreverent and curious strangers. Of course, the two blocks of townspeople ranged on either side of the steps—the women carrying shopping-baskets, the men with hands in pockets, but all, however bucolic-looking, seething with desire for drama—these spectators were much more interested in the other two than in me. Jim Ullstone they knew; I noticed him exchange a gruff greeting with one or two of the men bystanders, and nobody passed any audible remarks on him except to utter his name in tones of respect; but Marcel, as he climbed the steps without hurrying, with his usual easy grace, came in for a distinct murmur, the basis of which was unfriendly. He took no notice, but strode on and up and through the large doors, with his head in the air and a look of "*Canaille!*" which was no doubt traditional in his family. As for me, my appearance lightened the atmosphere and put everybody in a good humour: they found everything about me disarmingly funny, from my red hair to my thick shoes which unfortunately squeaked a little; and I suppose the hearty blush which spread over my face and down my neck completed their happiness. Never before had I felt so earnestly the truth of the Epicurean maxim, that in order to attain happiness, you must "live obscure."

The two girls had not been summoned. They were both still under the weather, and Mallett had agreed that nothing they could say at present would be useful in evidence. Aunt Susan and Uncle Biddolph, though not asked, had nevertheless come and were already seated in the body of the court when we entered. It was quite pleasant to see their familiar disagreeable faces among this sea of sensation-mongering strangers.

The policeman who had followed us up the steps guided us to

our places in the "decent, clean, commodious room" which as the law requires had been provided. We were seated opposite the Coroner's table with its pens and ink and blotting-paper, and at right-angles to the jury-box. Soon afterwards the jury entered and filed into their places from the back of the court. It struck me then, as it often has done since, that a jury is always an entity, no matter what individuals compose it. There is something about them always, as a body—a certain stodginess and consciousness of rectitude and determination to get the matter right which makes them as formidable as a steam roller; and this would be true if they were made up even of painters and poets. I looked at their faces—there were seven of them—and could see that they were all quite different; yet the impression made on me was that of a whole. I can think of no greater deterrent to would-be criminals than a few photographs, or better still, a close-up, of any British jury in action. As the seven took their places—there was one woman among them—they had a solemn and dedicated air, very natural as they had just viewed the body of Hugo. Last came the Coroner, accompanied by Sir Frederick Lawton and Superintendent Mallett. The Coroner was a small, bent, grey-haired man whose very way of handling his papers on the table before him, settling his spectacles on his nose, glancing round the court over the top of them, and returning to his papers, inspired confidence. I wondered if I should ever be as efficient and reliable in my job as he obviously was in his; and in all humility I had to confess that I didn't think so. He seemed to have been born like that, and I wished that I had, too.

After the preliminaries were completed, and the Coroner had explained to the jury what they were there for and how serious a matter it was, he proceeded to call witnesses. My heart beat fast, for I had thought that as the discoverer of the body I would be the first to be called; but to my surprise, it was Marcel. He stepped forward, neat, dark, debonair; he looked utterly alien, not merely in nationality but in his whole bearing and character, from these prosaic surroundings; but this time in the dignified atmosphere of the courtroom, there was no place for prejudice, or at least for its expression; and though the looks bent on him were full of lively interest, there was no sign of hostility. The Coroner, after another glance at his precept, gave him, over the top of his glasses, a look that corrugated his whole brow, and asked him very distinctly if he understood enough English to follow the proceedings; he seemed astonished when Marcel in his precise and almost accentless speech answered that he understood perfectly. The oath was administered, and the Coroner's equally precise, sometimes almost stupid-seeming questions began. It seemed that Marcel had been called first because he was the only person who could actually swear to the identity of Hugo Ullstone: nobody else here had ever seen him alive, and if they had, they could not have said who he was.

Marcel swore that the dead man was Hugo Ullstone, aged twenty-four. He knew that Hugo's age was twenty-four, he said in answer to the Coroner, because he remembered Hugo's twenty-first birthday party, three years before in February: 'There was a good deal of champagne,' he added solemnly (he pronounced "champagne" in the French manner: it was one of his few bits of linguistic obstinacy) and there was a murmur in court, too dim to be called laughter; for a British audience, great or small, always and in all circumstances laughs at the mention of drink, a habit that must be puzzling to people of other nationalities who take wine habitually with their meals. Marcel, I knew, had mentioned the champagne because it helped to fix the occasion in his mind. The Coroner asked:

'Were you acquainted with the father of the deceased?'

'I met him once or twice,' said Marcel. 'He came fairly often to see Hugo. But he seemed unwilling to meet Hugo's friends. In fact, Hugo said, his father never would meet his English friends at all: this was because he didn't want the fact of their relationship known. He never would let Hugo come to England.'

The Coroner stopped him. It was clear that he did not want Marcel to tell the whole story here and now.

'To come to the present occasion,' he said. 'This was his first visit to England?'

'So far as I know, yes,' said Marcel.

'And you accompanied him: at his request, or at your own suggestion?'

'At his request,' said Marcel indignantly. 'He not only requested, he insisted. I tried to dissuade him.'

Again the Coroner interrupted the flow of words: 'And his

expressed purpose was to see the property which he had inherited, and make the acquaintance of his relatives—his half-brother and half-sister?'

'Well,' said Marcel, pushing out his underlip, 'make their acquaintance—no, not necessarily. See them—yes. That was why I——'

'We shall come to that in due course,' said the Coroner. 'If you will kindly answer the questions—— So you crossed together on the eighth, and spent the night in London, travelling down to Chode next day.'

'Yes.'

'And you both spent the night of the ninth at the Chode Arms?'

'Yes.'

'Next day, on the afternoon of the tenth, you went on to the Hall, while the deceased remained at the hotel?'

'Yes.' Marcel, having been snubbed, was evidently determined to answer only in monosyllables, and sharply-bitten-off monosyllables at that.

'We need not, at the moment,' the Coroner said after a slight pause and consultation of his papers, 'go further into the reasons for your preceding him, and in fact impersonating him for a few hours. That would take us too far from our present purpose, which is to prove the time and place of death. I gather you dined with the deceased, in company with one of the ladies of the house, at the Inn that evening; and that you on that occasion made the arrangement with the deceased that he should present himself in or near the shrubbery at Ullstone Hall at some time on the following evening. That'—he glanced at the jury—'strikes the average man or woman as a very odd arrangement. Will you tell us, please, whether that suggestion came from you or from the deceased in the first instance?'

Marcel, deprived of his power to answer in a monosyllable, looked nettled. 'The suggestion was mine,' he said.

The Coroner cleared his throat: 'H'm. At what time did you suggest that the deceased should present himself at the rendezvous?'

Marcel frowned: 'I think I said after dinner, when the moon would have risen. I was not very certain what time the moon rose, and I had no calendar, but I thought he could find out.'

The Coroner consulted a pocket calendar. 'The moon was at the full at nine-fifteen p.m. on the evening of the eleventh.' He looked up inquiringly: 'Did you go to the rendezvous at that time?'

'Actually, no,' said Marcel, still frowning. 'I did not think it would be so early. I just knew that it would be bright moonlight some time after dinner, if the weather were fine.'

'You consulted no diary or calendar—though you expected your friend to do so?'

'I did not. There was no need. I knew from observation when the moon would be high.'

'At what time did you go to the meeting-place?'

'Oh, it must have been about half-past ten or later, I suppose. The moon was still bright then, and I thought he would be there.'

'Did you see him?'

'No, sir. He was not supposed to show himself then—while I was with Miss Ullstone. The idea was——'

'Yes, yes,' The Coroner again interrupted him decisively, and again I got the impression that for some reason he did not want Marcel to reveal the story. 'Did you see him at any time that evening? Think carefully, please, before you reply.'

But Marcel had no need to think. 'I never saw him,' he said. 'I went back there for a few minutes, some time between eleven-thirty and midnight, after I had returned to the house. But there was no sign of him. I thought he had got tired and gone off; but I realize now, he must have been dead.'

The Coroner looked pained. 'That is still a matter for investigation,' he said; and to the jury, 'Please ignore the witness's conjectures. They have no bearing whatever on this inquiry.' He turned back to Marcel: 'That is all for the present,' he said. 'You may stand down now. I may perhaps have to recall you later.'

Marcel looked astonished: he had evidently been prepared for a long examination, and this sudden dismissal nonplussed him. After a moment's hesitation, and a look at the Coroner as if he were prepared to challenge his decision, he gave way and stepped down.

The Coroner motioned to Mallett, and Mallett went to the

table and leaned over him while they held a whispered consultation. Again I thought it would be my turn next, surely; but this time Sir Frederick Lawton's name was called. The Coroner treated him with great respect, explaining that his evidence was being taken next in order not to waste his valuable time. Sir Frederick, erect and handsome, looked round at them all like a god weighing destinies, as he swung his eyeglass to and fro.

'I was summoned to the scene,' he said, in answer to the Coroner, 'at five minutes to six, and I arrived there some ten or fifteen minutes later. I found the body of the deceased lying half under a rhododendron bush near the shrubbery path. He was lying on his face, with the right hand grasping a handful of leaves, and the left arm doubled under his head. He had been dead for some hours. *Rigor mortis* was completely established.'

'You are not prepared to offer an opinion as to the time of death?'

'No. My examination was superficial only.'

'You recognized the deceased, I believe?'

'Yes.'

'You knew him?'

'No, I had never seen him before. I recognized him from his photograph which was in my possession.'

The Coroner leaned back with both hands on his table, as if a point had been reached at which Sir Frederick and he understood each other and were agreed that no more should be said.

'In the brief examination you then made,' said the Coroner, 'you were able to form a definite opinion as to the cause of death?'

'I was,' said Sir Frederick. 'I formed the opinion that the man had been shot from behind, by someone standing at some distance away. Beyond that, I did not think it proper to investigate then and there. I believed it my duty to get in touch with the police immediately.'

The Coroner bowed his head slightly in acknowledgment of the superior wisdom of Sir Frederick.

'And you therefore returned at once to the house and telephoned to the police? At what time?'

'At twenty-five minutes past six.'

'You were present at the post-mortem examination, I believe?'

'I was.'

'And you agree with the findings of the police-surgeon, Dr. Fitzbrown?'

'I do.'

'Is there any comment on those findings that you would like to record now, Sir Frederick, before we release you for your important duties elsewhere?'

'None whatsoever,' said Sir Frederick. 'My colleague and I were in complete agreement.'

'Then we need not detain you any longer—unless any member of the jury wishes to ask a question?'

The members of the jury stared rather stupidly at Sir Frederick, and then at one another. At last the only woman member spoke up: she was dressed in tweeds and a felt hat, and had the unmistakable air of a president of the Women's Institute.

'I take it,' she said in firm, clear, rather high-pitched tones, 'that the witness's evidence means that the deceased was undoubtedly murdered?' The way she completed the sentence, with an equally firm closure of the lips and a shake of the head, suggested: "If that is so, what are we wasting our time here for? Why don't we return a verdict and go home?"

Sir Frederick eyed her with benevolence, and I think he would have liked to agree; but he was too well experienced in the ways of Coroner's courts to answer directly. The Coroner looked shocked.

'The witness cannot be asked to answer such a question,' he said, his voice trembling a little with annoyance and the effort not to display it. 'That is a matter for the jury themselves to decide on the evidence when it is complete. The witness has told us that he formed the opinion that the deceased was shot from behind, by a person standing some distance away. It is for you to decide whether there is any possibility of accident, or whether the shot was fired with intent to kill. If the latter, then the verdict will be murder. But so far, on the evidence, all we can say is that there is no possibility that death was self-inflicted. And I must again warn members of the jury that they must consider the facts only; they must not abandon themselves to conjecture at this or any other stage.'

He gave the woman member a withering look; but she remained unabashed, and I could see she felt that if only she could have a few words with Sir Frederick and the police-surgeon outside the courtroom, she could settle the whole affair in five minutes, and return to her gardening.

'Very well, then, Sir Frederick.' The Coroner bowed again, and Sir Frederick stepped down. His benevolent smile embraced everyone and no one. Then he restored his eyeglass to the inner pocket of his waistcoat, patted the outside of his coat affectionately over the place, and after exchanging a couple of words with Mallett, left. We heard the sound of a car engine being started, and that was the last we knew of him. He seemed to have forgotten all about me.

Again I waited for my name to be called. Surely now, I thought, they must want to hear the tale of the man who discovered the body! But no: the next witness to be called was the great Mallett himself, who described how he had received the telephone message at six-twenty-six a.m., and how he had inspected the body in the place and position described by Sir Frederick. Marks on the path and on the shoes and clothing of the deceased showed that the body had been dragged from a point on the edge of the shrubbery to the place where it was found, a distance of about ten feet. The bullet had passed through the body, making its exit at a point just below the sixth rib, and embedding itself in the stump of a tree. On examination the bullet proved to be of American manufacture, of the kind usable in a Colt .38-inch revolver with one-and-a-half-inch cylinder. The revolver was subsequently found at the bottom of an ornamental pool in the grounds of Ullstone Hall.

Mallett's tone was non-committal and his evidence strictly factual; but I listened with interest to the many details which were unfamiliar to me. Slowly he built up his picture of what had happened: in his view, the deceased had been shot from a point within the shrubbery near to where his body was found. The person firing the shot must have aimed at him as he stood at the end of the path, silhouetted in the moonlight. The trajectory of the bullet was carefully reconstructed: diagrams were produced and shown to the Coroner and the jury.

'There is one point that I should like to mention here,' said Mallett, as the diagrams were handed back. 'The question arises, if the shooting was intentional, from what direction did the assailant approach? Presumably the deceased was standing at the end of the path, and looking towards the house, from which he expected those persons in whom he was interested to come. Anyone approaching him in front would be visible. Either the assailant was someone known to him, therefore, or else he contrived to get behind the deceased without being seen. This would mean a long détour by a path leading from the lodge gates and forming a loop in an arc to which the drive would be, as it were, the string to the bow.'

The Coroner looked up: 'Then you are inclined to rule out the possibility of accident, Superintendent?'

'Yes, sir, I am, most definitely,' said Mallett firmly. And to my surprise, this time the statement seemed to provoke no hostile reaction in the Coroner. I looked at my woman juror who had been so heavily sat upon for having called a spade a spade shortly before; but she did not seem to notice that she had made her point, nor to feel resentful. It seemed odd to me, but I supposed, human beings are never consistent, whatever else they may be, and that is why their affairs, though they don't run true to the rules, are perennially interesting.

Then, just as we were all getting keen, Mallett's evidence came abruptly to an end, as if by arrangement between him and the Coroner. A few more questions were asked. The jury were again offered the opportunity to put their own questions; and in a moment or two Mallett also had stepped down, leaving us all with our curiosity unsatisfied. This time I did not expect to be called, and I was right. The next evidence was that of the police-surgeon, Dr. Fitzbrown.

His evidence was succinct. The deceased, he said, was a young man of rather short stature, plump, not very heavy: the corpse, unclothed, weighed just under ten stone. The cause of death was internal hæmorrhage and shock, due to a bullet wound. The bullet had entered the back just below the heart and lungs, and had passed completely through, making its exit below the sixth rib, as Superintendent Mallett had said. External hæmorrhage had not been severe, and was confined to the exit wound. There was no scorching. Death had not been instantaneous: the deceased had fallen and had gripped a handful of leaves where he was lying; he had then been dragged to the position in which he was found, and must have died a few minutes later. The internal bleeding was severe. The person firing the shot had obviously aimed at the heart and missed; considering his intentions, the assailant was lucky to have achieved his object, for such shots often passed right through the body without fatal results. In the momentary shock of the impact, the deceased fell down, possibly in a state of paralysis, and was then dragged some ten yards to the place of concealment.

Dr. Fitzbrown was not prepared to conjecture any exact time of death; but in his opinion it had occurred at least eight hours before he began his examination of the body, which was at seven o'clock on the morning of the discovery.

The doctor stepped down. The Coroner folded his hands before him on the table and began:

'Well, members of the jury——'

I really thought he was going to address them without more ado and ask them to consider their verdict, when I saw Mallett rise and go over to him and whisper a few words in his ear again. "Ah," I thought, "Mallett at least hasn't forgotten my part," though even to me it now seemed a mere formality to ask me for my evidence. The others had sucked all the juice out of the story. I was bound to be the anti-climax. Still, I braced myself once more—only to hear the name "James Ullstone!" called.

Jim got up and walked slowly to the witness-box. He was trying to look nonchalant, but the muscle at the corner of his jaw was working. He took the oath in an unintelligible mumble; but his answers were sharp and clear.

'The deceased, your half-brother,' began the Coroner, 'met his end on the night of Wednesday, April 11th. I gather that you had never seen him, and in fact his existence was unknown to you until the death of your father.'

'Yes, unfortunately,' said Jim with venom.

The Coroner looked at him sharply. 'What do you mean by the expression "unfortunately"?'

'I mean,' said Jim, no less viciously, 'that if we had known about him, we could have prepared ourselves for the shock in store for us, when we found out that my father had made a will in his favour.'

The Coroner pursed up his lips with displeasure: 'That is not a matter for this inquiry,' he said.

Jim interrupted him rudely: 'Of course it is! The man who shot him did it to get rid of him, didn't he? And he wanted to get rid of him because he was the heir? That's why everybody at first suspected *me*, until I told the police——'

The Coroner held up his thin, veined hand. 'James Ullstone,' he said sternly, 'you will kindly remember that I am conducting this inquiry; and you will proceed to answer the questions put to you. It appears that you have a piece of information to give us which may help to establish the exact time of death. You did not disclose this to the police when you were first interviewed by them on the morning of the 12th. Why not?'

'Oh, well'—Jim looked down—'I was not sure—that is, I thought—I was afraid I might be incriminating somebody— somebody I didn't want to suspect, even, much less incriminate.'

The Coroner's severity was devastating and quite unfeigned: it was clear that he could see nothing but heinousness in any sentimental impulse to protect another person by concealing evidence. I looked at the jury: collectively they registered the same condemnation; and yet, I suppose, as individuals they would have sympathized with Jim, and probably have done the same themselves.

'It was your duty,' said the Coroner, 'to disclose all that you knew, at the earliest possible opportunity. However, subsequently you recognized your grave mistake, and—doubtless under the impact of a second tragedy'—he glanced round the courtroom over his spectacles: it was his first reference to Parmoor's death— 'you volunteered after all to give the police this important piece of information. It appears that at about five minutes to ten on the night of the 11th, you heard a shot, which seemed to you to come from the direction of the shrubbery. You looked out, and saw nothing.'

'Quite so,' said Jim.

'Where were you at the time?'

'I was in the billiard-room,' said Jim. 'I had been there for almost an hour by myself, practising shots.'

'Was the shrubbery visible from the windows of this room?'

'No. It faces south—that is, it is in the front of the house, on

165

the second floor; and the shrubbery is in a south-westerly direction from there. Besides, there are various trees and bushes along the drive and the paths, which would interfere with the view from the house.'

'Did you form any opinion as to the nature of the shot?'

'No. In fact, I wondered if I had been mistaken—if perhaps I had mistaken the click of the billiard-balls for a shot in the distance. It seems an absurd thing to say, but one can easily make mistakes, and it's difficult to remember afterwards exactly what one has heard.'

'And you saw nothing?' the Coroner pressed him.

'Nothing,' said Jim.

'And no one?'

'No one,' echoed Jim. 'At least, not then. Later I looked out once or twice.'

'And you saw——?'

'I saw various people coming and going—walking in the moonlight on the terrace, and so on. For instance, I saw my sister and de Souvigny—but that was later.' He looked down. 'They left the house about twenty to eleven, and walked off along the terrace in that direction.'

'But that was long after you heard the shot?'

'Oh, yes. I heard the shot, as I've told you, at five to ten.'

'And did you see anyone going or coming in that direction round that time?'

'Yes,' said Jim, while all hung on his words. 'I saw—I saw Dr. Parmoor.'

'Going or returning?'

'Both. I happened to look out, in between a couple of strokes, at about a quarter to ten, and I saw him going along the terrace in that direction. Then I lost sight of him. And at, say, about a quarter past ten, again I happened to look out, and I saw him coming back.'

'Was he alone?' said the Coroner.

Jim hesitated. Then he said, 'Yes.'

'Both going and returning?'

Jim fairly shouted 'Yes!' And then, as if breaking loose again from his leading-strings: 'Yesterday evening, when I heard he'd shot himself, I knew he must have been the killer. So I told the police about the shot I thought I'd heard. Till then, it hadn't seemed right to mention it.'

The Coroner regarded him long and gravely. 'Your judgment was at fault,' he said at last, 'and your conduct deserves censure. I hope that in future you will show a better sense of your duty to society, and more respect for the person injured than for the injurer. Would any member of the jury like to question the witness?'

A tall, dark, raw-boned man said: 'I should like to know whether this person the witness was protecting was Dr. Parmoor or somebody else.'

The look of malevolence which Jim directed to the raw-boned man was undisguised. This time, he turned to the Coroner for protection. The Coroner did not disappoint him.

'The question is not relevant to this inquiry,' he snapped. 'The witness need not answer it.'

Jim stepped down.

And now—and now——

The Coroner turned again to the jury. Then he looked back at his papers and turned one of them over.

'Ah, yes, of course,' he said. 'Perhaps for the sake of completeness we had better just take the evidence of the young man who happened to discover the body. Call John Jacob Seaborne.'

Quickly, in a sentence or two, I agreed that I had discovered the body of the deceased in the place where it was later seen by Sir Frederick Lawton and the police. The time was five-forty. What was I doing there so early? The Coroner asked this with a smile, and seemed quite satisfied with my answer that I had had a restless night and had got up early to go for a walk. Nobody took me seriously, and in fact even the jury hardly listened. In a few minutes it was over, and I was back in my seat again, with tingling ears and fast-beating heart.

The Coroner summed up the evidence at length and with care. Nothing seemed to have escaped him; but all that lay underneath was as much concealed as the base of an iceberg. I had the feeling that he knew all about it, and that that was the very reason why he was able to keep out everything irrelevant to his immediate purpose. He seemed to be leading up to a verdict; but at the very end, touching on Parmoor's death, he said that

167

another inquest now pending might prove to have a bearing on this one; and therefore he thought that the best course would be to adjourn the present inquiry to a later date when further evidence would perhaps be available.

And so, for the present, we were dismissed. It fell to Jim as the chief male representative of the Ullstone family, to wait behind and receive the warrant for the burial. So Marcel and I travelled back without him. We did not exchange one word all the way.

As we turned in at the gates, I glanced up at the three monkeys on one of the pillars: the one with his hand over his mouth seemed to be laughing.

23

The rest of that day—it was a Saturday—passed off gloomily.

I could not bring myself to leave the house, because I wanted to see Evelyn; and Evelyn did not appear. One gathered that she was still in her room, suffering from shock, and did not want to be disturbed. Ursula was present at meal-times, but she looked pale and withdrawn, and said very little. Jim was still absent, making arrangements for the burial of the half-brother he had never seen. Sir Frederick Lawton had left, one gathered, for town, and would not return for several days. I thought he might have spared time to say a word of thanks to me for what I had done for him; but of course that was an absurd idea. Marcel, like Evelyn, was missing, and did not turn up even to meals. So that whenever Ursula retired to attend to the household duties abandoned by Evelyn, or to rest in her room, I was left with the Biddolphs, who stuck closely together and ignored me.

In the afternoon, as I expected, a police constable arrived on a bicycle with a notice summoning me to attend at the Court at Chode on the following Monday, as a witness in the inquest on Hilary Parmoor. I asked the man in confidence if any of the others had to go; and he said he didn't think so. Wanting to talk to somebody, and since he seemed a friendly sort of fellow, I took him round to the kitchen and asked the cook for a couple of bottles of beer. Over the beer, he told me that he thought the inquest on Dr. Parmoor would not cause much trouble. Actually, he said, the Coroner was already satisfied with the police view that it was suicide following on murder, and the verdict would be *felo de se*. He said he didn't think the police were anxious to drag family matters into the inquiry: that the only other people present would probably be a relative of the deceased, and his wife's legal representative. I was needed as the one who had discovered the body and notified the police, but my part would be quite formal.

'I know that,' I interpolated rather bitterly. 'What about the young lady who was the last to see him alive? Aren't they calling her?'

'Oh, her evidence will be quite formal,' said the constable omnisciently. 'I think they've taken a statement from her already. She wants to get away.'

'What?' I said sharply. 'I thought she wasn't being called because she was ill.'

'Well, perhaps so,' said the constable, emptying his glass. He stood up and adjusted his belt. 'But I understood it was because she was leaving for abroad. Personally I don't believe in letting possible witnesses leave the district until inquiries are complete— but wealthy people like that can do as they please.'

He went off; and again I was left to my own devices, with something new to think about. By now I was getting restless and angry about Evelyn. I grasped pretty clearly that she had dropped me for Marcel, and on the whole I didn't blame her: after all, what had I to offer in comparison with him? He might even marry her if she played her cards carefully. I was sorry to lose her, and I was hurt; but mingled with my soreness was a certain relief. Now I could pursue my way unhampered, without the dragging inconvenience of having somebody else to think of and to miss when one couldn't see her. Also I should not have to explain and defend myself to my parents, who would certainly not approve. And even my reluctance to lose Evelyn herself was, I had to recognize, not so much for her own sake as for the sake of a pleasant dream. Nevertheless, I thought she owed me some explanation; I was getting a bit tired of being pushed around. So, though I felt rather nervous about it, I decided that I would give her till dinner-time that evening, and if she still did not appear and sent no message, I would go along to her room and try to see her, conventions be damned; for I was mightily upset and rattled by what the police constable had told me, and extremely suspicious at the continued absence of Marcel.

And yet, at the thought of breaking in on Evelyn, and finding her almost certainly in an unresponsive, possibly angry mood, my colour rose and my heart beat fast. I remembered what an odd little creature she was: how sometimes she seemed all sweetness and yieldingness and desirability, and at other times—well, frankly, as unresponsive as a brick wall. And I realized that always, although one part of me was sorry for her and touched by what seemed her need for protection, another part of me had been puzzled and afraid. And at the present moment I was, I considered, in a thoroughly false position: the position of one whose advances had been encouraged and accepted, and who suddenly finds all this denied and reversed without reason or explanation. If I ask for an explanation, I thought, I shall be accused of importunity. If I don't, she gets away with a piece of double dealing, and I am left standing, completely fooled.

I prowled about the house, along landings and corridors, up and down staircases and into unused wings with bedrooms shrouded in dust-sheets, the ceilings and walls showing sad signs of damp, and the carpets eaten by moths at the edges. What a place this must have been once! I thought. With a view to what lavish expenditure it was designed, and what armies of servants and what cohorts of guests! Four-fifths of it was now uninhabited, abandoned. Was this a pity, or not? It was hard to decide. A pity that such a fine house should fall into disuse and decay: yes. But a pity that Jim and Ursula couldn't find fifty servants, indoors and out, to look after them and their friends? I didn't think so. And what temporary insanity had made me think that I should like to possess and live among all this decayed splendour?

I drifted back to the inhabited part of the house. Nobody was about: they were all resting or brooding in their rooms. But I found myself doing a strange thing: everywhere I went, no matter what door I opened, I somehow expected to see Parmoor sitting there, perhaps sleeping, smiling to himself with his short, strong white hands linked across his chest, and his short, stout legs thrust out with the small feet crossed; perhaps leaning against the chimney-breast with a glass of whisky on the mantelpiece above him. And I realized that though I had not paid very much heed to him when he was alive, I was now looking for him, as it were, and missing him.

No, it was more than that: his image was haunting me, the twinkle of understanding in his eye, his perspicacious smile, his quiet and pleasant voice as he uttered his clear judgment of himself, and his despair—resigned, amused, yet nevertheless genuine despair. And then I would remember the still, dark form propped up in the corner of the stone seat by the lily-pool, and the toe of a polished shoe shining in the moonlight. He had seemed, for all his hopeless weaknesses, such a kindly sort of fellow. I could well understand how one day, tired of contemplating the wreck of his own life, he took a gun and shot himself; but I could not imagine him, of all people, creeping out and along the side of the house, down the drive and round by the path to the shrubbery, there to lie in wait for that other unfortunate, his fellow-misfit, the simple, guileless, melancholy Hugo; and there to shoot him in the back, so that he, Hilary Parmoor, should ensure to Ursula Ullstone, if it were possible, the continued joint possession of the white elephant, Ullstone Hall.

No: Parmoor was a waster, if it is wastrelly to be the permanent and unpaying guest of a woman who imagines herself in love with you; but if I was any judge of character, he was a kindly waster. His trouble was weakness, not meanness or treachery or cruelty or greed; and if he had gone on staying here—or should one say rather, postponing his departure?—it had been because Ursula wanted him to. Well, if she had ceased to want him, had he not gone, in his own way? And yet—again I seemed to see him, this time standing by the gramophone and smiling as we others danced—was that the whole simple answer? I doubted it.

Dinner-time came at last. Again neither Evelyn nor Marcel appeared. Ursula was there, and I wondered whether perhaps after all I wouldn't bother to seek out Evelyn, but would stay and talk to Ursula, sit with her on the terrace as I had done the evening before. But Ursula, immediately after the meal, retired, and was seen no more. Her eyes were red with weeping. I wondered whether she too, like me, was seeing Parmoor everywhere. Much against the grain, and because I could put it off no longer, I too, after the meal, went slowly upstairs, to seek out Evelyn.

Arrived at Evelyn's door, I tapped very gently, and laid my

ear to the panel. There was no reply. I tapped again, a little louder. Then, unwilling to make more noise or to wake her if she were asleep, I ventured to open the door. The bed was empty, and tidily made. Spread out over its counterpane were clothes: coats and skirts, stockings, silk underwear; and at the foot of the bed stood an open trunk, half-packed. I shut the door as if I had been stung by adders. Then it was true! She was going, without a word to me, who had been ready to jeopardize my whole career for her. What did they all take me for, I wondered. And were they right?

Hot and angry, I strode away and round the corner, back to Marcel's rooms, which were opposite my own. This time my knock was not gentle, and I did not wait more than a second or two for an answer. I was not surprised, when I opened the door, to find Marcel standing by the fireplace looking down at Evelyn, and Evelyn sitting in a chair gazing up at him. They both stared at me as if I were a stranger.

'Sorry to disturb you,' I said angrily, 'but I think I'm entitled to an explanation.'

Evelyn was staring at me with wide-open eyes, dark with fear. She looked terribly pale, but I did not feel sorry.

'Explanation of what?' said Marcel, scowling. 'It seems to me you are always bursting into here without warning and asking for explanations.'

'I'm not speaking to you,' I said. 'I'm talking to Evelyn.' I turned to her. 'Is it true you are leaving here quite soon?'

Evelyn still stared at me without speaking. The worried, almost appealing look she wore would have moved me a day ago; but now I only noticed what an odd expression it was, as if the make-up of a very old person, the lines and wrinkles, had been imposed on the face of a child. She had found life much too difficult for her, that was clear; and she was going to take the easiest way out, as she thought it. Well, it was also clear that her mind was made up, and that she was beyond persuasion. I stared back at her so hard that presently she averted her eyes and raised them to Marcel again; what I was thinking was, he was welcome to her. She was going to be, I fancied, a great nuisance to him. I wondered what I had ever seen in her, and if it had been transferred interest I had felt for her, why I did not feel it now, but only thankfulness at my escape. To think that I might have been burdened with her for life! There's no accounting for these aberrations.

Marcel stepped forward as if in her defence, and began to say something; but I stopped him.

'It's all right. It doesn't matter,' I said to him almost good-humouredly. 'It was rather a shock to me to find that Evelyn was leaving so soon. But it doesn't matter, it doesn't matter at all. I just thought she might have told me.' I noticed that I was talking about her over her head as if she were indeed a child or an irresponsible person of some kind.

Marcel did not like my tone. He liked it even less than when I had been angry. He drew himself up and said stiffly:

'Evelyn will leave here with me to-morrow. I have already told you that she will find refuge with my parents. I can assure you, she comes of her own free will.' He hesitated, and for the first time I thought he looked embarrassed. 'I am sure you will be glad to know,' he said, speaking with great precision, 'that I intend to make Evelyn my wife.'

'Oh, good!' I said heartily. 'That puts a very different complexion on it all. I thought you were doomed from the first.'

Marcel licked his lips, and I could see that he was exasperated by my choice of words.

'I mean,' I ran on cheerfully, 'since that first evening when you arrived, and you both went off together towards the rhododendrons.' It struck me that it was a rhododendron-bush under which Hugo's body had been found, and that the word would always have a sinister sound in my ears. 'Well,' I said, 'I wish you every happiness,' and turning to Evelyn and holding out my hand, 'Won't you say good-bye and wish me luck too?'

She placed her hand in mine; it was quite cold, and her fingers made no response to my friendly squeeze. She turned her eyes to my face for a moment, but they were blank and unfocussed, as if she looked at something beyond me, behind my shoulder. Before I released her hand, her eyes had returned to Marcel's face, and she was gazing at him with undisguised trust and adoration.

'All the best,' I said cheerfully, and turned away.

24

The next morning—Sunday—was bright and sunny, with a fresh breeze blowing, like the day on which I had taken Evelyn for that long car drive, and had thought that promises had been exchanged between us. Now I stood at the top of the steps with my hands in my pockets, and watched the chauffeur carrying Marcel's and Evelyn's trunks to the car. It was less than a week since I myself had arrived, in a thunderstorm; and it was as if I had always lived here and always been involved in these people's affairs. I had not seen Evelyn this morning; but Marcel had breakfasted with us, and had been at his most charming, as though nothing untoward had happened, and he was on the best of terms with all of us. At present he was exchanging a few last words with Ursula, and I had strolled out here through tactfulness. I wondered what he could find to say to her. In his place I would have felt guilty and ashamed. But when I passed them, he was leaning towards her solicitously and holding her hand in a long farewell grasp, while she, though she was looking down, obviously had not the heart to part with him on bad terms.

At last he appeared at the top of the steps and stood looking round, buttoning his light travelling-coat round him, so that it fitted his slim graceful figure. He looked like one who was used to travelling, and travelling alone; and it was difficult to see what possible advantage there would be to him in having Evelyn attached to him for life. I envied him, I had to confess, for his ability to move freely, to pick people up and drop them—and this though I knew I could never be the same. Yet, I thought, with Evelyn clinging to him he will be worse off than I am. I am luckier in one way than he is: there is nothing about me, neither riches nor good looks nor charm, to make people want to cling to me, whereas Marcel will always have to fight hard to escape from the attachments his personal magnetism will draw towards him. Would he escape this time, I wondered? It was strange how, from solicitude for Evelyn lest he should betray her, I had reverted to my old concern for him. I realized suddenly that it was he whom I was sorry to see going; I no longer cared about her at all.

He came towards me, gracefully and easily, with his most charming smile, a little sad, and his hand outstretched. I gladly gave him mine, and he pressed it hard with his, laying the other hand on my wrist.

'Good-bye,' he said. 'You do excuse me, don't you, if I've seemed a little *distrait* sometimes, and perhaps even irritable? But Hugo's death upset me a great deal. I felt he was in my care, you know. And until the murderer was discovered, or rather revealed himself, my mind could never have been at rest.'

I broke in: 'You're sure it was Parmoor who shot him?' I said.

'Of course,' said Marcel without hesitation. 'Aren't you? Why else should Parmoor kill himself?'

'I don't know,' I said doubtfully. 'Only I wouldn't have thought he was the kind of man who would do that sort of thing, that's all.'

Marcel shrugged his shoulders: 'No? For my part, I am content to leave it at that. Parmoor did kill himself, and that fact speaks for itself, I think.'

'Maybe,' I said. 'Well, I wish you every happiness—and Evelyn.'

'Thank you,' he said. 'You are very kind.' His charming voice sank a note or two, and ended in a half-sigh. 'You must come and see us some time. I shall send you my address. You will come, won't you?' His voice rose again with eagerness, and he gave my hand and arm a renewed shake with both his hands.

'I will,' I said heartily. But I knew I never would.

A moment later, Evelyn appeared at the top of the steps, and after a frightened glance round her, hurried down towards the car. The chauffeur held the door open, and she vanished into the rear. Marcel, with a last shake of my hand, followed. In a minute they were gone, and I was listening to the sound of the receding engine.

I wondered what the three monkeys would say to that pair's going off together, if they ever relaxed their rules and talked together at night of what they had seen and heard during the day.

PART THREE

THAT evening, I was sitting on the terrace with Ursula. The air was warm, and there was a splendid fiery-red sunset. Ursula was herself again, though rather pale and quiet; but there was a self-control about her and a hidden strength that I admired, and in fact I found I had come to like Ursula very much. I was not in love with her, and I knew that she was a thousand miles from being in love with me. But I also knew that my company was to-night of the utmost help and comfort to her, and this made me content and even happy. To-night, I knew, she could not have borne the drawing-room, where the Biddolphs sat playing bézique, nodding solemnly at the state of affairs that had developed in the house. The drawing-room was haunted by Marcel, singing *Au clair de la lune*; and by Evelyn, small and dark and mysterious, looking on, saying little, getting always her own way; and above all by Hilary Parmoor.

'You know, Jake,' she said to me as I held the lighter to her cigarette, 'I'm glad it's you who are going to the inquest to-morrow. I think—it's a queer thing to say—but I think Hilary would have liked you to be there. He liked you. He told me so.'

'I don't see how——' I was beginning laboriously, in the way one does, as being in duty bound to reject a compliment; but she interrupted me eagerly:

'Oh, yes, he did! He was very observant, you know—much more observant than anyone gave him credit for. But he usually kept his thoughts to himself. Even I didn't really know what he thought about—many things.' She inhaled her cigarette deeply, and I had not the heart to tell her she oughtn't to.

'Tell me,' I said, 'do you think his reason for shooting himself was—what the police seem to think?'

'You mean,' she said, 'do I believe it was he who shot Hugo? No, I don't. But I think'—she laid a hand on my arm—'I think he wanted the police to think so.'

I looked at her in amazement. The glow of the sunset sky had communicated itself to her face and her hair, and for the moment she looked singularly beautiful, even inspired.

'Oh, nonsense!' I said prosaically. 'No one would be so noble as that—not nowadays, anyhow.'

Ursula spoke rapidly, in a low passionate voice.

'You don't know Hilary,' she said. 'Nobody understood him. Everyone thought he was damned and lost because he had dropped his career and relapsed into what looked like indolence. But he was capable of great things—of tremendous self-sacrifice.'

'But why?' I said. 'Why on earth should he want to draw on himself such a terrible charge? And what about his family? Didn't he care about them?'

Ursula laughed. 'His wife, do you mean?' she said. 'He had no children. His wife wouldn't care about anything except insurance-money and things like that.'

'Well, she won't get even that,' I interpolated, 'apparently. But what about you? He knew you'd care—in spite of——'

I paused, not wanting to be tactless about Marcel.

'Yes,' said Ursula. 'He knew I'd care. But what if he thought there might be something even worse in store for me if he didn't do as he did.' Her voice was low. 'What if he thought he knew who killed Hugo? You see,' she hurried on, and her breath came fast, 'there *was* one person who left the drawing-room early that night, wasn't there? And don't you remember how Hilary went out later and left you at the gramophone? I never noticed at the time, I was so preoccupied with—the dancing. But afterwards, when I began to think, I remembered: first Jim going out, and then Hilary. What if Hilary saw something—heard something, in that half-hour while he was away?—something that would shatter my life if it were discovered?'

I looked round anxiously, gripping the arms of my chair, though she had spoken softly.

'Good heavens, Ursula!' I said. 'Where is he?—Jim, I mean.'

'He has gone away for the week-end, I think,' said Ursula. 'I haven't seen him since yesterday, but I believe he has been consulting solicitors and seeing friends, about this whole business—the will that was found on Hugo, and the rest. I don't know even if he knew that Evelyn was leaving. I don't suppose

177

she told him. She told nobody, not even me. It was Marcel who broke the news to me.'

'And you yourself—do you believe it was Jim, then?'

'Oh, I don't know, I don't know!' Ursula pressed her long slender fingers to her forehead. 'All my real knowledge of Jim tells me to say "no." He's violent, not treacherous. But of course, the police would say that that was just prejudice; and even I'm not convinced, or I wouldn't be so worried. They would say he stood to gain most by Hugo's death—or he thought he did.'

'Not more than you,' I said.

'Exactly!' Ursula was not at all displeased at this suggestion. She thought for a minute: 'No!' she said then, most emphatically. 'I'm *sure* he didn't do it. I *must* keep to that, whatever happens, or I shall go mad. But—I still think Hilary believed it was Jim, and that's why he shot himself. You see'—and there was a tremor in her voice as she said this—'he suffered from the delusion that he was no good—no good at life, and above all, no good at his job. He had not been the same since my father died. He blamed himself for not diagnosing the trouble earlier.'

'But that's crazy!' I said angrily.

'I know,' she said. 'From all that you and Sir Frederick have said, I've gathered that. But Hilary had high standards—too high, for himself at any rate.'

'Was he living here,' I said cautiously, 'when your father died?'

'No,' said Ursula. 'He had a house in Chode; but his practice was dwindling to nothing, and he didn't seem to care. He neglected the patients he had. And then, when he got to know us, he just gave up everything to come here. We took up all his time. We were rather selfish, I suppose. My father liked him at first, you see; my father was always trying new doctors, and Hilary was the latest. He used often to stay here for week-ends. He seemed to want to do nothing but play whatever game we were playing—golf, tennis, fishing, shooting—he was good at all of them——'

'Shooting!' I said.

Ursula gave me a curious sidelong look. 'Yes,' she said quietly, 'shooting. Hilary was a crack shot, especially with the revolver. He had lived for a year in South America. He taught us all to shoot: that is, he taught us things we didn't know, such as how to split a card sideways on. At one time we had quite a craze for it. There's a shooting-gallery on the top floor, you know. That's why nobody in this house—the servants, for instance—is very sensitive to the sound of shots. Not that we've done any of it for some time now.'

'But, Ursula!' I said, amazed at the studied casualness of her manner, 'surely all this is of the first importance? Do the police know it?'

'Oh, they know about the shooting-gallery,' said Ursula. 'Jim showed them that, as well as the gunroom. We haven't concealed anything. Everybody knows about the gallery: they'd have been bound to find out.'

'But did they know about Hilary—that he was a crack shot?— that he taught you all to shoot?'

'They do now,' said Ursula still imperturbably. 'We didn't tell them before. There was no need. We left it to Hilary to do so if he wished.'

'But, Ursula,' I protested again, 'if it wasn't Hilary who shot Hugo, or Jim, or you—and yet it was someone in this house— who was it? Marcel couldn't have known where there was a revolver, could he? Nor could I, apart from the fact that I had no motive. That leaves Sir Frederick, and——'

I gasped. We stared at each other in equal comprehension, Ursula quite calm, I in growing agitation. I was about to say something further, when there was the sound of a car coming up the drive. In the deepening dusk, we saw the small sidelights of the Ullstones' car. At the bottom of the steps, Jim emerged, and the car drove on towards the garages.

Jim came slowly up and into the porch. Ursula went to meet him. He did not seem to see me: I was sitting back in the shadow. Under the high stone porch with its Ionic columns at the outer angles, he stopped to light a cigarette; and I thought his face looked sharper and thinner, with two lines from nostrils to mouth, though it was as fresh-complexioned as ever.

Ursula began: 'Have you——?'

He nodded: 'They say it's not valid. It can be upset quite easily.' But there was no triumph in his tones. He sounded matter-of-fact and tired.

'Oh!' Ursula too sounded unexcited. 'How?'

'It wasn't properly witnessed,' said Jim. 'He wrote it on a scrap of paper and then signed it, apparently, and then called in Johnson and his wife and they signed. But they didn't see him sign. They didn't even know they were witnessing a will.'

Ursula laid a hand on his arm. 'Jim,' she said, 'is this true?'

He avoided her very straight gaze. 'God knows!' he said. 'But *I* didn't ask them to say it. They volunteered it, and they're prepared to swear to it. So if de Souvigny doesn't contest—or even if he does——'

There was a silence. Then Ursula said, 'Ah, well! It looks as if we're to be saddled with this place for the rest of our lives after all. I was beginning to think we might escape.'

Jim gave a scornful laugh: 'Don't worry! By the time we've got it back, minus death duties and lawyers' fees, we shan't be able to keep it up. We can hardly do that already. You'll get your wish.'

He moved towards the door. Ursula stopped him; and I knew from the way she spoke that she was frightened.

'Jim,' she said, 'do you know about Evelyn and Marcel?'

Jim said shortly: 'Thanks. O'Brien told me.'

O'Brien was the chauffeur.

I saw Jim pass on into the house, leaving Ursula staring after him. She came slowly back to me and sat down again. I gave her another cigarette and lighted it for her. At last she said:

'I wonder where they are now!'

The pain and fear in her voice were too much for me. Like Jim, I answered her shortly: 'In London, presumably. She'll have to get a passport—or has she got one?'

'She has one,' said Ursula. 'She came to Switzerland with us in December.—Jake!'

'Yes?' I said irritably, for her sudden grab at my arm and her change of tone had made me jump.

'*Why* did the police let them leave?'

'Because,' I said, as if explaining to a child—though I knew that she knew the answer—'they're sure it was Parmoor, and that suits them very well. What's the use of prosecuting a charge of murder against a dead man? They'll return a verdict of *felo de se*, and then they'll finish the other inquest with a verdict of murder against him.'

'But,' cried Ursula, 'he's innocent, and he can't defend himself!'

'He didn't want to defend himself,' I said. 'Can't we leave it as it is, if that's how he wanted it?'

Ursula was silent for a long time. Then she said, quietly and without visible emotion:

'I can't bear it.'

'You can't do anything about it,' I said.

We both looked up. There was a sound, faint at first, then growing—an ordinary enough sound, though somehow we both knew that it was significant: the sound of a car coming up the drive. Ursula grabbed my arm again. A taxi, driven at speed round the bend, pulled up with a squealing of brakes below. Even in the dusk, we knew at once who it was that stepped out. He was alone. He turned to pay the driver, and came running up the steps.

'Marcel!' called out Ursula.

He stopped in full flight, wheeled, and came slowly to us.

'Marcel!' said Ursula again, holding out both her hands; but he stood where he was, without responding; and when she got up and went towards him, he withdrew a step, fending her off with a gesture.

'I've come to warn you,' he said, and his voice, always pleasant, trembled a little.

I too got up and went to him. I thought I saw him sway slightly, and he put his hand to his head. I took his elbow.

'What's the matter?' I said, gently shaking him. 'Where's Evelyn?'

'I've left her,' he said.

'Left her?' I said. 'Where? What has happened? Have you had a quarrel? You should have brought her back with you.'

'I thought it best,' said Marcel, 'to get here first.'

He gave a sudden gasp, and sat down in one of the wicker chairs, and burst into tears. Ursula stood beside him, and her hand hovered over his head.

I left them together.

2

I waited up in my room. An unbearable curiosity about what had happened between Marcel and Evelyn kept me not only awake, but alert. I sat listening to every sound, not even reading, but hearing voices, footsteps, the opening and shutting of doors, the telephone. It was nearly midnight when there came a light tap at my door. I opened. It was Ursula.

'Jake!' she said. 'You're not asleep: I'm so glad! Marcel is much more himself now, but he's terribly strung up, and I don't think he'll sleep a wink unless he's given a sleeping-draught. But I don't know quite what to give him. He says aspirin doesn't suit him, and I think, too, it ought to be something stronger. Could *you* do something about it?'

'I haven't anything here,' I said.

'No, but—Hilary had, in his room. Would you care to come along with me and look in his medicine-chest and see if there's anything that will do?'

'Of course I will,' I said. I could see that her concern for Marcel was not quite strong enough to overcome her very natural reluctance to go alone to Hilary Parmoor's room and search among his possessions. It is always very painful to look at and handle the small personal belongings of the recently-dead. There they are, just as their owner left them, and to disturb the arrangement seems like sacrilege. I took Ursula's arm, and shepherded her down the corridor, round the corner to the left, past Evelyn's door. Parmoor's room was at the end of that corridor, where the west wing of the house jutted out beyond the façade. The door was locked.

'It's all right,' said Ursula, 'I have the key,' and she produced a ring of keys like the one I had seen Evelyn carrying. I switched on the light. The room was large, and carpeted in red, with white-painted fittings and furniture. There were tiers of shelves, and shallow drawers with brass handles, stretching from floor to ceiling, and cupboards, and long wardrobes, and mirrors let into doors, great and small. It was impossible to imagine anybody's ever having possessed enough clothes to need all this storage space; and yet, Ursula said, it was a guest-room. I thought of my own small attache-case containing handkerchiefs, pyjamas and tooth-brush, with which I could have travelled all over the world; and I marvelled that any man should want to saddle himself with what had evidently once been expected here. A door in the opposite wall led into a dressing-room and bathroom. Ursula went through, and I followed.

'Here it is,' she said, going up to one of the small white cabinets fixed on to the wall. 'This is where he kept his medicines. I suppose the police have ransacked everything. But it all looks quite tidy now, doesn't it?'

Her tone was casual, but I was not deceived by it. I knew that she remained here with the greatest effort, and that she talked in order to remind herself that I was there close behind her. She opened the medicine-chest with another smaller key from the ring, and the usual array of small bottles, pill-boxes and bandages wrapped in blue tissue-paper revealed itself.

'What exactly did happen between Marcel and Evelyn, Ursula?' I asked her. I thought it might help her to think of something other than Hilary; and, besides, I wanted to know.

'I don't know,' said Ursula, vaguely studying the contents of the medicine-chest. 'I dared not ask him.' She caught my look of incredulity, and added hastily, 'At least, when I did ask him, he just shook his head, and he looked so white and ill that I thought it best to make him go to bed. Now what shall I take him? Hilary used to have veronal, but I suppose you wouldn't advise that, and I don't see it now, anyway.' She picked up a box of sedative bouillon cubes. 'This is more the sort of thing, isn't it? Will this do?'

'But what is Marcel doing about it?' I persisted. 'Surely he's not going just to leave her there on her own.'

'I don't know at all,' said Ursula again, still rummaging in the medicine-chest. 'What about these capsules? Oh no, these are for 'flu, aren't they? Or is it indigestion?' She handed me several more boxes of pills and capsules, talking all the time more or less at random. 'Superintendent Mallett rang up to-night and told me to tell you that the inquest to-morrow would be postponed till next day. By the way, you know that poor Hugo's funeral is to-morrow at half-past two? Marcel says he will go. And Jim will have to go too, to represent the family. What a horrible farce!'

She laughed, with such sudden violence that I felt it was time to get her away from here.

'These will do all right,' I said, choosing a bottle of barbiturate tablets. 'They'll knock him out at once, and without after-effects.

She began putting the other bottles and boxes back into the medicine-cupboard; and as she did so, I noticed a small screwed-up piece of paper fall to the ground. I stooped and picked it up, and almost without noticing what I was doing, I unrolled it. It was a receipt for a registered postal packet. The pencilled name and address were scrawled as usual, and I hardly bothered to read them. I was about to crumple up the paper again and toss it away when suddenly I became aware that the name I had read was my own.

3

I looked again.

Yes, it was my own name, and my home address. The postmark was Chode. The date was perfectly clear: the thirteenth, the day of Parmoor's death. I took the slip to the wall-light over the wash-hand stand, and examined it again. There was no doubt—no doubt at all.

'Ursula!' I called.

She turned sharply, aware of something odd in my tone. I held out the paper slip. She read it, and looked up at me, as startled as I had been.

'How did he know my home address?' I said. 'I've had no letters forwarded on here, and I don't think I've mentioned it. Nobody knows where I am.'

'Probably out of the Medical Directory,' said Ursula musingly. 'He had one on his bookshelf in there. It used to give him pleasure to read it. Your father is a doctor, isn't he? Your name isn't very common.'

'As a matter of fact,' I said, 'we are the only Seabornes in the Medical Directory—my father and my brother, that is. So he'd know where to send it, even if I didn't give my address away. But what in heaven's name would he send me a registered packet to my home address for, when I was here in the house with him?'

Ursula came towards me. 'Jake,' she said earnestly, 'I think you ought to get hold of it at once. I feel sure it's important. Hilary must have had a reason for what he did. But—if I were you, I'd go and fetch it. I wouldn't have it redirected here. I think he meant you to read it somewhere else than in this house. And I don't think I'd tell Mallett about it—not yet, anyway.'

'I could get home in three hours by road,' I said. 'But first I'll 'phone my father and find out if it's there. He won't be pleased at being called in the middle of the night, but——'

'Come along to the extension in my room,' said Ursula.

4

Ursula's telephone was jade green. It stood beside her large double bed, on the edge of which I sat gingerly, for it seemed to me to be all covered with yellow silk or satin, with pink sheets, and a silk-smocked affair at the head like a reredos. On the small round table where the telephone stood, I noticed idly, as I waited for my number, all the things Ursula had to have near her even when she was in bed, such as powder, rouge, cream, lipstick, nail-files and nail-polisher and orange-stick, a couple of rings lying on an open book. At my feet were a pair of those extra-ordinary things women are so fond of—heel-less pink slippers ornamented with feathers and called, I believe, mules: they must be responsible for many a sprained ankle, if not a broken neck. My own heavy brown shoes looked like beetle-crushers beside them. The air one breathed here was faintly perfumed: it must have been the grains of face-powder floating about that titillated one's nose and made one want to sneeze. On the mantelpiece was a delightful ornamental clock, very tall and gilded and with a slender waist like a fine lady. On the dressing-table, which was low and had a long mirror, were what appeared to be masses of silver and cut-glass, and things in pots and bottles; and at the side was a great cut-glass vase of yellow tulips.

My observations were cut short by the operator's saying 'You're through,' and a moment later came my father's gruff voice giving our home number. I thought how, if I were a patient calling him at that time, I would be afraid; and then I thought how, in spite of his gruffness, his patients weren't afraid at all;

and they were quite right, for he was, under a rough exterior, a man of infinite patience and kindness. Luckily the 'phone was beside his bed.

'Oh, it's you, Jake,' he said, not at all put out. 'Where are you 'phoning from?'

I told him: that is, I said I was 'phoning from Ullstone Hall, but I didn't mention Ursula's bedroom. I wondered what he would say if he could see my actual surroundings. But nothing ever put him out.

'Oh, yes,' he said. 'We saw from the evening paper that you'd got involved in this shooting-affair. There was a report of the inquest—adjourned, I see. By the way, there are some letters for you. Do you want us to forward them?'

'Is there a registered packet?' I said, and my heart beat hard.

'Registered packet? Yes—yes, I think there is. Anyway, we'll send them on in the morning.'

'No, don't do that,' I said. 'I'm coming to fetch it—now. I'll be there in three hours.'

'Three hours? All right, my boy. Be careful, though: don't fall asleep at the wheel.'

I heard the click of the replaced receiver; and I knew exactly how that good man had sunk back on to his pillow and instantly fallen asleep again. He had that greatest of all virtues in fathers: having taught us all he knew, he then left us alone. He never pried.

I stood up, nearly upsetting the round table, and falling over the mules.

'Ursula,' I said, 'I'm going at once. You're sure about the postponed inquest?'

'Yes,' said Ursula. 'He said the official notice would be sent along in the morning. But you'll come back?'

'I'll come back,' I said.

She came towards me and put her two hands on my forearms. 'Oh, Jake!' she said, 'I told you he liked you.' Her eyes swam with tears. 'Don't you get the feeling, all the time, about the house, that he's watching from a little way off and smiling? He didn't believe in an after-life—and I suppose I don't either, though I'd like to—but I know he has something to tell us, and I'm glad he chose you.'

I kissed her on the forehead, and dried her eyes with my handkerchief. She brushed back her fair hair.

'You go and get out the car,' she said, 'and I'll get you a thermos of tea and some sandwiches.'

It was now a quarter past one in the morning.

5

I have never enjoyed a run so much as I did the drive home that night. My little car seemed to have benefited from its rest, and it went like a bird, answering to the throttle like a live thing. The roads were empty. There was still a gibbous moon high up, giving a lovely clear light; and the air was wonderfully mild. I had the hood down, and the wind rushed through my hair; there is no more exhilarating feeling in the world. As I passed through the tall gates with the three monkeys on the gate-posts, and left the great dark house and its trees behind; as I sped along the lane with its lacey shadows, on to the main road so clear and still, and through the suburbs and the old market square and past the church of sleeping Chode, I thought how I should really, by all rational reckoning, feel a sense of relief and a lightening of the heart; but the moment I said this to myself, I knew that the gaiety, the exhilaration that filled me was not that of escape: it was because I knew I would be returning. The speedometer rose to sixty-five . . .

It was a few minutes after four when, stiff but not at all tired, I drew up in front of our house and hauled myself out of the low driving-seat. The policeman passing by swung his torch at me, recognized me, called out, 'Working late, Mr. Seaborne?' and moved on. I ran up our asphalt path to the porch, which seemed very small, and opened the front door with my latch-key.

Nothing and nobody was stirring, for which I was thankful. I closed the door softly and hurried up the stairs to my room. Again the smallness of everything struck me; and yet I had been away for only a week. I reached my own room, which was at the back of the house, overlooking the garden. For a town garden it was quite big, with an oblong of grass and several old apple-trees and pear-trees, but to me it seemed no more than a handkerchief. Not that I could see it, for the moon had now set, and it was quite dark; but I was aware of what it looked like by day, with its black earth and sparse dark-green grass studded with daisies, and the gables at the backs of the houses in the next road parallel to ours and overlooking it. It was a good solid residential district, built in the latter half of the last century; yet what a strange thing to want to spend one's life here! My father had inherited his practice from his father, and we—my brother and I—would probably inherit it from him. "The burden of inheritance!" I thought. "Everybody ought to begin afresh, with his own capabilities and powers of production, and all inheritance should be put back into the common stock. The passion for inheritance," I thought, warming up to my theme as I crossed the room towards the big sash-window, "is one of the major curses of human life, and always has been. Carried to excess, it is a kind of insanity." I pulled down the spring blind, and recrossed the room, and switched on the light.

Yes, there it was, propped up on my desk: an oblong manilla envelope, with my name in heavy black hand-writing very suggestive of Hilary Parmoor. There was the blue and white registration label stuck across the corner. What had been this man's feelings as he handed the slightly bulging envelope over the counter at Chode and thought, "When this is opened, I shall be dead"? It was quite beyond my sanguine, life-loving nature to imagine how anyone could in cold blood take all these steps and make all these last arrangements. My small iron bedstead with its yellow cotton counterpane creaked as I sat down on the edge, and my hands shook as I drew out the triple-folded quarto sheets covered with the same stiff black handwriting. I propped up the pillow behind me, pulled myself together, and began to read.

6

My dear Seaborne,

You will, I am sure, be very much surprised to find this letter from me awaiting you on your return home from what will have been a remarkable holiday. I hate to be melodramatic, but of course, by the time you read this, I shall no longer be in existence, and you may even have attended my inquest as well as that of poor Hugo Ullstone—which will be good practice for you, though rather a bore.

You will wonder why I have chosen you, who five days ago were a complete stranger to me, as the recipient of this last communication. Well, it was not done, believe me, without considerable thought; and though it seemed hardly fair, on the one hand, to burden you with the responsibility, yet on the other hand I thought that the very fact of your being a stranger would make the business weigh on you less heavily. And again, the profession you have chosen—I hope you *have* chosen it, by the way, and aren't simply following in your father's footsteps— shows that you aren't afraid of responsibility, at any rate in prospect. Real responsibility is a very different matter, believe me.

As for my motive in writing at all, this is, so far as I can judge myself, mainly selfish. I can bear to leave the world, very easily; but I can't bear to depart without also leaving behind me a record of the truth: not on paper, because I most solemnly and strenuously direct you to destroy this letter as soon as you have read it, and to disclose the contents to no one—but on the mind of some living person. This will seem to you inconsistent when you have read my motive for doing away with my own life; but then, my dear fellow, human beings rarely are consistent; and I am inclined to think that complete consistency is as inhuman as complete irresponsibility, and is in fact a monstrosity. However, that is an academic question. To come to my narrative:

I first came into contact with the Ullstone family something over a year ago, when I was still practising actively in Chode. My wife had already left me, for reasons all of which are irrelevant except that she didn't really like me and never had. I don't blame her at all for that—it is all too understandable—but I think it was a pity she gave me to think otherwise: for I married her because I naively thought she was in love with me and would break her heart if I didn't do so, whereas what she wanted was a home. Contrary to the popular belief, I do not consider that this is an admirable attitude on the part of women: I think that if all they want is a home, they should seek out somebody willing to give them a home in return for their services—some widower with children, perhaps, or somebody ambitious to found a family or further his career by social activities; not someone young, romantic, serious, eager, easily-deceived and lacking in all worldly judgment like myself at twenty-four. When I discovered what had happened, the usual consequences followed: I felt myself very much left up in the air, with no object for my emotions—for we had no children, because my wife refused to have any—and since, as a doctor, I couldn't afford to let my feelings run away with me or attach themselves to the other women who came under my care, I took refuge in overwork. The overwork led to sleeplessness, and the sleeplessness to anxiety and nerves. The constant fear of making mistakes haunted me, and affected my health, or else I thought it did; and you know what followed—it's an all-too-common story in our profession—first of all drink, then drugs. By drugs, I don't mean dangerous things like cocaine and morphia: I never got that far. I just mean that I was constantly swallowing something for my health—a dispensary is a great temptation!—luminal, allonal, veronal and the rest, when I ought to have been dealing with the cause.

One effort to escape I did make: I went for a year to South America, to do a locum for a man who wanted to come home and put the finishing touches on an M.D. thesis, and who therefore needed to be near libraries. He took over my practice and ran it with the help of an assistant; and I went off, without my wife, and lived for a year in complete freedom and happiness on his ranch, which was about a hundred miles from Rio de Janeiro. Here I rode and hunted; here I perfected my shooting—for I had always been a good shot—and mixed with real men and women, and never took the lid off a pill-box or shook a capsule out of a bottle, either for myself or for anyone else. The only illnesses there were real illnesses, and nobody bothered about his or her nerves, and the drink one took as a matter of course didn't seem to do one any harm. Think twice, my boy, before you settle down in dull old dirty England, and give yourself up to looking down throats and doling out rhubarb mixture and tinct. camph. co. Give yourself a break first, before you marry the nice girl who lives on the corner, or the first pretty nurse who wants a fur coat and thinks you'll do to get it for her, and settle down to beef on Sundays and the smell of cabbage and gravy in the hall. Go west, young man, or go east; go anywhere, but don't stay put until you've seen what real sunshine is like and what some women mean when they say they love you. But I digress.

The year ended. The other fellow wanted to come back. And so I returned, to find that what had been a life of exasperating dissatisfaction had now become an unendurable hell of torment. I'm afraid I made it unendurable for poor Margeret too; anyhow, she left me, and all the neighbours sympathized with her.

However, I did not lose my practice. It's an extraordinary thing what people will put up with in their medical attendant if they have faith in him; and I was quite good at my job. In fact, I had a considerable flair for it when I wasn't too preoccupied with my own troubles. But the obsession that I would one day make a fatal mistake—an obsession I had entirely forgotten during my year in South America—now came back with redoubled force. I used to lie awake at night, going over and over the day's work, wondering if there had been anything I had failed to notice or omitted to do; and when patients died, instead of dismissing the matter from my mind as my colleagues did, I would go over and over the details of the treatment, wishing I had tried this new method or not risked that drastic dosage, until my head swam and I was driven again to the whisky decanter, or worse, to the medicine-cupboard in my room. At the same time, you understand, I was perfectly well aware with another part of my mind that this was an obsession: that actually, so far, I had never been to blame, and that my failures had all been due to the general limitation of human knowledge and not to negligence.

Then came my meeting with the Ullstones.

I had heard of them, of course, and had seen them occasionally in Chode; but I had never met any of them. They did not move at all in Chode circles, and Jim and Ursula were away at school and abroad for most of the time until last year. I was called in to see one of the stable boys who had been shot in the leg by one of their guests; and after that, I got friendly with them. I used to look in and drink a cup of morning coffee, nothing more, with Ursula. She was glad to see even me, poor girl, for she was very much bored after having lived most of her life in a community, and she found it very difficult to settle down in that great house with no one of her own age except her brother, and with a father who would have been hard to get on with in any circumstances, and who was now in the last stage—though we didn't know it—of a baffling and incurable disease. Ursula, you must understand, my dear boy, is actually, under all that scintillation, an affectionate, impulsive, intensely sociable creature. She loves play-acting in her life, it's true, but—paradoxical as it may seem to you—there's nothing false about her. Remember that, when you have a practice, and don't mistake a love of the poses and the graces for a love of lies.

My friendship with Ursula developed into a deep affection and regard on my side, and a generous gratitude on hers—gratitude for my sympathy and the help I was to her in her conflict with her father—for I was a help to her there, and I'm very glad to be able to remember it. I used to go and sit with him and talk to him for hours, or rather listen to him; and he fastened on to me like the ancient mariner, and kept me there for hours, telling me his life-story, which was strange—but then, I find, most life-stories are. It was, however, not so much the incidents of his life that interested me as the revelation of his character. I watched it, as one watches an organism under a microscope, and I very soon placed it in the enormous class of the egoists. At his age—the late forties—this man was no more capable of taking in a new impression than if he had been walled up in a tomb. Nothing interested him except his own past, round which he circled, and made one circle with him. Most people are egoists, of course, unfortunately for themselves, as every doctor knows; they worship themselves and everything about themselves, including their ailments, with an intensity which ought to be reserved for the supra- or extra-human entity they call God; but even so, this man's obsession with his past struck me as something out of the ordinary. He seemed to think that nothing interesting had ever happened to anybody except himself; and what interested him in his own life was the fact that he had once lived in India. He kept me there for hours and hours, talking to me about the Indian scene, the people—of whom I could see he certainly had special knowledge—the climate, flora and fauna, history, politics: all original and interesting in itself, but he spoilt it, as such people always do, by repetition. Still, I let him keep me there for hours, partly through a desire to help Ursula, partly because of my own boredom and inertia.

I shall not take you through all the stages of his development during the year. I shall come to the event which concerns us all most deeply. Shortly before Michaelmas last year, James Ullstone got worse. His temper, never very good, became quite ferocious, especially against Jim and Ursula, and he even changed towards me, Ursula thought because he had detected the friendship between us and was jealous; but I think now that it was just the progress of his disease. Anyway, his irritability was accompanied by an attack of acute arthritis, poor chap, and he had to take to his bed. I did the best I could for him, with diet, and so forth; but you know how obstinate these cases can be and how helpless one is unless nature lends a hand; and as he wouldn't have Ursula anywhere near him, I certainly thought it an excellent idea that we should get someone in to nurse him. Ursula explained about Evelyn Ross; she was written to, she accepted, she arrived.

At first, her arrival seemed the solution of Ursula's troubles. She was quiet, efficient, excellent in the sickroom, willing to relieve Ursula of the burdens of housekeeping as well. James Ullstone took to her at once, to our great relief. He fastened on to her as he had fastened on to me, and I was now discarded. He even conceived a hostility towards me, both as a doctor and as a man; and though Evelyn pretended to deplore this, I now believe that she encouraged it. Ursula disliked her from the first. Jim took rather a fancy to her, while pretending not to. As for me, I just thought she didn't count—and I was greatly mistaken. She counted, and still counts, enormously, as do all creatures of intense singleness of purpose, whatever their purpose may be, and her protective colouring is her quietness, her appeal to one's compassion, and a way she has of making one feel that whatever she may do out of a sense of duty, her real interest is oneself. Even I, though I disliked her, felt the power of that appeal once or twice; it's inexplicable unless one has been subjected to it, like the hypnotic eye, I suppose. You, too, have felt it, are feeling it still; so I need explain no further to you.

As for James Ullstone, you can imagine how it affected him in his mental and physical state. He was completely under her domination within a week. Ursula tried to pretend that she didn't mind; but she did mind, especially when she saw that her father would certainly marry Evelyn. Ursula is a generous creature, as I've said, but the thought of a stepmother of the same age as herself was rather too much to swallow. It made her feel ridiculous, for one thing; and I think also she was afraid: the domination was so rapid and so complete. Evelyn gave no sign of what her own reaction would be to a proposal of marriage; but her quiet, sedate manner was not reassuring. Yes, Ursula was afraid, and she clung to me all the more closely, not as a lover but as a friend.

Then came the affair with Jim Ullstone. Jim fell in love with Evelyn, to his own deep surprise, I'm sure. Jim is a rake, a thoroughly undisciplined, lazy, limited, self-indulgent little blighter with lots of vanity and no brains; and men like that, you'll observe, often fall for women of rather prim, repressive manners and inconspicuous appearance, no doubt as a contrast to their more exotic friends. Ursula encouraged him at first, hoping to break Evelyn's hold on her father, and not really believing that Jim was serious—for Ursula couldn't see where the attraction lay, and there she was at a disadvantage, since it made her underestimate her enemy. Evelyn too made a serious blunder here, from her own point of view: the power she had so easily acquired over James Ullstone made her a little careless, and perhaps too she was a little carried away by Jim, who is young and good-looking and apparently has a great appeal for women. Anyhow, Evelyn let James Ullstone see that she was interested in his son; and there she underestimated the man's egoism, for far from making him jealous and more devoted than ever, it enraged him past all bearing, and brought about the final disaster.

You know what happened. In a fury of destructiveness he burst all his bonds, and after some terrible scenes, he rushed up to London, unburdened himself to a stranger, discovered what was wrong with him, and before undergoing operation, altered his will. Let us hope that that last act of his, the final sacrifice of all he possessed in the present on the altar of the past, brought him peace of mind. As for me, when I heard Sir Frederick Lawton's diagnosis, I knew that I had made the mistake which had been lying in wait for me all my life. To an outsider, it would seem not to matter much perhaps, since probably nothing could have saved the man; but to me it mattered supremely, for it was the proof, the confirmation, of what I had long thought of myself. For months, ever since I had got to know the Ullstones, I had been neglecting my practice; and at last it had begun to suffer, since I was scarcely ever within call. It was dwindling and dwindling; and I didn't care. Now I gave up bothering, and just resigned from the panel and let the other fellows share out my patients between them, giving my own ill-health as the reason. You may think it curious, but that affair of James Ullstone was the breaking-point, and I knew it. I had arrived at that conclusion before you came. I had made up my mind just to wait and see Ursula through her meeting with her half-brother Hugo, and then pack up and go, possibly back to the Argentine, and try to recover that old happiness, living in obscurity till I died.

Events moved quickly, however. First you appeared, then the amazing Marcel de Souvigny, who swept us all off our feet, except perhaps Aunt Susan and Uncle Biddolph. Of what followed, you were for the most part a witness; what I have to tell you is merely what you didn't and couldn't see. For instance, you couldn't know, as I did, that Evelyn Ross, having lost one good chance of becoming mistress of Ullstone Hall, would naturally attach herself to the new heir, and would put out that peculiar hypnotic power she exercises from a distance like an electric current whenever she thinks it worth while. She immediately transferred her powers to the supposed Hugo, and even I, though I expected it, was amazed to see how easily it worked. Easily, yes—but too easily from her point of view; for Marcel, though he records all these things and responds, is as changeable as a barometer; in fact, he records everything and retains nothing. That is *his* protection.

Marcel, who can't keep a secret for two minutes—bless his heart, a charming fellow: I like him—at once revealed to Evelyn that he wasn't the heir; and that, of course, meant that she was no longer interested in him. My dear fellow, I do hope that this is not too much of a shock for you; but it is better that you should be shocked now than make the most appalling mistake of your

life, and it is to prevent you from doing that that I am bothering—
I don't quite know why—to write this letter.

Evelyn heard Marcel making his ridiculous arrangement with
Hugo to parade Ursula before him the next evening; and she
made up her mind—that very small, fiendishly-concentrated bit
of mechanism which can exclude all other considerations but its
own interest—that Hugo must be got rid of. She calculated that
he would probably not have had time to make a new will, and
that therefore the property would revert to Ursula and Jim, in
which event she would have returned to Jim as if nothing had
happened. That did not prevent her from planning to make Jim
look suspect, if it became necessary for her to use this in self-
protection; but of course she hoped that the first suspicion would
fall on Marcel, who planned the meeting. I am told that she
tried to suggest to the police that Marcel and Hugo were on bad
terms, when she was interviewed: she is the world's most competent liar, while constantly accusing others of the same thing.

On her return that evening, she told Jim of the meeting, while
pretending all the time to be afraid of his violence; and he played
into her hands by hitting you. There is no doubt that she was
responsible for this also: she knows just how to madden poor
Jim, who is not very clever. You can be sure also that she was
responsible for his leaving the drawing-room that evening at the
time when Hugo would be coming to the rendezvous. She left
the drawing-room herself some while later, didn't she?—and I
left some five minutes after her, to get a drink. It was what I saw
then that has led me to my present position, within an hour or
two of my end.

I was in my own room, with the door an inch ajar, when I saw
Evelyn coming down the staircase opposite, which leads to the
second floor. Of course there was no reason why she shouldn't
go up to the second floor at any time she chose. She was by now
the housekeeper, and the servants' rooms were up there as well
as box-rooms and the billiard-room and the gunroom and the
shooting-gallery. She might have been spying on the maids, or
quarrelling with Jim, or anything you please. I don't know even
now what there was about her appearance that arrested my
attention: she was wearing a dark coat, and had her hands in
the pockets, but what is there unusual in that? She went off in

the direction of her own room. I followed her. I saw her go in, and it was no surprise to me that she came out again a minute later and turned off down the service staircase which is near her room on the same side of the corridor. Again I followed, and I repeat, I don't know why I did this, except that my perceptions were once pretty acute, and still are when they are roused.

She left the house by one of the back entrances, I turned away; and I was about to get my drink and return to the drawing-room when something prevented me, some query in my mind. Instead, I walked out by the front door; and sure enough, when I rounded the angle, there she was, keeping in the black shadow of the house, then of the trees, and then making her way to the main drive and by a roundabout route to the shrubbery. I had no idea what she was up to. Even when she reached the beech-tree behind which she took her stand, and I saw Hugo pacing up and down in the moonlight at the end of the path—his face looked coppery-green, I remember, and he was watching the house—I still had no idea what she intended. I was absorbed in watching her, and him—I guessed, of course, who he was; but though my thoughts worked quickly, my will was paralysed, and I stood there behind my own beech-tree some thirty yards further back, watching as if at a play. It came as a complete surprise to me when she took aim and fired.

Hugo fell. Did I run forward and raise the alarm? Did I even go to the man's help? No. I watched still, without stirring. What was it that made me do this, in spite of all my training? Was it fear? I don't think so. I don't feel at all afraid now, and I don't remember even envisaging what would happen if I rushed up to her then. I will tell you the reason: it was the sudden failure, in an emergency, of all my powers, a sort of collapse of the will, if you understand me—but you won't. It was like being in the position of a man who was once an athlete, a famous sprinter, let us say, and who lets himself get gradually out of condition, through laziness. Then one day he is called upon to run quickly— it is a matter of life and death—and he finds that his muscles will no longer obey him. He is weaker than the ordinary man, who never learnt to run fast. So it was with me. I stayed where I was. It all happened very quickly. Hugo fell. Evelyn ran forward, and dragged him, apparently without difficulty, to the place where

197

he was found next day. Then she left, by the way she had come. She passed me quite close and was gone.

By now I was trembling—shaking from head to foot, though the evening was warm. When I could control myself, I went up to Hugo, and bent over him. He was dead. I realized then that I must not be found here—that if the shot had been heard, and I were caught, I should not be believed. Why should anyone take my word against Evelyn's? My motive for killing Hugo was as good as hers. But nobody came, nothing was stirring. So I too left, by the way I had come; and after reaching the house and giving myself a stiff drink, I rejoined you all in the drawing-room. Evelyn had already returned and was dancing with Sir Frederick. It was still only a quarter to ten; I had been absent just over half an hour. I thought how odd you all looked: the two couples dancing, Aunt Susan and Uncle Biddolph looking on, you still at the gramophone, everything just as I left it; and yet you all looked to me like automata. I could not believe that you had seen and heard nothing—that there was nothing to be read in my face or hers, that no echo of those violent minutes, and a man's death-agony, in the shrubbery, had penetrated here. I took over the gramophone from you again. Evelyn had retired. She passed me in the doorway, unaware that I knew her secret, still self-absorbed. She looked pale, but then she always does: it is one of her greatest assets. I wondered if I would follow her, speak to her; but you forestalled me. I expect she wasn't too pleased at that! However, you didn't return, and after a short while the party broke up. Marcel bethought himself of his arrangement, and asked Ursula to take a turn with him in the garden. Sir Frederick and the others went off. I stayed there in the drawing-room. I was there when you looked in at eleven, and when Marcel and Ursula returned.

Next morning, you found the body, and the police came. What was I to do? I had spent a sleepless night, wondering; and in the end I decided to see first how the investigations went. Perhaps she had left some clue, I thought; perhaps they would find out for themselves. If they didn't—well, what proof had I to offer? It seemed to me that if I came forward, nothing could save me from instant arrest and all the long-drawn-out business of a criminal trial, or at least endless questioning and nervous strain, which I was utterly unfit to bear. On this night my usual drugs, veronal and so on, had absolutely no effect on me, and I realized that I was faced with the possibility of insomnia such as even I had never yet experienced—unending nights with perhaps an hour or two of uneasy dozing in the small hours—or an increase in the dose that would reduce my whole waking life to a condition only just above stupor. How could I, in those circumstances, keep my mind alert and fresh enough to answer questions? As it was, nobody had noticed, apparently, that I had left the drawing-room; they had assumed, in so far as they assumed anything, that I had just gone for a few minutes to get a drink. You yourself assumed this, didn't you?—and you were the only one who had reason to notice the length of time I had been absent.

So when morning came and the inevitable investigations began, I just pretended, like the three monkeys, that I had heard and seen nothing and had nothing to say. I didn't even tell the police—and nobody else did, I notice—that Evelyn owed her skill in shooting to me, and that the cartridges she was using were probably mine: for after I got to know the Ullstones and they discovered that I was a first-class shot, they got me to give them lessons up there—target-practice in that shooting-gallery of theirs. Jim, Ursula, Evelyn and various guests from time to time took part; it was a craze with them for a month or two. I suppose I brought that box of cartridges along to illustrate some point about American ammunition's fitting the Colt revolver. Evelyn must have helped herself to a few, in case she should need them. She would have used them on Jim, or Ursula, or anybody, if it had been to her advantage.

So far as I was able, I followed her about the next morning. I was curious to see how she would dispose of the revolver. Would she put it back in the gunroom? She didn't. Would she try to plant it on someone else—on Jim or Ursula or even me? I had to watch out for that. What she actually did was to throw the thing into the lily-pool at some time, I don't know when; I imagine before we all met in Marcel's room that morning. I feel sure, from certain trifling indications, that it was already there when you had your interesting conversation—some of which I heard—with her beside the pool: when I gave you the police message and then took your place beside her. I watched her very carefully then, and her uneasiness, which wouldn't have been visible to you, was obvious to me with my special knowledge. By this time she knew that Hugo had after all made a will, in Marcel's favour; and it must have been a severe blow to her. I fancy that it was from then onward that she bent all her energies on suggesting that Jim was the most likely suspect. I stayed with her for a while after you left, and she contrived to let me know that she was deeply distressed about Jim. She was a consummate liar: she knew all the ways, direct and by implication, and she never ceased to use them.

You must have wondered why, this morning at breakfast, everybody looked at you so strangely. Poor fellow, you looked very much taken aback. You did not realize that Marcel as usual had announced to the whole company his intention of endowing *you* with the property, if it came to him by Hugo's will. He was full of this: he said that you had deserved it, because you alone had befriended him when he came. Ursula was naturally rather upset; but I assured her that Marcel would forget all about it by the next day, and that I didn't think you would accept the gift, anyhow. Sir Frederick Lawton, not so sure, promised Ursula that he would speak to you about it. And, crowning comedy from my point of view, Evelyn Ross went off with you for the day, and I've no doubt, was very nice to you. You returned an hour ago, looking solemn and yet exalted; and I am convinced you think that your future happiness is secure. You didn't know, and don't know, that Marcel has now returned from London and has told everybody that he has changed his mind. I don't know what his latest plan is, but it doesn't matter, because he won't carry out any of them, and probably Hugo's will isn't valid, anyway. I predict—and men about to die have sharp perception —that Marcel will vanish like a moonbeam, leaving no trace behind except a recollection of his charming personality, his pleasant voice and his graceful walk.

Now then: here comes the final event, which will lead presently to another shot being fired, down by the lily-pond this time, because that's where I've decided to go. While you were out with Evelyn, it seemed to me a heaven-sent opportunity to search her room. I did so; but of course I found nothing, though I gave myself up to it, feeling in mattresses and upholstery, probing into

200

drawers and cases and boxes, and in short, conducting a detailed search such as I have read about in crime stories. I found nothing except some carefully-preserved and labelled love-letters, including a few from James Ullstone and from Jim, and various bits of quite valuable jewellery stowed away in odd corners, some of which I think ought to belong to Ursula. When I gave up the quest and returned to my own room, I found a message asking me to ring up my own house in Chode; and on doing so I heard the very agitated voice of my housekeeper saying that the police had been there, and would I come, please, because she was not sure what was happening.

Well, I came; and that is where I am now. The police had indeed been, and while I had been ransacking Evelyn's room, they had been ransacking this house. They had found a box of cartridges, some of which were missing, of the same calibre as the one that shot Hugo Ullstone; and my housekeeper had gathered from their manner that this had greatly pleased them. They had asked her many questions about my habits: why I neglected my practice, if I drank, since when had I known the Ullstones, what were my relations with my wife. My housekeeper is a loyal soul, and she had said as little as she could; but I saw that she was much shaken. As for my locum, when he came in just now and saw me sitting here at my desk in the surgery, he started as if he had seen a murderer—and I'm convinced he thinks he has.

And now, Seaborne, I've decided to quit the scene. They are after me, they have evidence; and in Evelyn Ross I have a bitter enemy—an enemy I can't cope with because she acts not out of personal hostility but out of her own implacable purpose, and it suits her purpose that I shall be destroyed. It is possible that she has guessed that I know or suspect something about her; I think I may have given something away when I talked to her yesterday morning by the lily-pond. Anyway, I am in a net from which I cannot escape, and haven't the strength to struggle with. My death can affect no one: my wife will be glad; and Ursula, though she will be sorry, will be better without me. I have done all I can do for her, and my continued existence can only get in the way of her happiness. If I do as I intend, everybody will assume my guilt, and the matter will soon die down.

The police took away the box of cartridges; but I still have a loaded revolver in my trunk at Ullstone Hall. I must hurry back there now before they find it. First of all, though, I shall post this to you to your home address, from the post-office here. There is one precaution I shall take: the police will very probably find out that I have posted a registered letter to you at about four o'clock this afternoon, and they will get curious. Therefore I enclose another sheet briefly stating that I felt it best for various reasons to do away with myself, and wishing you luck in your profession and a few other banalities. This you can show if you are asked; and you can safely burn the rest. My reason for not wanting you to show this revelation to the police is that they would not believe it, and it would merely cause endless trouble to all concerned.

One last point: I don't care what happens to any of the others; but you must protect Ursula, from Evelyn, from Marcel, from herself. Evelyn will marry Jim, I suppose, and it will serve him right. Marcel will go, and Ursula if she doesn't go with him will be very unhappy for a time. This is where you come in. If you will stand by her and if possible take her away, she will, I'm certain, turn to you; and with you she will find a purpose in life that she at present lacks and needs. She is an enthusiast, and she will do well whatever she undertakes. As for you, you will get somebody who will make all the difference to you between success and failure—somebody who will smooth off all your rough edges, who will stimulate your ambition, who will take the trouble to alter you, not in things fundamental—you are all right there—but in externals, which matter a very great deal, whatever you may think now. Don't be afraid that she'll ruin you: she has a good business head, and she is more likely to make your fortune, even if she doesn't bring you one.

And now, my dear chap, accept the best wishes of a man who liked you at first sight, and who if he had been younger and not past his work and altogether beyond helping anybody, would have waited for you and made you his partner and successor. I would have been quite content to pass out without letting anyone know the reason, perhaps, if it had not been that I could not bear to think of *your* falling into the spider's web. Don't let considerations of your duty to society lead you to disclose the contents of this letter; it will only make trouble for all of you, and I don't think she'll do any further harm once she has what she wants.

Now I'm going to seal this and take it to the post. And then, after dark, to the lily-pond. I wonder which of you will find me. I shall try not to make too much mess of it. Good luck to you. Give my love to Ursula, and tell her to forget me. Good-bye.

7

I folded up the crackling sheets, and put them away into my breast pocket, mechanically. I could not yet think, nor see the consequences of what he had told me. The curious thing was that this revelation about Evelyn caused me no pain, not even surprise: it was, as he said, as if I had been hypnotized, and the effect had worn off, so that I could not even remember what I had been feeling during the hypnotic state. I could only dimly remember Evelyn's physical appearance; and in so far as I could recall it, it seemed to me to be utterly without attractive quality. Yet there was no denying that I had for a time believed myself in love with her—had asked her to marry me. No wonder Ursula had been afraid of her—Ursula, who was not given to being afraid—as she saw one man after another dancing like a marionette to Evelyn's will. Hilary Parmoor, it was true, had not succumbed, nor so far as I knew had Uncle Biddolph! but then, Evelyn had not taken any interest in Hilary; and Biddolph was immunized by a greater force, the fear of Susan. If either of them had turned out to be the heir, one could not say what would have happened.

But what a problem Parmoor had bequeathed to me! Did he really expect me to go to his inquest to-morrow and sit there while a false verdict was arrived at, knowing that the police thought the matter solved, while actually the murderer was still at large? It seemed to me a mark of the softening of his own powers of judgment and his moral sense that he could imagine that anyone would be satisfied to see truth thus sacrificed to comfort and convenience. And yet, if I showed them this letter, the whole agonizing business would be reopened, as he said, and the brunt of it would fall on Ursula. To think of Mallett and the rest reading all these intimate details, subjecting her to interrogation, making her one of the principal witnesses in the trial; to think of all the sensation-loving press and their readers gloating over her photograph, her clothes, her way of life, her outlook, so different from their own! But again: if Hugo's will proved to be invalid, was not Ursula herself in danger? Suppose Evelyn came back and married Jim: would not her first act be to eliminate Ursula? She could never really reign over the house she coveted while Ursula was there. Nobody, either servants or society, would regard Evelyn as anything other than the housekeeper in comparison with Ursula. As for me, what could I do, with three years still to go before I qualified? I could not make Ursula the only offer for which she might even consider leaving home; and if I tried to persuade her to leave, what explanation could I give if I were not allowed to tell her of her danger?

No, I decided: there was only one course open to me, and that was to go straight to Ursula and tell her the truth—show her Parmoor's letter. If she decided that it must be revealed, I would reveal it; if she decided against, it should be destroyed. My own belief was, she would want it to be revealed, or at any rate, measures to be taken to protect Jim; for though she had little in common with her twin brother, she was fond of him, I knew, and she would be horror-struck at the thought of his danger. Anyhow, the first step was to consult her. In that way, too, if at all, I would obtain an answer to the question that the latter part of his letter had raised in my mind: did Ursula want my friendship and my protection? Could I dare to hope for such a thing? Did Hilary Parmoor know something already that he laid this last charge on me to stand by her, to take her away if possible? I had told myself all along that I was not in love with Ursula; but was this true? Wasn't it perhaps based on pride, on a belief that she could not care for *me*? If this were not so, could I really say that she had no attraction for me? I thought of the mules beside her bed and the perfume that pervaded her room; I thought of the hours we had spent on the terrace together. I jumped up. . . .

And so, within less than an hour of my arrival, I found myself setting out again on the return journey.

8

When I drew up again before the porch of Ullstone Hall, it was a little after eight o'clock in the morning. The sun was shining, and the whole scene was peaceful. In the drive, I passed the milkman's rattling car; and at the back of the house, one or two tall chimneys were sending up a vertical plume of smoke against the blue sky. The gardener, crossing the wide gravel space between the house and the hot-houses, touched his hat to me as I shot past. I was already an accepted inmate, and this time my arrival was like coming home, I thought.

Ursula, to my relief, was alone in the breakfast-room. She started at the sight of me, and I imagined she blushed—but then, fair people blush readily, and I too felt my colour rising. Still, she seemed pleased to see me.

'Jake!' she said. 'I didn't think you'd be back so soon.' Her look of animation gave way to one of concern. 'But you must have been driving all night! Or didn't you get home after all?'

'I got home,' I said, sitting down heavily, while she poured out coffee and added cream.

'Did you get the letter?'

'Yes,' I said dully. Even now I was not sure if it were the right thing to do, to impose this burden of decision on her.

'Well, what did it say?' she said vehemently. 'Was there anything new in it?'

'Plenty,' I said.

'Well, give it me—give it me!' She stretched out her hand and waved it impatiently. 'Let me read it while you have breakfast.'

I shook my head. 'Ursula, you can't see it yet,' I said. 'It's in the highest degree secret. You mustn't even look at it till you've locked yourself in your room.'

From the distance, we both heard the telephone bell ringing in the hall; and we both started and turned to one another. In a moment a maid appeared. Neither of us was surprised when she said, 'For you, Miss Ursula: the Chode police on the 'phone.'

Ursula cast me a desperate glance. 'Come with me, Jake,' she said. 'I'm almost at the end of my tether.'

I followed her and stood beside her while she took up the

receiver as if it had been an adder. Her face was anxious as she began listening; but as the message proceeded, the look of anxiety changed to one of dismay. She said nothing except an occasional 'yes,' and at the end, 'Thank you.'

When she replaced the receiver and turned to me, I expected to hear something unpleasant. What I actually heard was:

'They say that they have had a message from the Paddington police that Evelyn has been found dead in the hotel where Marcel left her. They say she appears to have taken an overdose of veronal.'

9

Inquest followed inquest throughout that appalling week; and through it all I did my best, as Parmoor had asked me, to protect Ursula. Sir Frederick too arrived, and on his advice I went to the police with Parmoor's letter. I must say they behaved with extraordinary discretion, as did the Coroner. At Parmoor's inquest, parts of the letter were read, but only those parts which were relevant; Ursula's name was kept out of it entirely. I was greatly relieved to think that poor Hilary's name was cleared of guilt, even though he didn't know it. The verdict was 'Suicide during temporary insanity,' and the Coroner suggested that the shock of the scene he had witnessed, following upon a period of overwork and insomnia, had upset the balance of his mind. Two days later, at Paddington, a jury returned a verdict of murder and suicide against Evelyn Ross; and the following day, the adjourned inquest on Hugo Ullstone was brought to a corresponding conclusion.

Marcel, of course, had to be present at all three; and he went through the ordeal better than I had thought possible. The Paddington inquest was for him the most trying, though by now he had legal advice; but he bore himself with great dignity, explaining that he had undertaken to find Miss Ross a post as governess in his own family, at her request; but that on the first stage of their journey, her manner had become so strange that he had felt nervous about taking her any further and had tried to persuade her to think better of it and return home. She had, however, quite refused to do this; and so, not wanting to leave her quite to her own devices, he had returned to Ullstone Hall to warn her relatives of her condition and suggest that someone should go and fetch her back. She had, he said, in answer to the Coroner, threatened suicide, but as she would do nothing he suggested, he had no choice but to leave her there and go for help.

The Coroner thought it best to accept this explanation, and added that the deceased young woman was no doubt already driven to extremities by the knowledge of her crime; and so Marcel got out of the business without too close scrutiny.

A few days later, I was seeing Marcel off at Victoria Station. The train was waiting. The engine was getting up steam. His place had been found, his magazines bought, and he was leaning out of the window talking to me with his most charming smile. We had dined and spent the evening together; and he had already told me, with many shakings of the head, much of what had happened between him and Evelyn in that dimly-lighted hotel bedroom. He had, he said, by this time come to the conclusion that he could never marry her, that she must not take advantage of his impulsive, generous nature, but must accept with gratitude his original offer of the protection of his family and a post as governess in a distinguished household. When she realized this—when she grasped that he had been moved by pity and not by love—her real nature, he said, emerged: the nature of a murderess. . . . His dark eyes flashed as he told me this over the chicken and the wine; his face was pale, and his voice vibrating with the horror of that scene.

And now, as he leaned out of the window, and I, aware that probably I would never see him again, was studying his features earnestly, suddenly against the darker background of the compartment I saw him as I had seen him once before, leaning against the mantelpiece with the strange plaster figures dangling behind him. . . . The whistle blew, the train began to move. As I watched him, he leaned out towards me and said, smiling:

'She would have taken it in any case, I think. I just—guided her hand.' And as the train gathered speed a little, he seized my hand and gripped it hard, and his tone changed to ferocity, though he still smiled: 'She killed my friend, you know.'

He released my hand; and as the distance between us widened, I heard him call out in an ordinary social tone:

'By the way, you know that Ursula is going to marry Sir Frederick Lawton? Yes, really! She told me so herself yesterday. Well, good-bye! Be sure to come over and see me when you have the time.'

We were too far apart for any words of mine to reach him in answer. In a moment, after a last wave of the hand, he left the window. I was left standing there while more demonstrative people ran down the platform trying to keep waving handkerchiefs in sight. There was a buzzing in my head and a tingling at the tips of my ears.

10

I have never been inside Ullstone Hall again. Once, a year or so later, I visited Sir Frederick and Lady Lawton at their town house by invitation, and sat uncomfortably on a low gilt chair with other guests, while Lady Lawton sparkled and made us feel very much the reverse of at home. Sir Frederick came in to tea for a short while and swung his eyeglass at me and asked after my brother; but they both behaved as if nothing out of the ordinary had ever happened between us, and I'm inclined to think they had forgotten my part in the affair. By now I knew that Hugo Ullstone's will had been ruled invalid, and that the Hall had been sold and the estate divided between Jim and Ursula, who had gone their separate ways.

Once only, after I qualified, occasion brought me in that direction again, and I could not resist making a détour down that lane along which first I had passed in a thunderstorm. Whatever other changes there might have been, the new owner had not removed the two groups of monkeys on the gateposts. As I stood looking up at them, the one who his hand over his eyes seemed to be peeping at me, the one who has his hand over his mouth seemed to be guffawing, and the one who has his hands over his ears seemed to be stopping them against anything I might say.

But I had nothing to say. It was all just the past to me: a murmur of pleasant voices.

A CATALOGUE OF
SELECTED DOVER BOOKS
IN ALL FIELDS OF INTEREST

A CATALOGUE OF SELECTED DOVER BOOKS IN ALL FIELDS OF INTEREST

CELESTIAL OBJECTS FOR COMMON TELESCOPES, T. W. Webb. The most used book in amateur astronomy: inestimable aid for locating and identifying nearly 4,000 celestial objects. Edited, updated by Margaret W. Mayall. 77 illustrations. Total of 645pp. 5⅜ x 8½.
20917-2, 20918-0 Pa., Two-vol. set $9.00

HISTORICAL STUDIES IN THE LANGUAGE OF CHEMISTRY, M. P. Crosland. The important part language has played in the development of chemistry from the symbolism of alchemy to the adoption of systematic nomenclature in 1892. ". . . wholeheartedly recommended,"—Science. 15 illustrations. 416pp. of text. 5⅝ x 8¼. 63702-6 Pa. $6.00

BURNHAM'S CELESTIAL HANDBOOK, Robert Burnham, Jr. Thorough, readable guide to the stars beyond our solar system. Exhaustive treatment, fully illustrated. Breakdown is alphabetical by constellation: Andromeda to Cetus in Vol. 1; Chamaeleon to Orion in Vol. 2; and Pavo to Vulpecula in Vol. 3. Hundreds of illustrations. Total of about 2000pp. 6⅛ x 9¼.
23567-X, 23568-8, 23673-0 Pa., Three-vol. set $27.85

THEORY OF WING SECTIONS: INCLUDING A SUMMARY OF AIRFOIL DATA, Ira H. Abbott and A. E. von Doenhoff. Concise compilation of subatomic aerodynamic characteristics of modern NASA wing sections, plus description of theory. 350pp. of tables. 693pp. 5⅜ x 8½.
60586-8 Pa. $8.50

DE RE METALLICA, Georgius Agricola. Translated by Herbert C. Hoover and Lou H. Hoover. The famous Hoover translation of greatest treatise on technological chemistry, engineering, geology, mining of early modern times (1556). All 289 original woodcuts. 638pp. 6¾ x 11.
60006-8 Clothbd. $17.95

THE ORIGIN OF CONTINENTS AND OCEANS, Alfred Wegener. One of the most influential, most controversial books in science, the classic statement for continental drift. Full 1966 translation of Wegener's final (1929) version. 64 illustrations. 246pp. 5⅜ x 8½. 61708-4 Pa. $4.50

THE PRINCIPLES OF PSYCHOLOGY, William James. Famous long course complete, unabridged. Stream of thought, time perception, memory, experimental methods; great work decades ahead of its time. Still valid, useful; read in many classes. 94 figures. Total of 1391pp. 5⅜ x 8½.
20381-6, 20382-4 Pa., Two-vol. set $13.00

DRAWINGS OF WILLIAM BLAKE, William Blake. 92 plates from Book of Job, *Divine Comedy, Paradise Lost,* visionary heads, mythological figures, Laocoon, etc. Selection, introduction, commentary by Sir Geoffrey Keynes. 178pp. 8⅛ x 11. 22303-5 Pa. $4.00

ENGRAVINGS OF HOGARTH, William Hogarth. 101 of Hogarth's greatest works: *Rake's Progress, Harlot's Progress, Illustrations for Hudibras, Before and After, Beer Street and Gin Lane,* many more. Full commentary. 256pp. 11 x 13¾. 22479-1 Pa. $12.95

DAUMIER: 120 GREAT LITHOGRAPHS, Honore Daumier. Wide-ranging collection of lithographs by the greatest caricaturist of the 19th century. Concentrates on eternally popular series on lawyers, on married life, on liberated women, etc. Selection, introduction, and notes on plates by Charles F. Ramus. Total of 158pp. 9⅜ x 12¼. 23512-2 Pa. $6.00

DRAWINGS OF MUCHA, Alphonse Maria Mucha. Work reveals draftsman of highest caliber: studies for famous posters and paintings, renderings for book illustrations and ads, etc. 70 works, 9 in color; including 6 items not drawings. Introduction. List of illustrations. 72pp. 9⅜ x 12¼. (Available in U.S. only) 23672-2 Pa. $4.00

GIOVANNI BATTISTA PIRANESI: DRAWINGS IN THE PIERPONT MORGAN LIBRARY, Giovanni Battista Piranesi. For first time ever all of Morgan Library's collection, world's largest. 167 illustrations of rare Piranesi drawings—archeological, architectural, decorative and visionary. Essay, detailed list of drawings, chronology, captions. Edited by Felice Stampfle. 144pp. 9⅜ x 12¼. 23714-1 Pa. $7.50

NEW YORK ETCHINGS (1905-1949), John Sloan. All of important American artist's N.Y. life etchings. 67 works include some of his best art; also lively historical record—Greenwich Village, tenement scenes. Edited by Sloan's widow. Introduction and captions. 79pp. 8⅜ x 11¼. 23651-X Pa. $4.00

CHINESE PAINTING AND CALLIGRAPHY: A PICTORIAL SURVEY, Wan-go Weng. 69 fine examples from John M. Crawford's matchless private collection: landscapes, birds, flowers, human figures, etc., plus calligraphy. Every basic form included: hanging scrolls, handscrolls, album leaves, fans, etc. 109 illustrations. Introduction. Captions. 192pp. 8⅞ x 11¾. 23707-9 Pa. $7.95

DRAWINGS OF REMBRANDT, edited by Seymour Slive. Updated Lippmann, Hofstede de Groot edition, with definitive scholarly apparatus. All portraits, biblical sketches, landscapes, nudes, Oriental figures, classical studies, together with selection of work by followers. 550 illustrations. Total of 630pp. 9⅛ x 12¼. 21485-0, 21486-9 Pa., Two-vol. set $15.00

THE DISASTERS OF WAR, Francisco Goya. 83 etchings record horrors of Napoleonic wars in Spain and war in general. Reprint of 1st edition, plus 3 additional plates. Introduction by Philip Hofer. 97pp. 9⅜ x 8¼. 21872-4 Pa. $4.00

THE PHILOSOPHY OF HISTORY, Georg W. Hegel. Great classic of Western thought develops concept that history is not chance but a rational process, the evolution of freedom. 457pp. 5⅜ x 8½. 20112-0 Pa. $4.50

LANGUAGE, TRUTH AND LOGIC, Alfred J. Ayer. Famous, clear introduction to Vienna, Cambridge schools of Logical Positivism. Role of philosophy, elimination of metaphysics, nature of analysis, etc. 160pp. 5⅜ x 8½. (Available in U.S. only) 20010-8 Pa. $2.00

A PREFACE TO LOGIC, Morris R. Cohen. Great City College teacher in renowned, easily followed exposition of formal logic, probability, values, logic and world order and similar topics; no previous background needed. 209pp. 5⅜ x 8½. 23517-3 Pa. $3.50

REASON AND NATURE, Morris R. Cohen. Brilliant analysis of reason and its multitudinous ramifications by charismatic teacher. Interdisciplinary, synthesizing work widely praised when it first appeared in 1931. Second (1953) edition. Indexes. 496pp. 5⅜ x 8½. 23633-1 Pa. $6.50

AN ESSAY CONCERNING HUMAN UNDERSTANDING, John Locke. The only complete edition of enormously important classic, with authoritative editorial material by A. C. Fraser. Total of 1176pp. 5⅜ x 8½.
20530-4, 20531-2 Pa., Two-vol. set $16.00

HANDBOOK OF MATHEMATICAL FUNCTIONS WITH FORMULAS, GRAPHS, AND MATHEMATICAL TABLES, edited by Milton Abramowitz and Irene A. Stegun. Vast compendium: 29 sets of tables, some to as high as 20 places. 1,046pp. 8 x 10½. 61272-4 Pa. $14.95

MATHEMATICS FOR THE PHYSICAL SCIENCES, Herbert S. Wilf. Highly acclaimed work offers clear presentations of vector spaces and matrices, orthogonal functions, roots of polynomial equations, conformal mapping, calculus of variations, etc. Knowledge of theory of functions of real and complex variables is assumed. Exercises and solutions. Index. 284pp. 5⅝ x 8¼. 63635-6 Pa. $5.00

THE PRINCIPLE OF RELATIVITY, Albert Einstein et al. Eleven most important original papers on special and general theories. Seven by Einstein, two by Lorentz, one each by Minkowski and Weyl. All translated, unabridged. 216pp. 5⅜ x 8½. 60081-5 Pa. $3.50

THERMODYNAMICS, Enrico Fermi. A classic of modern science. Clear, organized treatment of systems, first and second laws, entropy, thermodynamic potentials, gaseous reactions, dilute solutions, entropy constant. No math beyond calculus required. Problems. 160pp. 5⅜ x 8½.
60361-X Pa. $3.00

ELEMENTARY MECHANICS OF FLUIDS, Hunter Rouse. Classic undergraduate text widely considered to be far better than many later books. Ranges from fluid velocity and acceleration to role of compressibility in fluid motion. Numerous examples, questions, problems. 224 illustrations. 376pp. 5⅝ x 8¼. 63699-2 Pa. $5.00

TONE POEMS, SERIES II: TILL EULENSPIEGELS LUSTIGE STREICHE, ALSO SPRACH ZARATHUSTRA, AND EIN HELDEN-LEBEN, Richard Strauss. Three important orchestral works, including very popular *Till Eulenspiegel's Marry Pranks,* reproduced in full score from original editions. Study score. 315pp. 9⅜ x 12¼. (Available in U.S. only)
23755-9 Pa. $8.95

TONE POEMS, SERIES I: DON JUAN, TOD UND VERKLARUNG AND DON QUIXOTE, Richard Strauss. Three of the most often performed and recorded works in entire orchestral repertoire, reproduced in full score from original editions. Study score. 286pp. 9⅜ x 12¼. (Available in U.S. only)
23754-0 Pa. $7.50

11 LATE STRING QUARTETS, Franz Joseph Haydn. The form which Haydn defined and "brought to perfection." *(Grove's).* 11 string quartets in complete score, his last and his best. The first in a projected series of the complete Haydn string quartets. Reliable modern Eulenberg edition, otherwise difficult to obtain. 320pp. 8⅜ x 11¼. (Available in U.S. only)
23753-2 Pa. $7.50

FOURTH, FIFTH AND SIXTH SYMPHONIES IN FULL SCORE, Peter Ilyitch Tchaikovsky. Complete orchestral scores of Symphony No. 4 in F Minor, Op. 36; Symphony No. 5 in E Minor, Op. 64; Symphony No. 6 in B Minor, "Pathetique," Op. 74. Bretikopf & Hartel eds. Study score. 480pp. 9⅜ x 12¼.
23861-X Pa. $10.95

THE MARRIAGE OF FIGARO: COMPLETE SCORE, Wolfgang A. Mozart. Finest comic opera ever written. Full score, not to be confused with piano renderings. Peters edition. Study score. 448pp. 9⅜ x 12¼. (Available in U.S. only)
23751-6 Pa. $11.95

"IMAGE" ON THE ART AND EVOLUTION OF THE FILM, edited by Marshall Deutelbaum. Pioneering book brings together for first time 38 groundbreaking articles on early silent films from *Image* and 263 illustrations newly shot from rare prints in the collection of the International Museum of Photography. A landmark work. Index. 256pp. 8¼ x 11.
23777-X Pa. $8.95

AROUND-THE-WORLD COOKY BOOK, Lois Lintner Sumption and Marguerite Lintner Ashbrook. 373 cooky and frosting recipes from 28 countries (America, Austria, China, Russia, Italy, etc.) include Viennese kisses, rice wafers, London strips, lady fingers, hony, sugar spice, maple cookies, etc. Clear instructions. All tested. 38 drawings. 182pp. 5⅜ x 8.
23802-4 Pa. $2.50

THE ART NOUVEAU STYLE, edited by Roberta Waddell. 579 rare photographs, not available elsewhere, of works in jewelry, metalwork, glass, ceramics, textiles, architecture and furniture by 175 artists—Mucha, Seguy, Lalique, Tiffany, Gaudin, Hohlwein, Saarinen, and many others. 288pp. 8⅜ x 11¼.
23515-7 Pa. $6.95

THE AMERICAN SENATOR, Anthony Trollope. Little known, long un-
available Trollope novel on a grand scale. Here are humorous comment
on American vs. English culture, and stunning portrayal of a heroine/
villainess. Superb evocation of Victorian village life. 561pp. 5⅜ x 8½.
23801-6 Pa. $6.00

WAS IT MURDER? James Hilton. The author of *Lost Horizon* and *Good-
bye, Mr. Chips* wrote one detective novel (under a pen-name) which was
quickly forgotten and virtually lost, even at the height of Hilton's fame.
This edition brings it back—a finely crafted public school puzzle resplen-
dent with Hilton's stylish atmosphere. A thoroughly English thriller by
the creator of Shangri-la. 252pp. 5⅜ x 8. (Available in U.S. only)
23774-5 Pa. $3.00

CENTRAL PARK: A PHOTOGRAPHIC GUIDE, Victor Laredo and
Henry Hope Reed. 121 superb photographs show dramatic views of
Central Park: Bethesda Fountain, Cleopatra's Needle, Sheep Meadow, the
Blockhouse, plus people engaged in many park activities: ice skating, bike
riding, etc. Captions by former Curator of Central Park, Henry Hope
Reed, provide historical view, changes, etc. Also photos of N.Y. landmarks
on park's periphery. 96pp. 8½ x 11. 23750-8 Pa. $4.50

NANTUCKET IN THE NINETEENTH CENTURY, Clay Lancaster. 180
rare photographs, stereographs, maps, drawings and floor plans recreate
unique American island society. Authentic scenes of shipwreck, light-
houses, streets, homes are arranged in geographic sequence to provide
walking-tour guide to old Nantucket existing today. Introduction, captions.
160pp. 8⅞ x 11¾. 23747-8 Pa. $6.95

STONE AND MAN: A PHOTOGRAPHIC EXPLORATION, Andreas
Feininger. 106 photographs by *Life* photographer Feininger portray man's
deep passion for stone through the ages. Stonehenge-like megaliths, forti-
fied towns, sculpted marble and crumbling tenements show textures, beau-
ties, fascination. 128pp. 9¼ x 10¾. 23756-7 Pa. $5.95

CIRCLES, A MATHEMATICAL VIEW, D. Pedoe. Fundamental aspects
of college geometry, non-Euclidean geometry, and other branches of mathematics: representing circle by point. Poincare model, isoperimetric property, etc. Stimulating recreational reading. 66 figures. 96pp. 5⅝ x 8¼.
63698-4 Pa. $2.75

THE DISCOVERY OF NEPTUNE, Morton Grosser. Dramatic scientific
history of the investigations leading up to the actual discovery of the
eighth planet of our solar system. Lucid, well-researched book by well-
known historian of science. 172pp. 5⅜ x 8½. 23726-5 Pa. $3.50

THE DEVIL'S DICTIONARY. Ambrose Bierce. Barbed, bitter, brilliant
witticisms in the form of a dictionary. Best, most ferocious satire America
has produced. 145pp. 5⅜ x 8½. 20487-1 Pa. $2.25

YUCATAN BEFORE AND AFTER THE CONQUEST, Diego de Landa. First English translation of basic book in Maya studies, the only significant account of Yucatan written in the early post-Conquest era. Translated by distinguished Maya scholar William Gates. Appendices, introduction, 4 maps and over 120 illustrations added by translator. 162pp. 5⅜ x 8½.
23622-6 Pa. $3.00

THE MALAY ARCHIPELAGO, Alfred R. Wallace. Spirited travel account by one of founders of modern biology. Touches on zoology, botany, ethnography, geography, and geology. 62 illustrations, maps. 515pp. 5⅜ x 8½.
20187-2 Pa. $6.95

THE DISCOVERY OF THE TOMB OF TUTANKHAMEN, Howard Carter, A. C. Mace. Accompany Carter in the thrill of discovery, as ruined passage suddenly reveals unique, untouched, fabulously rich tomb. Fascinating account, with 106 illustrations. New introduction by J. M. White. Total of 382pp. 5⅜ x 8½. (Available in U.S. only)   23500-9 Pa. $4.00

THE WORLD'S GREATEST SPEECHES, edited by Lewis Copeland and Lawrence W. Lamm. Vast collection of 278 speeches from Greeks up to present. Powerful and effective models; unique look at history. Revised to 1970. Indices. 842pp. 5⅜ x 8½.   20468-5 Pa. $8.95

THE 100 GREATEST ADVERTISEMENTS, Julian Watkins. The priceless ingredient; His master's voice; 99 44/100% pure; over 100 others. How they were written, their impact, etc. Remarkable record. 130 illustrations. 233pp. 7⅞ x 10 3/5.   20540-1 Pa. $5.95

CRUICKSHANK PRINTS FOR HAND COLORING, George Cruickshank. 18 illustrations, one side of a page, on fine-quality paper suitable for watercolors. Caricatures of people in society (c. 1820) full of trenchant wit. Very large format. 32pp. 11 x 16.   23684-6 Pa. $5.00

THIRTY-TWO COLOR POSTCARDS OF TWENTIETH-CENTURY AMERICAN ART, Whitney Museum of American Art. Reproduced in full color in postcard form are 31 art works and one shot of the museum. Calder, Hopper, Rauschenberg, others. Detachable. 16pp. 8¼ x 11.
23629-3 Pa. $3.00

MUSIC OF THE SPHERES: THE MATERIAL UNIVERSE FROM ATOM TO QUASAR SIMPLY EXPLAINED, Guy Murchie. Planets, stars, geology, atoms, radiation, relativity, quantum theory, light, antimatter, similar topics. 319 figures. 664pp. 5⅜ x 8½.
21809-0, 21810-4 Pa., Two-vol. set $11.00

EINSTEIN'S THEORY OF RELATIVITY, Max Born. Finest semi-technical account; covers Einstein, Lorentz, Minkowski, and others, with much detail, much explanation of ideas and math not readily available elsewhere on this level. For student, non-specialist. 376pp. 5⅜ x 8½.
60769-0 Pa. $4.50

HOLLYWOOD GLAMOUR PORTRAITS, edited by John Kobal. 145 photos capture the stars from 1926-49, the high point in portrait photography. Gable, Harlow, Bogart, Bacall, Hedy Lamarr, Marlene Dietrich, Robert Montgomery, Marlon Brando, Veronica Lake; 94 stars in all. Full background on photographers, technical aspects, much more. Total of 160pp. 8⅜ x 11¼. 23352-9 Pa. $6.00

THE NEW YORK STAGE: FAMOUS PRODUCTIONS IN PHOTO-GRAPHS, edited by Stanley Appelbaum. 148 photographs from Museum of City of New York show 142 plays, 1883-1939. *Peter Pan, The Front Page, Dead End, Our Town,* O'Neill, hundreds of actors and actresses, etc. Full indexes. 154pp. 9½ x 10. 23241-7 Pa. $6.00

DIALOGUES CONCERNING TWO NEW SCIENCES, Galileo Galilei. Encompassing 30 years of experiment and thought, these dialogues deal with geometric demonstrations of fracture of solid bodies, cohesion, leverage, speed of light and sound, pendulums, falling bodies, accelerated motion, etc. 300pp. 5⅜ x 8½. 60099-8 Pa. $4.00

THE GREAT OPERA STARS IN HISTORIC PHOTOGRAPHS, edited by James Camner. 343 portraits from the 1850s to the 1940s: Tamburini, Mario, Caliapin, Jeritza, Melchior, Melba, Patti, Pinza, Schipa, Caruso, Farrar, Steber, Gobbi, and many more—270 performers in all. Index. 199pp. 8⅜ x 11¼. 23575-0 Pa. $7.50

J. S. BACH, Albert Schweitzer. Great full-length study of Bach, life, background to music, music, by foremost modern scholar. Ernest Newman translation. 650 musical examples. Total of 928pp. 5⅜ x 8½. (Available in U.S. only) 21631-4, 21632-2 Pa., Two-vol. set $11.00

COMPLETE PIANO SONATAS, Ludwig van Beethoven. All sonatas in the fine Schenker edition, with fingering, analytical material. One of best modern editions. Total of 615pp. 9 x 12. (Available in U.S. only) 23134-8, 23135-6 Pa., Two-vol. set $15.50

KEYBOARD MUSIC, J. S. Bach. Bach-Gesellschaft edition. For harpsichord, piano, other keyboard instruments. English Suites, French Suites, Six Partitas, Goldberg Variations, Two-Part Inventions, Three-Part Sinfonias. 312pp. 8⅛ x 11. (Available in U.S. only) 22360-4 Pa. $6.95

FOUR SYMPHONIES IN FULL SCORE, Franz Schubert. Schubert's four most popular symphonies: No. 4 in C Minor ("Tragic"); No. 5 in B-flat Major; No. 8 in B Minor ("Unfinished"); No. 9 in C Major ("Great"). Breitkopf & Hartel edition. Study score. 261pp. 9⅜ x 12¼. 23681-1 Pa. $6.50

THE AUTHENTIC GILBERT & SULLIVAN SONGBOOK, W. S. Gilbert, A. S. Sullivan. Largest selection available; 92 songs, uncut, original keys, in piano rendering approved by Sullivan. Favorites and lesser-known fine numbers. Edited with plot synopses by James Spero. 3 illustrations. 399pp. 9 x 12. 23482-7 Pa. $9.95

PRINCIPLES OF ORCHESTRATION, Nikolay Rimsky-Korsakov. Great classical orchestrator provides fundamentals of tonal resonance, progression of parts, voice and orchestra, tutti effects, much else in major document. 330pp. of musical excerpts. 489pp. 6½ x 9¼.   21266-1 Pa. $7.50

TRISTAN UND ISOLDE, Richard Wagner. Full orchestral score with complete instrumentation. Do not confuse with piano reduction. Commentary by Felix Mottl, great Wagnerian conductor and scholar. Study score. 655pp. 8⅛ x 11.   22915-7 Pa. $13.95

REQUIEM IN FULL SCORE, Giuseppe Verdi. Immensely popular with choral groups and music lovers. Republication of edition published by C. F. Peters, Leipzig, n. d. German frontmaker in English translation. Glossary. Text in Latin. Study score. 204pp. 9⅜ x 12¼.
                                               23682-X Pa. $6.00

COMPLETE CHAMBER MUSIC FOR STRINGS, Felix Mendelssohn. All of Mendelssohn's chamber music: Octet, 2 Quintets, 6 Quartets, and Four Pieces for String Quartet. (Nothing with piano is included). Complete works edition (1874-7). Study score. 283 pp. 9⅜ x 12¼.
                                               23679-X Pa. $7.50

POPULAR SONGS OF NINETEENTH-CENTURY AMERICA, edited by Richard Jackson. 64 most important songs: "Old Oaken Bucket," "Arkansas Traveler," "Yellow Rose of Texas," etc. Authentic original sheet music, full introduction and commentaries. 290pp. 9 x 12.   23270-0 Pa. $7.95

COLLECTED PIANO WORKS, Scott Joplin. Edited by Vera Brodsky Lawrence. Practically all of Joplin's piano works—rags, two-steps, marches, waltzes, etc., 51 works in all. Extensive introduction by Rudi Blesh. Total of 345pp. 9 x 12.   23106-2 Pa. $14.95

BASIC PRINCIPLES OF CLASSICAL BALLET, Agrippina Vaganova. Great Russian theoretician, teacher explains methods for teaching classical ballet; incorporates best from French, Italian, Russian schools. 118 illustrations. 175pp. 5⅜ x 8½.   22036-2 Pa. $2.50

CHINESE CHARACTERS, L. Wieger. Rich analysis of 2300 characters according to traditional systems into primitives. Historical-semantic analysis to phonetics (Classical Mandarin) and radicals. 820pp. 6⅛ x 9¼.
                                               21321-8 Pa. $10.00

EGYPTIAN LANGUAGE: EASY LESSONS IN EGYPTIAN HIERO-GLYPHICS, E. A. Wallis Budge. Foremost Egyptologist offers Egyptian grammar, explanation of hieroglyphics, many reading texts, dictionary of symbols. 246pp. 5 x 7½. (Available in U.S. only)
                                               21394-3 Clothbd. $7.50

AN ETYMOLOGICAL DICTIONARY OF MODERN ENGLISH, Ernest Weekley. Richest, fullest work, by foremost British lexicographer. Detailed word histories. Inexhaustible. Do not confuse this with Concise Etymological Dictionary, which is abridged. Total of 856pp. 6½ x 9¼.
                                               21873-2, 21874-0 Pa., Two-vol. set $12.00

A MAYA GRAMMAR, Alfred M. Tozzer. Practical, useful English-language grammar by the Harvard anthropologist who was one of the three greatest American scholars in the area of Maya culture. Phonetics, grammatical processes, syntax, more. 301pp. 5⅜ x 8½.   23465-7 Pa. $4.00

THE JOURNAL OF HENRY D. THOREAU, edited by Bradford Torrey, F. H. Allen. Complete reprinting of 14 volumes, 1837-61, over two million words; the sourcebooks for *Walden*, etc. Definitive. All original sketches, plus 75 photographs. Introduction by Walter Harding. Total of 1804pp. 8½ x 12¼.   20312-3, 20313-1 Clothbd., Two-vol. set $70.00

CLASSIC GHOST STORIES, Charles Dickens and others. 18 wonderful stories you've wanted to reread: "The Monkey's Paw," "The House and the Brain," "The Upper Berth," "The Signalman," "Dracula's Guest," "The Tapestried Chamber," etc. Dickens, Scott, Mary Shelley, Stoker, etc. 330pp. 5⅜ x 8½.   20735-8 Pa. $4.50

SEVEN SCIENCE FICTION NOVELS, H. G. Wells. Full novels. *First Men in the Moon, Island of Dr. Moreau, War of the Worlds, Food of the Gods, Invisible Man, Time Machine, In the Days of the Comet.* A basic science-fiction library. 1015pp. 5⅜ x 8½. (Available in U.S. only)
20264-X Clothbd. $8.95

ARMADALE, Wilkie Collins. Third great mystery novel by the author of *The Woman in White* and *The Moonstone.* Ingeniously plotted narrative shows an exceptional command of character, incident and mood. Original magazine version with 40 illustrations. 597pp. 5⅜ x 8½.
23429-0 Pa. $6.00

MASTERS OF MYSTERY, H. Douglas Thomson. The first book in English (1931) devoted to history and aesthetics of detective story. Poe, Doyle, LeFanu, Dickens, many others, up to 1930. New introduction and notes by E. F. Bleiler. 288pp. 5⅜ x 8½. (Available in U.S. only)
23606-4 Pa. $4.00

FLATLAND, E. A. Abbott. Science-fiction classic explores life of 2-D being in 3-D world. Read also as introduction to thought about hyperspace. Introduction by Banesh Hoffmann. 16 illustrations. 103pp. 5⅜ x 8½.
20001-9 Pa. $2.00

THREE SUPERNATURAL NOVELS OF THE VICTORIAN PERIOD, edited, with an introduction, by E. F. Bleiler. Reprinted complete and unabridged, three great classics of the supernatural: *The Haunted Hotel* by Wilkie Collins, *The Haunted House at Latchford* by Mrs. J. H. Riddell, and *The Lost Stradivarius* by J. Meade Falkner. 325pp. 5⅜ x 8½.
22571-2 Pa. $4.00

AYESHA: THE RETURN OF "SHE," H. Rider Haggard. Virtuoso sequel featuring the great mythic creation, Ayesha, in an adventure that is fully as good as the first book, *She.* Original magazine version, with 47 original illustrations by Maurice Greiffenhagen. 189pp. 6½ x 9¼.
23649-8 Pa. $3.50

UNCLE SILAS, J. Sheridan LeFanu. Victorian Gothic mystery novel, considered by many best of period, even better than Collins or Dickens. Wonderful psychological terror. Introduction by Frederick Shroyer. 436pp. 5⅜ x 8½.   21715-9 Pa. $6.00

JURGEN, James Branch Cabell. The great erotic fantasy of the 1920's that delighted thousands, shocked thousands more. Full final text, Lane edition with 13 plates by Frank Pape. 346pp. 5⅜ x 8½.
                                                        23507-6 Pa. $4.50

THE CLAVERINGS, Anthony Trollope. Major novel, chronicling aspects of British Victorian society, personalities. Reprint of Cornhill serialization, 16 plates by M. Edwards; first reprint of full text. Introduction by Norman Donaldson. 412pp. 5⅜ x 8½.   23464-9 Pa. $5.00

KEPT IN THE DARK, Anthony Trollope. Unusual short novel about Victorian morality and abnormal psychology by the great English author. Probably the first American publication. Frontispiece by Sir John Millais. 92pp. 6½ x 9¼.   23609-9 Pa. $2.50

RALPH THE HEIR, Anthony Trollope. Forgotten tale of illegitimacy, inheritance. Master novel of Trollope's later years. Victorian country estates, clubs, Parliament, fox hunting, world of fully realized characters. Reprint of 1871 edition. 12 illustrations by F. A. Faser. 434pp. of text. 5⅜ x 8½.   23642-0 Pa. $5.00

YEKL and THE IMPORTED BRIDEGROOM AND OTHER STORIES OF THE NEW YORK GHETTO, Abraham Cahan. Film *Hester Street* based on *Yekl* (1896). Novel, other stories among first about Jewish immigrants of N.Y.'s East Side. Highly praised by W. D. Howells—Cahan "a new star of realism." New introduction by Bernard G. Richards. 240pp. 5⅜ x 8½.   22427-9 Pa. $3.50

THE HIGH PLACE, James Branch Cabell. Great fantasy writer's enchanting comedy of disenchantment set in 18th-century France. Considered by some critics to be even better than his famous *Jurgen*. 10 illustrations and numerous vignettes by noted fantasy artist Frank C. Pape. 320pp. 5⅜ x 8½.   23670-6 Pa. $4.00

ALICE'S ADVENTURES UNDER GROUND, Lewis Carroll. Facsimile of ms. Carroll gave Alice Liddell in 1864. Different in many ways from final Alice. Handlettered, illustrated by Carroll. Introduction by Martin Gardner. 128pp. 5⅜ x 8½.   21482-6 Pa. $2.50

FAVORITE ANDREW LANG FAIRY TALE BOOKS IN MANY COLORS, Andrew Lang. The four Lang favorites in a boxed set—the complete *Red, Green, Yellow* and *Blue* Fairy Books. 164 stories; 439 illustrations by Lancelot Speed, Henry Ford and G. P. Jacomb Hood. Total of about 1500pp. 5⅜ x 8½.   23407-X Boxed set, Pa. $15.95

AN AUTOBIOGRAPHY, Margaret Sanger. Exciting personal account of hard-fought battle for woman's right to birth control, against prejudice, church, law. Foremost feminist document. 504pp. 5⅜ x 8½.
20470-7 Pa. $5.50

MY BONDAGE AND MY FREEDOM, Frederick Douglass. Born as a slave, Douglass became outspoken force in antislavery movement. The best of Douglass's autobiographies. Graphic description of slave life. Introduction by P. Foner. 464pp. 5⅜ x 8½. 22457-0 Pa. $5.50

LIVING MY LIFE, Emma Goldman. Candid, no holds barred account by foremost American anarchist: her own life, anarchist movement, famous contemporaries, ideas and their impact. Struggles and confrontations in America, plus deportation to U.S.S.R. Shocking inside account of persecution of anarchists under Lenin. 13 plates. Total of 944pp. 5⅜ x 8½.
22543-7, 22544-5 Pa., Two-vol. set $12.00

LETTERS AND NOTES ON THE MANNERS, CUSTOMS AND CONDITIONS OF THE NORTH AMERICAN INDIANS, George Catlin. Classic account of life among Plains Indians: ceremonies, hunt, warfare, etc. Dover edition reproduces for first time all original paintings. 312 plates. 572pp. of text. 6⅛ x 9¼. 22118-0, 22119-9 Pa.. Two-vol. set $12.00

THE MAYA AND THEIR NEIGHBORS, edited by Clarence L. Hay, others. Synoptic view of Maya civilization in broadest sense, together with Northern, Southern neighbors. Integrates much background, valuable detail not elsewhere. Prepared by greatest scholars: Kroeber, Morley, Thompson, Spinden, Vaillant, many others. Sometimes called Tozzer Memorial Volume. 60 illustrations, linguistic map. 634pp. 5⅜ x 8½.
23510-6 Pa. $10.00

HANDBOOK OF THE INDIANS OF CALIFORNIA, A. L. Kroeber. Foremost American anthropologist offers complete ethnographic study of each group. Monumental classic. 459 illustrations, maps. 995pp. 5⅜ x 8½.
23368-5 Pa. $13.00

SHAKTI AND SHAKTA, Arthur Avalon. First book to give clear, cohesive analysis of Shakta doctrine, Shakta ritual and Kundalini Shakti (yoga). Important work by one of world's foremost students of Shaktic and Tantric thought. 732pp. 5⅜ x 8½. (Available in U.S. only)
23645-5 Pa. $7.95

AN INTRODUCTION TO THE STUDY OF THE MAYA HIEROGLYPHS, Syvanus Griswold Morley. Classic study by one of the truly great figures in hieroglyph research. Still the best introduction for the student for reading Maya hieroglyphs. New introduction by J. Eric S. Thompson. 117 illustrations. 284pp. 5⅜ x 8½. 23108-9 Pa. $4.00

A STUDY OF MAYA ART, Herbert J. Spinden. Landmark classic interprets Maya symbolism, estimates styles, covers ceramics, architecture, murals, stone carvings as artforms. Still a basic book in area. New introduction by J. Eric Thompson. Over 750 illustrations. 341pp. 8⅜ x 11¼.
21235-1 Pa. $6.95

CATALOGUE OF DOVER BOOKS

GEOMETRY, RELATIVITY AND THE FOURTH DIMENSION, Rudolf Rucker. Exposition of fourth dimension, means of visualization, concepts of relativity as Flatland characters continue adventures. Popular, easily followed yet accurate, profound. 141 illustrations. 133pp. 5⅜ x 8½.
23400-2 Pa. $2.75

THE ORIGIN OF LIFE, A. I. Oparin. Modern classic in biochemistry, the first rigorous examination of possible evolution of life from nitrocarbon compounds. Non-technical, easily followed. Total of 295pp. 5⅜ x 8½.
60213-3 Pa. $4.00

PLANETS, STARS AND GALAXIES, A. E. Fanning. Comprehensive introductory survey: the sun, solar system, stars, galaxies, universe, cosmology; quasars, radio stars, etc. 24pp. of photographs. 189pp. 5⅜ x 8½. (Available in U.S. only)
21680-2 Pa. $3.75

THE THIRTEEN BOOKS OF EUCLID'S ELEMENTS, translated with introduction and commentary by Sir Thomas L. Heath. Definitive edition. Textual and linguistic notes, mathematical analysis, 2500 years of critical commentary. Do not confuse with abridged school editions. Total of 1414pp. 5⅜ x 8½. 60088-2, 60089-0, 60090-4 Pa., Three-vol. set $18.50

Prices subject to change without notice.

Available at your book dealer or write for free catalogue to Dept. GI, Dover Publications, Inc., 31 East Second Street, Mineola, N.Y. 11501. Dover publishes more than 175 books each year on science, elementary and advanced mathematics, biology, music, art, literary history, social sciences and other areas.